A BAD VIBE

Just moments later, while taking a restorative breath of brine-scented air, Salome heard tires crunching the gravel drive above her. That would be Phyl . . .

At least, she *hoped* it was Phyl. But what if it wasn't? What if the killer had returned, having no idea she'd discovered the body and that the police were on their way.

She started to call out, then thought better of it. If it wasn't Phyl, she'd be a fool to announce herself.

She ran to the nearest tree, a huge acacia at the edge of the lawn and hid among the drooping branches heavy with tiny yellow flowers. She heard first one then another car door slam.

What if there had been two killers? She glanced to her right. Less than a foot away was the steep embankment, now her only means of escape.

Then she heard feet running down the steps on the north side of the house, where she herself had descended roughly fifteen minutes ago. Her grip tightened on the trunk of the acacia. Her eyes were riveted to the far side of the mansion. At the first sight of anyone but Phyl, she'd have to make her way silently down the embankment, where any misstep could result in a broken neck on the narrow walkway far below.

A DEADLY ARRANGEMENT

Denise Osborne

BERKLEY PRIME CRIME, NEW YORK

This is a work of fiction. Names, characters, places, and incidents either
are the product of the author's imagination or are used fictitiously, and
any resemblance to actual persons, living or dead, business
establishments, events, or locales is entirely coincidental.

A DEADLY ARRANGEMENT

A Berkley Prime Crime Book / published by arrangement with
the author

PRINTING HISTORY
Berkley Prime Crime mass-market edition / September 2001

Visit our website at
www.penguinputnam.com

ISBN: 0-425-18184-7

Berkley Prime Crime Books are published
by The Berkley Publishing Group,
a division of Penguin Putnam Inc.,
375 Hudson Street, New York, New York 10014.
The name BERKLEY PRIME CRIME and the BERKLEY PRIME CRIME
design are trademarks belonging to Penguin Putnam Inc.

PRINTED IN THE UNITED STATES OF AMERICA

10 9 8 7 6 5 4 3 2 1

*This book is lovingly dedicated to
my husband, Chris J. Osborne, and my mother, Alberta Barker,
who both have an uncanny knack for attracting good ch'i*

Acknowledgments

Many thanks to the feng shui practitioners who shared their wisdom and insights, especially Cathleen Rickard, cherished friend and mentor, and to Madhu Brodkey and Nancy Santo Pietro.

Thanks must also be extended to Professor Lin Yun, who established the Black Sect Tantric Buddhist Feng Shui School, and Grace Jagchid for guidance at the Yun Lin Temple in Berkeley, California.

To family members for support and tireless promotion: Mom, Diane Barker, Harrison Barker, Signe Nelson, Dana Richmond, Lorraine Kessler, Dolores Osborne, Phil Osborne, Steve Osborne. To Judy Osborne and Chris Osborne for tech support.

To friends across the country who helped with research: Beverly Hogg, Marilyn and Mike Fitzgerald, Kathryn and Tony Gualtieri, Dianne Day, Mara Wallis and Richard Recker, John Barlow, Charlotte Morrison, Kevin Bransfield and Kathy Ball.

Special mention to the Capitola Women of Mystery for delightful conversation, and Julie, Deborah, Kathy, and Shannon at Dominican Hospital for their medical insights.

Without the blessings bestowed by the aforementioned, this book could not have been written. Without the spirited efforts and dedication of my agent, Don Gastwirth, the book would not have been published. For their efforts on behalf of the book, thanks to the staff at Berkley Prime Crime, especially my fine editor, Samantha Mandor.

While the book is a work of fiction and all characters creations of an active imagination, all material concerning the practice of feng shui is, to the best of the author's knowledge, factual.

1. *Out of clutter, find simplicity.*
2. *From discord, find harmony.*
3. *In the middle of difficulty lies opportunity.*

—Albert Einstein
Three Rules of Work

THE BAGUA

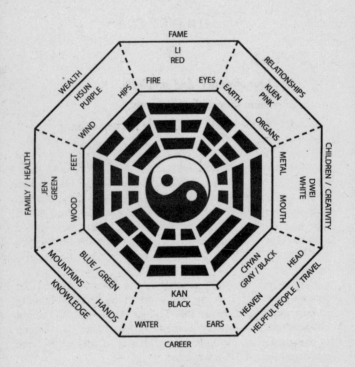

THE MOUTH OF CH'I

Chapter 1

SALOME Waterhouse recoiled from the sight of Palmer Fordham's battered body, the once finely formed torso and handsome face reduced to a thick stew of blood and pulp. For an instant she wondered if she'd been set up, had walked in on a joke. His Halloween parties were legendary, this old mansion the perfect venue for staging the macabre. But it was now nearly the end of January and the corpse she'd stumbled on all too real. She shivered as morning fog slipped in silently through the French doors and under the curtains behind her.

Pulling her eyes off the corpse, she glanced around the shadowy, two-story living room, absorbing details, straining to hear any sound, aware that besides the corpse, she might not be alone. An eternity seemed to pass as she stood frozen in place, eyes searching for some clue as to who might have murdered the well-known artist.

Finally, when the dead stillness became unbearable, she spun around and left the way she'd entered, through the tall French doors, the diaphanous curtains swaying in her wake.

In the short time she'd been in the house, the fog had slithered out of the nearby trees and now shrouded the veranda in what appeared to be old, tattered chiffon. She passed through it, heading for the clear green patch of lawn on a slight rise, feeling as if she'd been transported into someone else's nightmare.

In the east, spikes of amber and pink sunlight shot through dark turgid clouds heralding the coming storm. She finally started breathing again when she felt grass cushion her footsteps, unaware of the single trail of bloody footprints marking her passage across the veranda, now diminishing to beads of crimson on the dewy lawn. She finally stopped at the fence about a foot from a sheer seventy-foot drop. Below, a narrow roadway wound around the promontory.

The flat, gray bay spread out before her. To her left and past the nearby creek the village of Holyrood-by-the-Sea still slumbered beneath its blanket of fog. Behind her loomed the grand Spanish-style mansion and a terraced garden that rose about fifty feet to the circular drive at the front.

Feeling a little dizzy, she gripped the top slat of the fence with both hands. The action made her aware that sometime in the last few moments she'd dropped her briefcase. She started to turn, but stopped. No way was she going back. Abruptly, she patted the pockets of her long black robe, a garment similar to a priest's cassock, and sighed in relief when she felt the little cell phone she always kept it in her pocket during a consultation. Under the circumstances, she excused herself for a certain amount of confusion as to its whereabouts.

She called the home of Holyrood's chief of police, her cousin, Phyllis Waterhouse. Instead of soothing her, Phyl's groggy voice only added to the rich mix of sensations, stirring up a lifetime of petty, unresolved quarrels. Still, had she simply called 911 she could expect to be chastised for not calling her cousin directly.

"Are you in the house?" Phyl asked.

"No, on the lawn by the cliff."

"You see or hear anyone in the vicinity?" Phyl asked.

"No, everything's quiet."

"Stay put. And don't go back to the scene. I'll be right there."

Salome returned the phone to her right pocket then raised her hands to gut level, palms up, the left hand covering the right. With her thumbs nearly touching, she began to chant the heart-calming mantra to prepare herself for the upcoming confrontation. Life was over for Palmer Fordham, but for the living the effects of his murder were just beginning.

"Gatay, gatay, para gatay, para sam gatay, bodhi swaha . . ."

Silhouetted against the dawn-tinted pewter sky, Salome appeared to be little more than an inky stroke from an Asian calligrapher's brush. At least that was the image conjured by the one person watching.

JUST BEFORE SUNRISE, SALOME HAD BEGUN HER day by chanting the same heart-calming meditation nine times, the first step in priming herself for the upcoming feng shui consultation. So ingrained were the words and timing, she automatically stopped after the ninth chant.

She ate some fruit, showered, dusted her angular cheekbones with blusher, added maroon lipstick, then twisted her shiny black mane into a bun. Though in her fifties, she had no gray. Her Japanese-American mother hadn't sprouted gray until her midseventies.

Moving into the adjacent dressing room, she pulled one of several identical "uniforms" from the closet. Of her own design, the black robe was of a lightweight wool and silk blend and had a stiff Chinese collar, black satin frogs securing the bodice, long tight sleeves, a full, ankle-length skirt, and two roomy pockets.

While securing the frogs, she slipped on a pair of butter-soft black leather walking shoes with lightly pebbled interiors and thick soles. Now in her fifth year as a feng shui practitioner, she knew well the importance of comfortable footwear as she spent most of the consultation on her feet.

Of the many practitioners she knew—and their numbers were burgeoning as feng shui caught on in the U.S. and Europe—all wore western attire. But she believed that dressing like the ancient Chinese practitioners augmented both her credibility and clients' respect for her knowledge and advice.

Finally, she strapped on a small watch, a black and white *tai chi*, or yin yang symbol, on the face. It was 7:01 A.M. and the appointment was for 7:30. Enough time to walk to the consultation.

Salome left her cliff-side cottage via the patio, locked the slider then dropped the keys into the lightweight black leather briefcase containing her varied and unusual tools. She'd taken but a few steps when dread broke into her calm. The client's celebrity didn't bother her—a number of her clients were famous—but the circumstances surrounding this particular consultation, and indeed, the venue itself, did.

During his five-year tenancy, Salome had had no reason to visit her tenant, Palmer Fordham, nor the mansion. Since she wintered in Holyrood from late October until March, she always received an invitation to his Halloween parties but had never attended, believing it unwise to socialize with a tenant. Then, three days ago, a padded envelope arrived sporting a local postmark but no return address. Inside were two thousand dollars cash and a sheet of ordinary paper with typed instructions. She was to appear at the Perfume Mansion on this date at 7:30 A.M. for a feng shui consultation. *Do not call ahead. This is to be a surprise birthday gift*, the mysterious sender concluded.

She took a calming breath of the cool morning air and glanced out past the neat lawn to Monterey Bay. In the still dawn, with hardly a ripple on the surface, the water resembled a sheet of metal able to support anyone wanting to walk across it to the misty blue headlands to the south. Feeling steadier, she crossed the patio then followed the curving path of nine stepping stones imbedded in the grass to the redwood arbor where a little wind chime with five prongs hung motionless. She gave it a swat as she passed through to Sea Horse Lane, enjoying the brief tinkling sound that broke the quiet.

Just as she was rounding the high shrubbery at the intersection of Sea Horse Lane and Dolphin Way, she and an early morning jogger nearly collided.

"Salome! Good morning," Janelle Phillips said brightly.

"Good heavens, Janelle, you nearly knocked me down!"

"Sorry. Maybe I should install headlights and a horn."

Janelle's thick blond ponytail swung from side to side as she jogged in place. At nearly six feet, she topped Salome by about six inches. Despite the cold, she wore a pink sports bra, fuchsia spandex shorts, and white running shoes. Though probably in her midforties, she looked just north of thirty, a testament to the staying power of a former Miss America contender with access to the best cosmetic surgeons in the country.

Just last month Salome had feng shuied the four-bedroom "hideaway" that Janelle and her oil baron husband used whenever they tired of Houston's heat and humidity and wanted the more bracing air common to the central Pacific coast.

"You off to a consultation?"

Being a client entitled Janelle to a bit more than a curt good-bye. But before Salome could reply, Janelle exclaimed, "You won't believe this—but of course you will—Tommy puts the toilet seat and lid down after he pees! Twenty years I've been tryin' to get him to do that and *you* made it happen. Hope you're ready to travel, honey, 'cause I told all my friends in Texas about you. Don't worry, though, I haven't breathed a word about the toilet secret. Let them pay for it."

Salome had to smile. What Janelle called the "toilet secret" had probably done more to increase her client base than any of the many house enhancements in her repertoire. Her female clients invariably passed the word that Salome Water-house had the answer to the age-old problem of how to get men to put down the toilet seat and lid.

"Must be good money in fing shuey," Janelle went on, mangling the words. "Since you can afford to live up here and all. Maybe I should take it up—just in case Tommy's wells dry up."

"It's pronounced fung shuway," Salome corrected, finally able to get a word in. But she didn't have time for a chat.

"Fung shuway," Janelle repeated slowly without a trace of embarrassment.

"Well, I'd best be going," Salome said already moving away. "Have a good—"

"Maybe I could stop by, get the name of a school or some-thin'," Janelle called out.

"Yes, do that." Salome increased the speed and length of her stride.

"Fog's rollin' into the village—if you're headed that way."

Without turning, Salome lifted her hand and waved. While always a talker, Janelle seemed somewhat manic this morn-ing, her eyes unnaturally bright as if she'd taken a stimulant. But Salome didn't know her that well and could be she was projecting her own unease onto the other woman.

Janelle watched Salome until she disappeared around the next corner onto Starfish Lane.

Moments later she reached the overlook marking the west-ern boundary of the Bluff, as this residential section of Ho-lyrood was known. Set among wild rosemary, lavender, and dainty primroses were several benches from which to enjoy an unobstructed view of Holyrood-by-the-Sea's natural and man-made attractions. Nearby, steep concrete steps provided a shortcut down to the village.

Just below was the Sebastian Theater and beyond it, the wharf that stretched out into the bay, a restaurant and boat-house at the end.

Like a natural amphitheater, the village itself swept up

from the wide crescent of beach to Holyrood Church on Holyrood Hill. Close to shore were expensive beachfront restaurants, art galleries, vintage lodgings, and quaint shops. Further back were the whimsical cottages nestled in the trees and shrubs that seemed to have been transported from the pages of a fairy tale. Built early in the twentieth century, they defined the character of Holyrood.

As Janelle mentioned, morning fog rolled from the sea all the way up to the church green. On sunny days and clear nights one could imagine elves and fairies cavorting around the storybook houses and shops. In fog, though, one's imagination turned to more sinister beings—trolls, witches, and evil-spirited imps.

Salome paused for a moment, her gaze traveling across roof and treetops to the Perfume Creek, so named for a cannery that long ago stunk up its shores. Wisps of fog spiraled off the surface. On the steep opposite bank, fat acacias, stylishly slim eucalypts, and sturdy pines shielded most of the solitary Spanish mansion from sight. But from her vantage point, Salome could see the red-tiled roof and top-floor windows which, reflecting the orangey pink dawn light, shone like sheets of copper. This was the Perfume Mansion, so named because of its proximity to the creek. It was a property she had inherited from her grandfather, Joshua Waterhouse, one of Holyrood's founding fathers.

An incident in childhood had left her with an unshakable—and what some thought, unreasonable—fear of the place. On her seventh birthday, while exploring the Perfume's underground rooms, she and her cousin Phyllis had become separated. Alone, Salome had stumbled into a chamber that appeared to be filled with screaming children. Terrified, she'd blindly fled and somehow ended up in the Perfume Creek. She might have drowned had Phyllis not heard her thrashing and sputtering and dragged her out of the water and up onto the creek-side walkway. She'd begged her parents and grandparents to look for the room with the frightened children but her grandfather had sternly refused. He had built the mansion and declared that no such room existed—except in her imagination.

The Perfume was also, on this morning, her destination. Last night while studying the mansion's blueprints in preparation for the consultation, she'd felt the old fear stirring even though nothing on paper indicated a hidden room. Since inheriting the mansion when her grandfather died, she'd been in the subterranean chambers a few times, always in the company of the housekeeper—but not since becoming a feng shui practitioner. Now it seemed the time had come to put the old fear to rest. If there really was a secret room, maybe she'd find it today.

Feeling both excitement and trepidation, Salome gripped the cold metal handrail and scurried down the stairs, her black skirt billowing in her wake. A moment later, like one of those imagined witches, she vanished in the fog.

BY THE NINTH AND FINAL CHANT, SALOME'S voice was strong and even, testament to the mantra's power. Just moments later, while taking a restorative breath of brine-scented air, she heard tires crunching the gravel drive above her. That would be Phyl. At this hour, there was no need of a siren. Short of a fire, the city fathers would not be pleased by any superfluous noise disturbing those few tourists who chose to spend their dollars in Holyrood in winter.

At least, she *hoped* it was Phyl. But what if it wasn't? What if the killer had returned, having no idea she'd discovered the body and that the police were on their way.

She started to call out, then thought better of it. If it wasn't Phyl, she'd be a fool to announce herself.

She ran to the nearest tree, a huge acacia at the edge of the lawn and hid among the drooping branches heavy with tiny yellow flowers. She heard first one then another car door slam.

What if there had been two killers? She glanced to her right. Less than a foot away was the steep embankment, now her only means of escape.

Then she heard feet running down the steps on the north side of the house, where she herself had descended roughly fifteen minutes ago. Her grip tightened on the trunk of the acacia. Her eyes were riveted to the far side of the mansion. At the first sight of anyone but Phyl, she'd have to make her way silently down the embankment, where any misstep could result in a broken neck on the narrow walkway far below.

Chapter 2

SEEING her cousin rounding the north side of the mansion, Salome muttered a prayer of thanks, then feeling a bit foolish, she stepped out of her hiding place.

Even dressed casually in running shoes, jeans, a white sweatshirt, her badge attached to the collar, and a blue windbreaker, Phyllis Waterhouse looked every bit a stern, authority figure as she trotted up the five steps to the veranda. Short, wiry, gray-blond curls framed sharp features on a tanned face. Though three months younger than Salome, Phyllis looked older, the result of a life in law enforcement. In one hand she carried a police radio.

Limping a few paces behind her, came Sergeant Ralph Blue, also wearing civvies. In his early thirties, he had longish sun-streaked brown hair, broad shoulders, and the long fluid muscles of a swimmer. He'd only just returned to duty after being attacked by a Great White while surfing the rougher waters north of Holyrood. The shark "bite" required over three hundred stitches in his left buttock and thigh, and a new board and wetsuit. Having faced white death, Ralph probably wouldn't flinch at the sight of Palmer Fordham's corpse.

Salome started forward. "Phyl—"

"Stay there, Mei!" Phyllis barked, her blue eyes darting around, finally resting on the open French doors and drawn curtains. "You said the body's just inside, right?"

"Yes."

Through the thinning fog, the bloody shoeprints leading from the doors to the lawn were clearly visible.

"Yours?" Phyl asked, indicating the prints.

Salome frowned. "I—I guess so."

With Ralph at her heels, Phyl moved to the doorway, and avoiding the bloody tracks, parted the curtains and peered inside.

As if her own eyes were looking out of Phyl's head, Salome mentally revisited the crime scene. Palmer's body lay parallel to and about a foot from the French doors on the bloody parquet floor. While his head and torso were severely battered, below the faded blue Hawaiian motif shorts, his legs and feet appeared untouched.

Randomly, she recalled other details: the glass-topped coffee table supported by a cannily sculpted piece of driftwood, upon which were a clear vase of lavender tulips, a bottle of wine, and two partially filled wineglasses; a large L-shaped navy sectional sofa, and two end tables with matching ginger jar lamps. The furniture faced the fireplace. A mirror above the green marble mantel reflected some of the two dozen or so framed prints of sea goddesses hanging on the two-story north wall. Everything was in place, nothing overturned or shattered.

Salome now remembered a quick impression—that the corpse had been *posed*. Or had Palmer simply lain down near the door and without putting up a struggle allowed himself to be brutally murdered? An absurd notion to be sure but how could one account for the neatly arranged furnishings?

Phyl dropped the curtain and turned to Salome.

"There's a briefcase just inside. Yours?"

Salome groaned. A rather incriminating detail but at least now she knew its location.

"Would you get it for me?"

"No can do, Mei. It's part of the crime scene. Any other doors unlocked?"

"I don't know."

"You have keys?"

"No, but Dora will," Salome said, referring to house-keeper, Dora Whalen.

"I need to gain entry now! Someone else might be inside," she said, not specifying killer or another victim. Obviously, she wouldn't further taint the scene by entering through the French doors.

"Maybe the kitchen door's unlocked," Salome suggested.

Phyl turned to Ralph and the word POLICE seemed to shout at Salome from the back of Phyllis's windbreaker, an unsettling reminder that she'd entered dangerous territory.

Now, looking back at Salome, Phyllis said, "Given the death of your tenant, and since you're the owner, I need your permission, a consent to search the house."

"Of course! Just do it!"

While Ralph stayed on the veranda, Phyllis headed back down the steps to the kitchen door at the far end of the mansion. She pulled a latex glove from the inside pocket of her windbreaker, slipped it on, and tried the brass knob. It didn't give. She then took a credit card from her wallet. In seconds, she had the door opened. She pulled a Glock 9mm from the small of her back and gripping it in both hands, slipped sideways into the kitchen and disappeared.

Salome's stomach tightened. *Oh no,* she suddenly thought, *what if Phyllis comes upon the killer—or worse, vice versa?* There were so many rooms in which to hide and whoever hacked Palmer had to be a nut case.

"Shouldn't you be backing her up?" Salome called out to Ralph, tension escalating.

"Just chill, all right? She can handle herself."

He parted the curtains and glanced inside, part of his attention on Salome. She wondered if he remained on the veranda to keep an eye on her. A few tense moments passed.

Salome tried to find solace in Ralph's declaration—*She can handle herself.* Indeed, no one could doubt Phyllis's competence, especially confronting crazies. The lion's share of her career had been with the San Francisco Police Department, working her way up through the ranks to homicide detective. She'd seen it all and then some.

Apparently, Phyl had made it to the living room. Salome heard her talking to Ralph about whom to immediately contact: the fire department, county coroner, photographer, crime scene techs, and local cops to set up a perimeter.

Salome rubbed her arms in the cold morning air. She had "chilled" all right.

After a while, Salome heard more vehicles arrive and the sounds of chatter and the crackle of police radios. Phyllis must have opened the mansion's front door to provide access to the arrivals.

Finally, Phyllis appeared, moving around the hedges bordering the gravel drive and making her way down the terraced garden to the lawn. She motioned for Salome to join her at a bench in the shape of a sleeping bear. Nearby, a palm tree stood like a lone sentinel.

When their grandparents were alive and the tree smaller, Salome and Phyllis had sat on this very bench and watched Fourth of July fireworks, compared candy-filled Easter baskets, played with birthday and Christmas gifts; one little girl dark-haired and with an Asian cast to her features, the other blond and blue-eyed. Yin and yang.

"You find anyone else?" Salome asked anxiously.

Phyllis shook her head perfunctorily then said, "So, what the hell were you doing here at the crack of dawn?" Nothing of Salome's former playmate was in Phyl's harsh, biting tone.

"A feng shui consultation," Salome replied.

"Good Christ, playing house witch at this hour?"

Salome regarded her cousin stoically. At the beginning of

her professional practice, Phyl began referring to her as "the house witch." Though intended to be offensive, Salome considered the reference more amusing than rude.

Of course, feng shui at any time surprised Phyl, a skeptic who said she didn't believe the fish tank Salome had given her two years ago had anything to do with her appointment as chief of police. The twenty-gallon tank and nine orandas provided tranquility; admittedly an improvement over the stacks of old newspapers and magazines it replaced in what Salome said was the "career" position in her living room. Still, a week after the fish tank arrived, the city manager appointed her top cop.

Salome told her of the anonymous letter and cash that came by mail three days ago.

"You still have it?"

"Well, not the cash."

"Spent before you earned it?" Phyl remarked.

Salome knew the question was meant to rattle her and put her on the defensive.

"I don't like having that much money lying around," Salome said evenly. "Nothing unethical about depositing cash into a business account as soon as it's received."

"Unless it's laundered money."

"How am I supposed to know that? I don't know who sent it."

"That's another question we'll have to answer, won't we. Do you have the envelope and letter?"

"I'll have to look."

"Don't tell me there's *clutter* in your house. I thought you feng shui people were clutter-free."

Salome shifted her eyes to the south, where the building clouds now blocked the sun. But sun or not, the temperature around the bench was dropping swiftly.

"So, tell me about this morning—and you can skip what you had for breakfast. Your car's not here so I assume you walked. Anyone see you?"

Now Salome was grateful for the near collision with Janelle. *Thank the Goddess for small favors*, she thought. She told Phyl of the early encounter then moved on to her arrival at the mansion. When no one answered the bell, she said, she decided to check around back, thinking Palmer might be on the veranda painting one of his sea goddesses.

"Why would you think that?"

"Why not? He *is* a painter."

"You're familiar with his work habits?"

"Not at all. I wanted to put a little more effort into being here than just ringing the front door bell."

"You didn't try the front door?"

"No."

"But you did open the French doors."

"No, I didn't. The one was already open but the curtains were closed."

"And?"

"I called out. With the door open, I figured he was up and about even though he didn't answer."

"So why'd you enter?"

"Because, damn it, I was here to do a house reading." She paused to collect herself.

"Seeing his body didn't shock you? Any normal person—"

"I didn't see him, Phyl," Salome interrupted. "The curtains were in the way." She took a breath. "Look, the first thing I do when I arrive for a consultation is stand on the threshold for a moment and clear my mind. Then I enter with my eyes closed to get a feel for the energy. That way my first impression isn't altered by anything I see."

Phyllis shook her head as if to say *what idiocy*.

"Normally, I'm met at the door and I tell whomever answers that I need to enter with my eyes closed. It's simply part of the way I work. It's never been a problem."

"Until now. Were you in love with him?"

Right out of left field. But Salome had a good arm, too.
"Absolutely. For paying his rent on time."

"Where were you last night?"

"Home. Studying the Perfume's blueprints, preparing for
the consultation."

"Anyone with you?"

Salome smiled. "Shishi."

"Well, I'll definitely do the follow-up on him. Any two-
legged critters?"

"Had dinner at Otter Haven with Mother and Dad."

"When'd you get home?"

She shrugged. "Oh, I guess about nine-thirty, ten."

"When was the last time you spoke to Palmer?"

"Actually, he called me a few days after Dad's heart attack, just after Christmas. Wanted to be sure he was first on
the list to buy the Perfume. He probably figured the closer
Dad was to death, the sooner I'd be willing to sell. As you
probably know, he's wanted to buy the place since he moved
in."

Salome sensed something menacing uncoil within Phyllis.
Her cousin had always loved the Perfume. In the early 1980's
when their grandfather died, Phyllis had hoped her affection
for the property would translate into an inheritance even
though her Uncle Reggie, Salome's father, might be the more
likely candidate. But Reggie already owned Otter Haven, the
twelve-acre resort on the east side of The Bluff. Phyllis's
parents were dead (her father being Reggie's brother) and it
only seemed fair that she should be given the second major
piece of Waterhouse real estate. But Joshua Waterhouse had
surprised everyone and left it to his first-born grandchild,
Salome. Phyllis's disappointment quickly degraded into re-
sentment of her cousin.

"And were you planning to sell it to him?"

"Of course not. While Dad's alive, I won't sell." Like
Phyllis, her father felt a deep attachment to the Perfume,

having been raised in the mansion. He'd begged Salome to always keep it in the family.

"How many sets of keys are there?"

"Let's see—the property management firm keeps a set, Dora has a set. Dad, too." She shrugged. "That's all as far as I know. Oh yes, and Palmer, of course."

"What about yours?"

"I don't have keys."

"Why not?" Phyllis looked genuinely surprised.

"No reason. Dad's property management firm takes care of everything," Salome said, feeling as if she were talking to a stranger.

The conversation underscored the poor communications that existed between the cousins. Salome couldn't remember the last time they'd sat down and talked, though she imagined it had been before their grandfather's death. It was hard to believe they'd once been close. Even occasional cards and gifts—like the fish tank—never bridged the gap. She felt the familiar dull ache that gripped her chest whenever she thought of their estrangement.

Phyllis said nothing for several moments, increasing the pressure. Whatever had uncoiled within her cousin was positioning itself for a strike.

"I'm having a real problem with your story." Phyllis looked down for a moment then abruptly gave Salome the full force of her arctic eyes.

"Why would you even come here to do a consultation— given the anonymous letter and cash is true. Aside from the monthly income it generates, it's no secret you loathe the Perfume."

"I'm a professional," she said, her tone bristling. "Personal considerations do not keep me from fulfilling an obligation. Furthermore, I could certainly understand any parts of the mansion where Palmer might feel uncomfortable. In particular, the subterranean rooms. And 'loathe' is too strong a word. Let's just say there's too much negative energy here."

Phyllis resumed the silence. Was she rehearsing procedure, preparing to arrest Salome for murder? Salome worked to quiet rising apprehension.

"In what denominations were the bills?"

"As I recall, twenties."

"New or used?"

"Gosh, used, I guess."

"So who do you suppose sent you on this errand?"

Salome shook her head. "I can't imagine."

But actually she could. Something she'd seen at Barbara Boatwright's in December. Still, to mention a friend to take the heat off herself would be the worst kind of betrayal. What she'd seen *implicated* but proved nothing. Too many variables existed, one being that Barbara considered feng shui a bunch of hocus-pocus. Her words.

"You realize, of course, that someone who knows you pretty well could have set you up."

"I can't imagine anyone doing that."

"First on the scene makes you a prime suspect."

Another silence followed. Hands clenched in her lap, Salome pursed her lips, straining to hold back tears, certain that she was about to be arrested.

Phyllis abruptly stood, regarding Salome coldly.

Salome shivered.

"I'm finished for the moment but you have to go into the station and give a formal statement. Today, preferably, while everything is fresh in your mind. I'll also need your fingerprints, and hair and blood samples. And I don't want you leaving town for a while."

Though thankful she wasn't about to be locked up, there were other matters she considered too important not to mention.

"I have appointments in San Francisco."

"Cancel." Phyllis paused, then said, "Now I want your shoes."

"What?"

"To match them to the prints on the veranda and the floor. Didn't you learn anything working for that ex-husband of yours?"

Salome's throat tightened as she swallowed her anger. She pulled off her shoes and handed them over. Not having any evidence bags handy, Phyllis placed the pair, topside down on the bench.

"And your uniform."

"If you think I'm going to strip out here, you're nuts!"

Phyllis finally cracked a smile. "Ralph'll drive you home. You can give it to him then. It'll have to be tested for blood splatter. To eliminate you as a suspect." But the look on her face said quite the opposite.

Salome rose from the bench, her thin socks quickly soaking up moisture from the damp grass. "My house keys are in the briefcase. Would you get them for me?"

"Come on. You know I can't do that."

"I just thought—"

"That I'd do you a favor because you're my cousin? Not for anyone will I disturb a crime scene," *especially you* she seemed to imply.

Then Phyl nodded toward the steep, terraced slope. "Leave by the garden. And don't forget to look for that envelope and letter. And while you're at it, the deposit slip."

Phyllis turned, moving toward the veranda.

"Just how long am I supposed to stay in town?"

"Until I say otherwise."

"Look, it's only a two-hour drive to San Francisco. I can be up and back in no time."

"You heard me. Stay . . . in . . . town."

Phyl brought up Salome's ex-husband, and now Salome mentioned Phyl's. "Manderson's one of those clients I'm scheduled to see."

Phyllis spun around, her body tense. A hissing curse escaped before Phyl could contain it. "When?"

"Today at four." Salome watched Phyl's jaw clench and

unclench. "He needs me to augment the health sectors in his flat. Shouldn't take long. I could be back by seven. Eight at the latest."

Phyl stared at her shoes. She sniffed a time or two then, raising her head, said, "Sorry, it'll have to wait."

Salome stared at her cousin with dull eyes, unable to comprehend such a lack of compassion. Because of his illness, Manderson needed all the help he could get. Suddenly overwhelmed by negative energy, Salome couldn't wait to get out of her uniform and under a cleansing shower. Then she remembered she didn't have keys to get in the house.

"Feng shui can't help him," Phyl remarked.

Salome turned her back on Phyllis and holding up her skirt, began awkwardly picking her way up the incline. Then, raising her right hand, she flicked her two middle fingers against her thumb while concentrating on deflecting the negative energy that had been building all around her.

"And, Salome," Phyllis called out "don't go sticking your nose where it doesn't belong. You could get yourself in more trouble."

The warning didn't penetrate; it slid off Salome like water down a slab of polished marble. Focusing intently, she'd connected with something emanating from the mansion and could almost see sharp spikes piercing the walls, hurled from a core in the sublevel. She dropped her hand; deflecting the energy had about as much effect as blowing into a strong wind to turn it around. Beyond negative, this force was evil. And, she sensed, a long-term tenant.

But whatever evil prompted the killing of Palmer Fordham had a human hand attached.

She plopped down at the top of the garden, the gravel drive and assorted vehicles at her back. While waiting for Ralph Blue, her thoughts drifted back to an evening in early December, a night during which she may have been in the presence of the killer.

Chapter 3

☯

Second Tuesday, the previous December

AROUND 7 P.M., professionally attired and clutching her briefcase, Salome rang the bell at Barbara Boatwright's cliff-side house, where Star Fish Lane met Bayview.

A moment later, Barbara answered, looking elegant in a beige silk hostess ensemble of tunic and wide-legged pants accented with gold jewelry, her medium length blond hair neatly coiffed and colored to hide the gray.

"Make yourself comfortable in the library, Salome," she said briskly. "It'll be a few minutes before we start. I've still got things to do but you should know some of the women."

In the two-story library, a number of the Women of Mystery book club members had marked places on various chairs and sofas with jackets, handbags, and notebooks and were helping themselves to chocolate mocha cheesecake and a hot beverage. The cheesecake, the size of a tire on a midsize truck, attested to Barbara's belief that all nineteen members would show up for tonight's soiree as did the restaurant-sized coffee urn borrowed from Billie Ruth's Bakery. Packaged teas, both herbal and black, filled a silver bowl.

Not wanting to mingle, Salome acknowledged various women with a nod then slipped upstairs. Just off an alcove on the second floor, she climbed another set of stairs to the third and topmost floor of Barbara's house.

She'd been in this room many times and always particularly liked it at night, which is why she'd come up to assemble her thoughts and more or less quiet herself before the presentation Barbara had asked her to give.

The curtains were hung in tight clusters of fine linen, allowing a spectacular three-hundred-sixty-degree view of coastal mountains and sea. Beneath the wraparound windows were fitted cabinets. Enough ambient light allowed her to move around without bumping into anything.

The large room was furnished with sun-faded futon couches draped with woolen throws, assorted tables and reading lamps, portable electric heaters, and huge floor pillows. On the nearest coffee table were stacks of mysteries and books on Asian, pre-Columbian and South American art. The Boatwrights owned World Wide Imports. Their stores were scattered along the West Coast and featured upscale decorative and household items from South America and Asia.

She was about to sit on one of the futon couches when she noticed the telescope on a tripod in front of a ladder-back chair. After setting her briefcase on the couch, she went over for a look at the moon and stars. Nearby was an ashtray, a box of Barbara's preferred Sherman cigarettes, and a gold lighter.

Without disturbing the telescope's position, she sat down and put her eye against the cushioned cup. Almost immediately she jerked away, uttering a cry of surprise. Then she looked again to confirm the sighting.

Sure enough, the studio of local artist Palmer Fordham appeared at what seemed to be arm's length. A jumble of sketchpads and artists' paraphernalia cluttered the surface of a long table. Of greater interest though, was the artist himself. Naked to the waist, he wore only a pair of low-slung faded jeans that looked ready to fall off. Thick, champagne-colored hair brushed his shoulders as he stood at an easel, sketching with a piece of charcoal. She could even make out smudges on his flat torso, where he'd absently wiped his hand.

She felt a chill, imagining Barbara sitting in this chair, puffing a Sherman while watching Palmer's every move.

Of friends nearest her age, Barbara seemed the least likely to succumb to any loopy expression of middle-age madness.

"Damn it, Salome!"

Salome jumped out of the chair as if it had been electrified. Barbara punched a button and the curtains automatically *whooshed* across the windows, shutting out the view.

While the mechanism hummed, she marched toward Salome, put the chair in a corner, then tucked the tripod and telescope in the cupboard beneath the window. "I don't appreciate your snooping!"

"I thought I'd be seeing stars. In a sense, I suppose—"

"Everyone's here," Barbara snapped.

"Look, I just came up to collect my thoughts."

"Well it's time to present the collection."

In a flurry of beige and gold, Barbara hurried down the stairs. In black, Salome trailed behind her.

Though somewhat unnerved by the encounter with Barbara, Salome calmed herself by silently chanting a simple mantra—*"om ma ni pad me om"*—in preparation for the presentation and stood in the shadows, waiting for Barbara's introduction. Looking out at the assembled crowd, she noted a light dusting of young faces among the majority of well-nourished females between forty and seventy.

Then Barbara began. "We've all derived pleasure from reading Gabriel Hoya's wonderful mysteries. And other than the author himself, who better to talk about his work than his former researcher and wife of twenty years."

In the shadows, Salome stiffened. She didn't mind promoting Gabe's books and had done so plenty of times but always casually. She'd agreed to appear only if half the time would be spent on feng shui. Barbara had assured her the women expected that exactly. The silent mantra picked up speed.

"For those of you who don't know our speaker, she was born and raised right here in Holyrood. She's bicoastal now, spending half her time in the Georgetown section of Washington, D.C. and the other half—the better half, I must say—just a block away on Sea Horse Lane. If anyone knows where Gabriel Hoya buried the bodies, she does."

Barbara spread her hands then, and with a slight smirk on her face, glanced back toward the Salome. "So, ladies, I'm pleased to present tonight's speaker, Gabriel Hoya's ex-wife."

To scattered applause, Salome stepped out, working her facial muscles into a smile, annoyed that Barbara had not said a word about feng shui, and further, that Barbara hadn't even introduced her by name. Barbara might have been nervous but Salome wondered if this was some sort of retribution for the discovery of the telescope's point of interest.

"Thank you." Salome glanced around the room. "I see a number of familiar faces but for those who don't know me, I'm Salome Waterhouse.

"These days, I'm more often asked to talk about feng shui. I've been a practitioner for over five years now. When I first took up the study of feng shui, known to many westerners as the art of placement, Gabriel Hoya and I were married and living in McLean, Virginia."

A hand shot up attached to a petite woman with custom-dyed auburn hair and sharp green eyes. Salome well remembered those eyes and the malice they once shot her way back in high school. But those days were long past and now curiosity seemed to have replaced enmity.

"Yes, Billie Ruth?" Though 'Ruth' was her surname, she'd always been called Billie Ruth.

"I did some research and learned that your ex went to Georgetown with Bill Clinton and that Gabriel Hoya is a pseudonym. What's his real name?"

Go with the flow, she told herself.

"Sounds like you're something of an investigator yourself," Salome remarked. That garnered a few laughs and comments.

"You've got that right!"

"Billie Ruth's a frustrated P.I.!"

"Sorry, I'm sworn to secrecy. Gabe doesn't like his real name. But, I can tell you that he used his grandfather's first name and being an avid fan, tacked on Georgetown's basketball team, the Hoyas."

"Did you party with the Clintons?" Billie Ruth interjected. Salome thought she detected envy in the question.

"We went to the White House a few times. Like all of you, Bill Clinton's a mystery fan and likes Gabe's books but they were just acquaintances in college."

A young woman wearing oversized tortoise shell glasses in the front row interrupted, looking as if she found the personal probing inappropriate. "I've always been impressed with how well he writes his female characters, especially private investigator Antoinette de Beauharnais."

A ribald character if ever there was one, Salome had to smile as a vision of wide-bodied Antoinette with her big red hair and little feet in stiletto heels filled her mental screen.

"For those unfamiliar with the books, Antoinette has the distinction of being the illegitimate daughter of a New Orleans underworld figure and a wealthy Creole madame— folks who, Gabe likes to say, make Caligula look like Mickey Mouse."

Hands stopped popping up and now the women simply called out questions.

"Even though you're divorced, do you still work together?"

Ah! Just the question she'd been waiting for.

"Not since I started my own feng shui practice. However, after the divorce he hired me to feng shui the house he'd just bought. He'd heard Donald Trump, among others in the corporate world, take feng shui very seriously.

"Anyway, his new house wasn't far from the one we shared for many years. Gabe became a true believer when, a couple weeks later, his agent finalized a seven-figure, three-book contract with a new publisher."

By the hush and wide-eyed expressions she knew she'd found the hook.

"That's the wonderful thing about feng shui—it works."

Another silence followed.

"I know what you're thinking—if feng shui works then why did we end up divorced? Well, our marriage had been going the way of the DoDo bird before I began my feng shui studies. We'd primarily become partners in crime, as it were. Working together and sharing the same house, but that's about it.

"When I decided to become a practitioner, my mentor told me to get rid of nine items a day for nine weeks. At the end of the nine weeks I felt indescribable freedom and could see my life with absolute clarity. And I finally realized the time had come for Gabe and me to go our separate ways."

"So, he went out with the trash."

"I wouldn't put it that way, Billie Ruth."

One woman called out, "Why nine?"

"Nine's the magic number in feng shui. Now let me give you a brief overview and then I'll take questions.

"Feng shui has been practiced in China for millennia. But you don't have to be a student of eastern culture to understand the principles. It's all about *ch'i*: positive, lively energy, and *sha*: negative, stagnant energy. Good ch'i being the energy we want to attract in our homes and work environments."

She reached into her briefcase and held up a sheet of paper on which was printed an octagon with a black and white yin yang symbol in the center, embraced by eight trigrams from the I Ching. Life situations, colors, and elements were printed at each side.

"This is a Bagua, my most important tool. From it I determine the location of the significant areas of life in an apartment, a house, a room—any structure for that matter. Each particular area is called a *gua*.

She turned to Barbara. "There're copies in my briefcase. Would you mind handing them out?"

Barbara's eyes hurled a few darts—proving she hadn't cooled off since Salome discovered her little vice—then fulfilled the request.

"Let's first look at the bottom of the Bagua, where we find career in the middle, knowledge on the left, and helpful people slash travel on the right. At one of these points will be the entrance to the residence—called the mouth of ch'i. Let's use Barbara's house as an example."

Out of the corner of her eye, Salome noticed Barbara freeze as if preparing for Salome to reveal what she'd seen on the third floor.

"Barbara's front door is in the middle of the west side of the house thus in the career gua. After we entered the house, we turned left and headed for the library, which is here in the knowledge gua—a perfect, harmonious position for a library. Both floors above us are also in the knowledge gua." And how appropriate, she thought, that Barbara's telescope would be so placed for spying.

"Moving on, clockwise from knowledge," she continued, "we next come to family and health, followed by wealth, then fame-one's reputation-then relationships which includes marriage, then children and creativity, and finally helpful people and travel.

"In the ninth area, the center of the Bagua, we find the tai chi or yin yang symbol, which represents wholeness, balance, and harmony."

Looking at the Bagua, she went on. "You will note that

each area is also represented by an I Ching trigram with its respective Chinese name, then specific colors, body parts and natural elements: wood, fire, water, earth, metal and mountains, wind and heaven."

She lowered the paper. She had her audience and now she had to hold their interest before someone asked another question about Gabe and his mysteries.

"As a practitioner, I first ask a client what area of their life they would like to improve." She looked directly at her former adversary.

"Billie Ruth. How about you? What area of your life needs improvement?"

Without hesitation, Billie Ruth said, "My sex life. But I don't see it here on this Bagua thing." That brought laughs and chatter. Billie Ruth, always the clown.

Someone called out, "Hell, you don't need a Bagua. Just give Palmer Fordham a jingle."

Billie Ruth laughed. "Honey, been there, done that."

Salome saw Barbara leave her chair and slip out of the room, carrying her cup. Before things got out of hand, Salome interjected, "Sex is covered in the relationship gua so first thing to do is look at that area of your house. If a bedroom is there, you're in luck. If not, adjustments can be—"

Billie Ruth interrupted, now more serious. "Actually, my bakery could stand to make more money."

"Right," Salome said. "Then you'd want to feng shui the bakery itself, concentrating first on the career gua, then wealth then fame—and by fame, I mean your bakery's reputation in the community. And finally, helpful people, which no one in business can do without."

"So how can feng shui increase my sales?"

"By attracting good ch'i; energizing those guas I mentioned. And that's done by implementing what are known as the nine basic cures or enhancements."

Using it like a magician's bag of tricks—this, after all, was a presentation, and a little dramatic flair wouldn't hurt—

she began pulling items out of her briefcase: a small round mirror, a multifaceted crystal hanging from a nine-inch red cord, a small wind chime, a bamboo flute, a square of vibrant red silk, a polished stone, a small, battery-operated fan, some pink silk flowers, and a three-inch bronze Kwan Yin statuette.

"These are just a few of the many items you could place in various guas to stimulate the flow of ch'i. One of the best for the career gua is a fish tank—couldn't fit one into my briefcase. You'll often see a fish tank near the entrance of Chinese restaurants.

"Computers and any electrical appliances also stimulate ch'i. But when they break they have to be discarded, otherwise they create negative effects."

Billie Ruth stared at Salome. "I don't like fish."

There were a few nervous twitters but Salome easily deflected the negative energy Billie Ruth shot her way.

"That's just the sort of thing we'd determine during the initial interview." Then she moved on.

"After determining the location of each section of the Bagua in the floor plan of your residence or business, then you do the same in each room. Again, the entrance will be in either knowledge, career, or helpful people."

Blanche Goodfellow, a lanky septuagenarian dressed in a tailored blue pantsuit said in a husky voice, "Salome, dear, you make it all sound so easy. I thought feng shui was a complicated science, requiring compasses, complex astrological calculations and such."

"I follow Black Hat sect feng shui, which does not employ the traditional compass, and is easy to understand.

"You see, feng shui has undergone a sort of revolution in the past twenty years or so—having gone from a relatively obscure science to one rapidly approaching mainstream worldwide. And that is because, as I said before, it works. My method may seem simple but, in fact, I studied and apprenticed with a mentor for four years before I opened my practice. And I'm still learning and always will be."

For the next hour she went through each gua, answering questions about specific problems. Because residences come in all shapes and sizes, the homes of some women had various guas missing. Salome addressed those concerns and suggested enhancements.

"Though I've given you the basics and some quick fixes, I haven't even touched on the transcendental applications involving intentions—a powerful aspect of feng shui. By melding your intention with the ch'i, you can generate greater fulfillment in those areas of life you want to improve."

A short time later, Barbara rose from her chair and on behalf of the group thanked Salome then whispered, "Mind staying after for a drink?"

"All right."

From Barbara's alcohol-scented breath, Salome could tell she'd already started; had probably been lacing her coffee during those times she left the room.

Salome handed out business cards to those with more than a passing interest and chatted briefly with those who thanked her for coming, Billie Ruth noticeably not among them.

By nine-fifteen, Salome and Barbara were settled on a leather sofa now turned back around to face the crackling fire in the fireplace.

"Charles and I are having financial and, well, other problems."

"Would you like to set up a consultation?"

"Good heavens no! You know I don't believe in that hocus-pocus. Besides, at the moment, I can't afford any extra expenses."

"Oh come on, Barbara. I'd be glad to help at no cost."

"You probably got yourself a client or two tonight. I should ask for a percentage. Still, I need the business, too. Which is why I lobbied to host the December meeting. Frankly, I just wanted them all to think about World Wide

Imports when they went Christmas shopping."

Barbara stared into the fire for a moment then suddenly laughed. "Oh my God! I introduced you as Gabriel's ex-wife!" Then she shrugged. "But you're probably used to that; having lived so long in the shadow of someone famous."

Salome felt a nuclear glow on her cheeks and set her coffee cup on the nearby end table. "Why don't you call me? We can get together when you're feeling better."

Suddenly Barbara reached over and grabbed Salome's sleeve.

"Don't go yet. Charles is off in South America on a buying trip. Won't be back till March. He does love to shop at Christmas. Unfortunately on another continent. God, how I hate this time of year." She finished her brandy and poured another.

"Why don't you join him?"

"I hate flying. The glamour's been sucked out of it."

After a moment, Barbara sighed. "Look, don't tell anyone about the telescope . . . and, uh, whatever you saw."

"Of course not."

"Thing is, we're having an affair."

"For how long?"

"Been going on two weeks."

"Why him? I mean, he's gorgeous but—"

Barbara jerked her head around. "—he's twenty years younger than me?"

"It's not the math, Barbara. He's a known womanizer. Good grief, I saw how you reacted when someone mentioned him after Billie Ruth joked about her sex life. I'm sure I'm not the only one. How serious is this?"

Instead of answering, Barbara polished off the brandy and added yet another refill to the snifter.

"Maybe you should get away for a while, spend a few days at your condo up at Lake Tahoe."

"Sold it last month. And anyway, I can't leave the store. Not at Christmas. The only pleasure I have is when I'm with

Palmer. When we're not together, I love to watch him work."

Barbara managed World Wide Imports flagship store in San Jose and because of the season surely was under a lot of pressure. Salome wondered when she even had time for an affair.

After a few moments of silence, Salome spoke. "You know, it wouldn't hurt if you stocked feng shui supplies. Believe me, the feng shui business is on the verge of a boom. There are special candles now, wind chimes, fountains, all sorts of items. Just having them there would attract good energy. I could give you some catalogues."

"Ah! Always thinking of business, aren't you?"

Salome took a breath. "Didn't I just hear you mention financial problems? You could use feng shui right now and I can help."

"Maybe after Christmas," Barbara interjected. She spun the delicate gold bracelet watch on her bony wrist then held the timepiece, the action drawing Salome's attention.

Salome noticed age blooming on Barbara's large elegant hands. Her eyes traveled up to Barbara's face as her friend squinted at the watch. Her upper lip was losing its fullness. Shrinking from bitterness and discontent? The makeup beneath her eyes had long faded, revealing translucent gray pillows.

Then suddenly Barbara stood up as if aware of Salome's scrutiny. "Early day tomorrow and I need rest."

As they stood at the front door, Barbara wore a mask with a fixed smile.

"Thanks for the presentation. Despite manipulating the evening to your own ends, the women enjoyed it. Good night, Salome."

She swayed slightly then closed the door, leaving Salome stung by the rebuke.

Instead of going home, Salome took a brisk walk around the Bluff. Critics of feng shui often accused practitioners of being charlatans spouting psychobabble intended to separate any and all from their money. Salome had learned to live with it. After all, everything good in life would always attract those determined to bring it down. Fortunate enough to enjoy financial security, she could have become a woman of leisure. But she had chosen her business and believed completely in feng shui as a natural science. Ch'i exists. The idea is to attract the good ch'i and dissipate the bad ch'i. The art came after. When someone accused her of simply wanting to make money, she took it to heart.

By the time she opened her rounded red front door, Salome couldn't shake the feeling that she'd lost an old friend. Still, Barbara's interest in a friendship had diminished after the divorce. The lively dinner parties the Boatwrights had once hosted whenever Gabe and Salome were in town were now replaced by an occasional lunch date.

Loss of a friend always produced the same hollow sensation. Some friends she'd lost because they simply wanted to disengage all associations with the past. Others simply drifted off into other lives. But this was different—she sensed Barbara felt betrayed now that Salome had knowledge of her private life, gained however inadvertently.

Chapter 4

AT last, Ralph Blue arrived to escort her home. She tried to believe that Phyl hadn't left her to wait in the cold over thirty minutes simply out of spite; that Ralph must have had things to do before Phyl would let him leave.

With her arms wrapped around her chest, Salome huddled on the passenger seat of the police car. Sensitive enough to know she didn't want to talk, Ralph kept quiet during the short drive to her cottage. That Phyl hadn't ordered her arrest was enough for him; his only task was to take her home. He assumed she was brooding over the horrific sight of the dead man.

He would have been surprised by the truth.

For Salome's thoughts weren't on Palmer Fordham but now on the mansion itself. At some point, she'd have to perform an exorcism and blessing ceremony. Just the idea chilled her to her soul. But no way would she permit anyone to move in until the evil had been removed.

House exorcisms were not common. She knew the procedure but even during her four-year apprenticeship with Madame Wu, she'd never even been in a house requiring such a rigorous spiritual cleansing. The thought of performing one herself seemed overwhelming, exacerbated by the irony that the very property so in need belonged to her. But feng shui practitioners had been providing the service for thousands of years and that gave her some comfort.

Determined not to let anticipation immobilize her, Salome compartmentalized the problem. Besides, there was no telling how long it would be before Phyl released the Perfume. Given that this was the first time Phyl could legally take possession of the mansion, Salome figured her cousin would keep it under her control as long as possible.

AS RALPH PULLED INTO THE DRIVE, EMILY HAR-kin suddenly appeared and picked up her morning paper. The timing couldn't have been worse considering Emily's ravenous appetite for gossip. The editor-in-chief of *The Holyrood Echo*, she also wrote the paper's gossip column. Seeing Salome with her hair half falling out of the bun, exiting a police car—shoeless, no less—driven by good-looking Ralph Blue early in the morning, and trying to break into her own house would provide Emily with a juicy tidbit. At least until news about the murder broke.

Salome groaned.

"What?"

"The town crier's watching."

Ralph glanced up at the rearview mirror. "Won't be long before everyone hears you and me were out all night having it on." He smiled sweetly as if the idea wasn't altogether unpleasant. Such insinuations were rare these days and she had to smile, too. Her glum mood lightened.

"Well, let's see about breaking and entering," Salome said.

"You're sure none of the doors are unlocked?"

"Right now, Ralph, I'm not sure of anything."

Finding the front door locked, they headed toward the east side of the stone cottage, away from Emily, who was acting as if she always read the paper out on the street in her robe.

A lovely Japanese-style garden was located between the

kitchen and the small detached garage. They tried the kitchen door but it was locked along with the windows.

"Haven't you got a spare hidden in a flower pot or something?"

"My parents have a set but I refuse to bother them right now. I'd rather break in."

The glass slider and all the south side windows were locked tight.

Salome's feet were soaked and, if possible, even number as they approached the west side of the house. Salome hoped the cold had sent Emily back into her house. Not that it would matter much. She'd simply station herself at a window.

They turned the corner and there stood Emily, paper open, her eyes focused like a camera above the top. Times like this, Salome missed the ten-foot hedge she'd replaced with a short ranch-style fence. But hedges had always reminded her of coffins and then, in particular, of the death of her marriage.

The bedroom window on this side was closed so they moved on to the windows of the last room, the study. *Maybe,* she thought, *just maybe, I didn't close them last night before going to bed.*

Of the two windows, the one located behind the thick camellia bush was open about an inch. Feeling some relief, she pulled it out another six inches then confronted the screen. In the tight space, she exchanged places with Ralph. Using a pocketknife, he cut through the mesh and undid the two lowest latches but couldn't reach the two at the top of the window. But by bending the aluminum frame he was able to swing it inside about six inches.

"Should be enough room for you to crawl through," he said. "I'll give you a boost. Keep clear of the screen's edge. Looks pretty wicked."

They maneuvered awkwardly for a moment, the camellia bush, lush with red blooms, pushing against them. Salome struggled up over the side, with one hand against the screen, trying to avoid the sharp edge.

So glad to be gaining access, she'd quite forgotten the shrine with the Kwan Yin statue and small fountain bubbling just beneath the window.

"Wait a sec!" she cried out. But at that very moment, Ralph gave her a final shove. Her head connected with the screen's pointed edge. As she hit the shrine, the statue and fountain toppled over onto the hardwood floor with a resounding crash.

"Salome! You okay?"

Stunned, Salome sat in a puddle of water, polished stones, and pieces of the Kwan Yin Goddess scattered all around. When she moved her head, something tugged her hair, sending pain ricocheting through her skull.

Ralph peered over the side of the window. "Holy shit! Don't move." Hauling himself up onto the ledge, he reached out and carefully removed a hank of hair, most of it still connected to her head, from the edge of the screen.

"Go open the front door. I'll be right there."

She wiped something wet from her left eye. Her hand came away covered in blood. As she slowly got to her feet, she spied a box of tissues on the nearby desk. She grabbed a handful and pressed the wad against her head. On trembling legs, she went to open the front door.

"Let me see that," Ralph said and gently took her hand from her head. The tissues were already soaked through.

"Where's the bathroom?"

"Down the hall on the right."

"Wait right here."

In a moment, he returned with a couple of towels, instructing her to hold one to her head.

"Gotta get you to the hospital. You need stitches."

"Oh hell," she groaned. "I need to put something on my feet."

While she stood keeping the pressure on her wound, Ralph

retrieved a pair of fleece-lined Ugg boots from the hall closet. He pulled off the wet socks then helped her into the boots.

"What do you say we leave the front door unlocked?" he said, taking her arm.

"Wish I'd thought of that earlier," she remarked.

As Ralph sped out of the drive, Emily Harkin's eyes widened. "My, my, aren't you a busy girl this morning, Salome," she muttered.

Folding her *San Jose Mercury News*, she waited until the cruiser disappeared around Dolphin Way, a slight smile lifting her thin lips. She then hurried across the street toward the camellia bush to have a peek. Salome herself was always going on about "synchronicity," things coming into one's life when needed. Maybe there was something to it, thought Emily. For days she'd been looking for something to wake her readers from winter ennui. A nice scandal had been too much to hope for. Until now.

Two hours and a dozen stitches later, Salome stepped out of the cruiser at her front door and into the pouring rain. She glanced over at Emily's house, glad the weather had sent the news hound inside.

While Ralph waited, she entered the house, carrying the bloody towels she'd used en route to the emergency room about ten miles away. In the foyer, she dropped the towels on the floor then took the cell phone from her pocket and set it on the Korean chest, avoiding her image in the mirror above it. She felt woozy enough without having to confirm the fact.

She stripped off the damp uniform, thinking it ironic that now there really was blood on it, and folded it neatly.

From the coat closet, she retrieved her trusty Drizabone, an Australian oilskin coat, and put it on.

Still wearing the Ugg boots, she dashed through the rain to the squad car, holding the ankle-length coat closed with one hand. Ralph lowered the passenger window. She put the folded uniform on the passenger seat.

"Thanks for your help, Ralph," she said. "Sorry to keep you from all the excitement."

"Already filled my excitement quota," he said and patted the thigh scarred for life by the Great White's razor-sharp teeth. "You need anything give me call."

She gave the door a swat and ran back into the house.

Minutes later, she stood beneath the stinging needles of a hot shower, hoping her head wouldn't hurt too much when the local anesthetic wore off. She'd refused a script for pain-killers, determined to keep her mind free of pharmaceutically induced brain clouds. She had too much to do today.

After gingerly toweling and combing out her hair, she examined the wound. The emergency room doctor, a friend of Ralph's, had taken extra care. Though neatly done, it still looked grotesque, something she'd have to live with for the next seven to ten days. She daubed on antiseptic and applied a smaller dressing.

Somewhere in the house Shishi, a fluffy black and white cat, had slept through all the activity. Or maybe he was visiting friends. The kitty was named after the Japanese Guardian Lion and like Salome, Shishi had two homes. When Salome wintered in Holyrood, Shishi stayed with her. The remainder of the year, Shishi lived with Salome's parents at the Otter Haven Resort three blocks away. From time to time, he'd wander over to her parents' apartment in the huge Victorian lodge to make certain everything was running smoothly then return, using his personal entry at the bottom of the cottage's kitchen door.

After dressing in jeans and a maroon sweater that zipped up the front, she gathered dirty towels from the utility room where the washer and dryer were housed and carried them into the study, wishing Shishi would appear. She could use some kitty comfort and consolation.

"Jeeze!" she shouted, seeing the rain pour in through the open window, there to join the mess on the floor. She dropped the towels on the enlarging puddle, removed the screen, and closed the window.

Salome tried calling Manderson Monroe for the second time, having first telephoned him from emergency only to reach his answering machine. Besides being Phyl's ex, he was an old and dear friend, and she wanted to tell *him*, not his machine, why she couldn't make their appointment at four. Again, his machine kicked in.

"Mandy! If you're there, pick up!" She paused. "As I said before, I can't come to the city today. I'll try you again later."

The remainder of the week's appointments were scattered over the next few days. She'd wait to call. The possibility existed that Palmer Fordham's killer would be quickly caught and she wouldn't need to change her schedule.

Through her work with Gabe, she knew the first twenty-four hours of a murder were crucial in finding the perpetrator. Too, she knew that battering wounds to the face and upper torso indicated a personal relationship between victim and killer. Though Holyrood swelled to well over ten thousand souls in the summer, especially on weekends, in winter, the population stabilized at around five thousand. She figured Phyl would apply her bulldog talents to the investigation and come up with a short list of suspects in no time. And, of course, the mayor would pressure Phyllis to make an arrest before the AT&T Pro-Am golf tournament scheduled to start next week.

What Salome needed to do was remove herself from the short list.

She found the bank deposit slip and the letter and envelope from Palmer's mysterious gifter among other papers in a wire "catch-all" basket on her desk. She shuddered to think that the same person might have killed him, setting her up as a suspect. She carefully slipped them into a large plastic bag, even though her prints were already on each item.

From the top middle drawer of her desk she pulled out an

extra set of car keys. She'd never even thought to keep an extra set of house keys *in the house*. Instead, after purchasing the cottage, originally owned by her grandmother and namesake, she'd simply asked her parents to keep a set of keys for her.

Back in the utility room she dumped the bloody towels in the washing machine to soak in cold water and left via the kitchen door.

Despite all that had happened this morning, she found pleasure in the sight of her Japanese garden. Rain pocked the surface of the small pond and slicked the tiny arced bridge, a red pagoda on one side, a ceramic Asian fisherman on the other, his line bobbing along the surface. She would have liked to stock koi but that would have been the same as opening a fresh fish restaurant for the local raccoons. Fortunately, they were too big to fit through Shishi's little door.

With some reluctance, she pulled herself away and hurried off to deal with realities beyond the tranquil garden.

Chapter 5

A different world existed on the other side of Holyrood Hill. On the north side, "town," as it was known, driving turned into combat. While drivers didn't suddenly acquire intelligence, good manners, or keener eyesight upon entering the narrow streets of the village, at least there they were forced to slow down.

Salome always felt the energy change from an even flow to jagged and manic. One reason was town's proximity to the constant blasts of energy from Highway 1. Also, there were no signal lights at the four-way intersections. Drivers contemptuous of a mere stop sign, sailed through without waiting their turn. But perhaps no one could read anymore and needed colored lights for instruction.

To protect herself and her little pickup truck, she kept a small, faceted crystal on a nine-inch red ribbon hanging on her rearview mirror and, of course, drove defensively, spit out the window a lot (to rid herself of negative energy) and exercised her horn.

After about three blocks, she came to the shopping center—two outdoor areas positioned on either side of the four-lane street. The west side housed chain grocery, drug, and video stores and local retailers: a dry cleaner, a pizza place, a theater, and the best bookstore for miles, Holyrood Book Café. Unfortunately, the developers in their greed-inspired zeal neglected to provide enough parking. At times, traffic backed up a quarter of a mile to the highway where trees that could have absorbed much of the erratic energy had been thoughtlessly chopped down.

Taking up most of the space on the east side was O'Kelly's Hardware and Garden, O'Kelly's submarine sandwich shop, and a couple of barnacle stores that were mostly occupied in the summer and vacant in the winter. Behind O'Kelly's was the post office and set even further back were the new city government offices, including the police station on a lot landscaped with palm, pepper, eucalyptus, and acacia trees. She wondered if Phyl missed the old police station located down in the village across from the fire station. There, she'd had both home and the best restaurants within walking distance. At least plenty of trees surrounded this new building.

Salome parked in a visitors' slot behind the only black and white in the lot, all the others, no doubt, at the Perfume. She pried her fingers off the steering wheel and switched off the ignition. Leaning against the seat, she took a moment to relax, cupping the damaged part of her head.

The short drive had taken nearly twenty minutes when it should have taken five. But the rain had brought out hordes to shop for supplies. An all-news radio station spouted flood warnings, whipping up the frenzy.

You'd think, Salome thought, *people would simply prepare for winter before its arrival.*

Then she reminded herself, many of these people had never before lived in California, wouldn't even be here if the boom in Silicon Valley, just over the Santa Cruz Mountains, hadn't lured them with the same kind of lust as the 1849 Gold Rush. Now they arrived almost instantly, pouring off jets from all parts of the world. When San Jose popped its seams, any place within a radius of a hundred miles started feeling the pressure. The computer had turned the central coast into another Los Angeles. Housing was at a premium and traffic a nightmare. . . .

Suddenly Salome sat straighter, remembering the young woman who'd showed up at her door one recent morning.

Hello, she'd said brightly. She wore an expensive black suit and silver jewelry. As if accessorizing her stylish image, a shimmery silver Lexus was parked in the drive. "I'm looking for Salome Waterhouse."

"I'm Salome." Just moments before, she'd finished showering. Her long black hair streamed over the blue and white cotton yukata, a kimono-style robe.

Without preamble, the woman came right to the point. "My company is interested in buying the Perfume Mansion."

"It's not for sale."

The woman then handed Salome a business card. "We're prepared to pay the price on the back of the card."

Salome flipped the card over and looked at the astonishing sum.

"I told you it's not for sale. How did you find me?"

"Jason Twitchell sent me on up here."

Salome made a mental note to wring Jason's neck. He was not supposed to give out her name, let alone her address, to anyone. But maybe he hadn't been told. He'd only been with the property management firm a few months. And no doubt he was an easy mark for an attractive young woman.

Salome glanced briefly at the front of the card: Blair Farrell & Associates. An address and phone number in San Jose followed. Oddly, there was no reference to the sort of business they were in.

"Are you Blair Farrell?"

"One of the associates, Susan Truro." She pointed out her name on the card, then held out her hand.

Instead of a handshake, Salome returned the business card.

Undaunted, Susan continued. "It's our understanding that the mansion will soon be on the market."

"If Jason told you that, he's mistaken."

"Look, why don't we discuss this over coffee?"

"There's nothing to discuss. Now if you'll excuse me," Salome concluded and closed the door.

She had immediately telephoned Jason Twitchell. He blubbered an apology for sending Susan Truro to Salome's house but flatly denied saying the mansion was for sale.

Over the past couple of years people had begun appearing on her doorstep, offering to buy her cottage. She quickly sent them on their way and even, for a time, considered putting up a NOT FOR SALE sign. But this was the first time someone had come about the Perfume.

The umbrella sheltering her, Salome hurried across the lot, the police station indistinct behind the gauzy curtain of rain. Why, she wondered, would anyone at Blair Farrell & Associates, believe the Perfume was going to be on the market? And who the hell were they?

A moment later Salome entered the sterile, unfurnished lobby and pressed a buzzer beside a narrow bulletproof window, the stainless steel trough beneath it kept polished by the many parking tickets and payments that passed through en route to the city coffers. Soon, she hoped, some of that money would be spent on traffic lights at the swollen, lethal intersections.

Britta O'Kelly trotted up to the window, her hefty bosom stretching the daisies on the bodice of her cotton dress. In her early sixties, Britta was nearing retirement. Despite thirty-plus years of secretarial wages and constant exposure to the dark side of human nature, she always brought an ambassadorial attitude and smile to work. Replacing her would be next to impossible.

"Salome, dear! Didn't expect you so soon. Here, let me buzz you in."

Salome moved to the door to her left. Painted the same institutional gray as the walls rendered it nearly invisible.

The buzzer blared and she entered the large, newly carpeted squad room, a maze of gray partitions separating each desk. It was unnaturally quiet. The prevailing odor reminded her of the smell of a new car.

"Good heavens, what happened to you?"

"Just a bump."

"Phyl said you'd be coming in. If you would, honey, just pop down the hall and we'll get your necessaries: prints, hair, and blood. Frankly, I thought you'd need some time to recover. What a terrible ordeal for you," Britta said. Salome was relieved Britta didn't treat her like a suspect but then, Britta would have been just as gracious to Jack the Ripper.

After the "necessaries," Salome left her rain gear on a rack alongside Britta's yellow slicker and umbrella and sat down in a comfortable chair.

"Guess everyone's up at the Perfume," Salome commented, still wiping ink from her fingers with tissues.

"Been a while since we've had a murder. Everyone wants to get in on the action. Oh, by the way, Phyl said to tell you you're free to go up to the city but to check in when you leave and return."

So, Salome thought, not all compassion had been burned out of her cousin. "She happen to mention why she changed her mind?"

"Heavens no. But just between you and me? This is her first murder as police chief. She must have thought the county sheriff would be breathing down her neck but Sheriff Martinez is fishing in Cabo San Lucas. Won't be back for another week. The deputies are busy with those drive-bys up in Santa Cruz. She can pretty well run the investigation as she pleases.

"Can I get you something to drink, dear? Coffee? Tea?" She pulled out a bottom drawer and nodded toward it. Inside, Salome saw a bottle of Bushmill's Irish whiskey and two shot glasses.

"No thanks, but I appreciate the offer," Salome said, wondering if the libation supported Britta's cheerful attitude.

Salome removed the deposit slip, envelope, and letter enclosed in plastic from a leather portfolio. "Phyl wants these."

Britta set the plastic bag to one side. She placed a small tape recorder on the desk and handed Salome a lapel mike to attach to the front of her sweater.

"Well, let's get this unpleasant business out of the way, shall we?" Britta said, her fingers poised on the keyboard the tape recorder her backup.

"First I want to mention an incident that occurred, oh, maybe a week or so after Dad's heart attack. Around the new year. I'm not really sure of the date."

Salome told of the encounter with Susan Truro and Blair Farrell & Associates' interest in purchasing the Perfume. "Possibly someone in the company heard about Dad and figured he wouldn't survive. They might have assumed he owned the place since his firm has been handling the property for so many years.

"On the other hand, that someone might have been plotting to do away with Palmer. I know it's far-fetched. I hadn't even thought about it until just a few minutes ago. It just seems suspicious and I thought Phyl would want to know."

From there, Salome segued into her reason for being at the Perfume and the discovery of Palmer Fordham's body. Britta's fingers flew across the keyboard, her unflinching blue eyes glued to the monitor.

Salome concluded by noting that she'd given her uniform to Ralph Blue and that Phyl not only took her shoes but retained her briefcase at the scene.

"And that's it." She took a pen from her purse in anticipation of signing the printout of her statement. Though her head had begun to throb, she didn't consider the pain enough of a deterrent to keep from driving up to San Francisco. She was anxious to get to a phone and inform Mandy of the change in plans. With so much on her mind, she'd forgotten to pick up her cell phone on the Korean chest in the foyer.

Britta finally looked at Salome. But her fingers remained on the keyboard, a clue that she wasn't finished.

"Do you recall anything else, dear? Even the tiniest detail could prove helpful—like the woman offering to buy the Perfume."

Salome sighed. She placed the pen on Britta's desk then looked up toward the ceiling.

"Tell you what," Britta prompted. "Why don't we back up a bit. You began with an explanation of why you went to the Perfume, arriving at seven-thirty." Clearly, she hadn't just typed the words but listened carefully. "Tell me about when you left your house, no doubt excited about plying your most unusual skills on our most famous landmark."

She'd been so anxious to get the statement out of the way, she'd overlooked the early morning encounter with Janelle Phillips. Taking her time now, she included her personal feelings about the Perfume. She told of ringing the front door bell half a dozen times, half expecting Dora Whalen, the housekeeper, to answer.

Dora lived in the caretaker's cottage on the other side of Perfume Creek. A footbridge provided easy access to the mansion and had been worn smooth by several generations of Dora's family, her great-grandparents starting the tradition when the Perfume was first built.

"Even if Palmer was asleep, I planned to ask Dora if she wouldn't mind my going ahead with the consultation. After all, the two-thousand-dollar cash fee gave me extra concern about getting the job done."

"Are you familiar with Dora's schedule?"

"No."

"So you didn't know if she would be there at seven-thirty?"

"No, but given the size of the place, I just figured she probably starts early."

Finally, she came full circle to the beginning of her statement. Now she added a few details she'd automatically edited because of Phyl's skepticism about feng shui.

". . . how long I looked at him, I don't really know. As I

said before, the room was dim. Still, it's automatic with me, I immediately know the position on the Bagua of whatever I'm looking at. He was in the fame position of not only the living room but the house itself. Fame, reputation—" She stopped. Britta probably didn't have a clue what she was talking about.

"May I have a blank sheet of paper?"

Britta handed one over. As Salome drew a large octagon, she explained, "You see, the Bagua is a sort of template with fixed positions representing life's conditions."

As she'd done for the Women of Mystery, Salome automatically went into her spiel, though this time providing just a brief reference to each gua.

"The front door determines the starting point and will always be here"—she pointed to the bottom of the Bagua—"at either knowledge, career, or helpful people. Overall, when doing a house reading, you start with the front door, even if the occupants more often use another entrance. Then, you do the same with each room, using the entrance of the room or the door's position as the starting point. You still with me?"

"Oh yes. It's quite interesting. When you're finished, I'll attach it to your statement. Phyl just might find it helpful."

Salome doubted that. "Anyway," she continued, pointing to "fame" at the very top of the Bagua, "this is where I found Palmer." She then pointed to "career," directly opposite at the bottom of the sketch. "And this is where the front door to the Perfume is located.

"Naturally, I'd have to do a complete reading of the house to determine areas of his life where he might be having problems—*including*," she said with emphasis, "the sort of people he might be having problems with." That spurred the memory of the foul energy she'd sensed coming from the sublevel—an enemy of the house itself.

Britta's eyes widened. "Hmm. That could be useful."

"Makes me wonder: Did his fame, his reputation as an

artist have anything to do with his death? Certainly fame has been an integral part of his adult life. These days, it's all too common for fame to attract stalkers.

"Further, though metaphorically, art is in his blood and it is in the fame position that his blood was spilled. Now, this may sound, well, over the top, but his blood may provide a clue to whoever killed him."

Salome waved her hand. "I don't expect Phyl to go along with my impressions, no matter how strong they are . . . and one more thing. His legs looked relatively free of splatter. Granted, there wasn't much light, but given the excessive head and chest wounds, one would expect blood to be all over the place, which leads me to wonder if he was dead *before* he was so viciously attacked."

Britta seemed to take Salome's speculations seriously. "Well, we'll just have to see what shows up on the photographs and in the coroner's report. But you have a good eye for detail. Must be all those years doing research for your husband."

Salome tried to look pleasant.

"He's one of my favorite mystery writers. Anything forthcoming?"

Salome exhaled a long breath. "He has a new research assistant," she remarked, the unwelcome image of a thirty-year-old woman with thick blond hair and a voluptuous shape appearing in her mind crisp as a photograph.

Britta winced then patted her hand. "Sorry, dear. I forgot you're divorced."

A short time later, Salome initialed each page of the printout, then signed and dated the last page.

She collected her rain gear and Britta walked her to the door.

"And how is your father doing?"

"Very well, considering. Doesn't move quite so fast since the heart attack but at least he's moving."

"And your mother?"

"Just fine. Never learned the meaning of 'retirement.' "

"Oh how I envy her having you close."

"Well, only during the winter. Georgetown's still home base."

"At least she gets you part of the time. I rarely see any of my kids and grandkids—and they're not on the other side of the country."

A widow for the past two years, Britta was too people-oriented to care for single living. But she'd married into the ubiquitous O'Kelly clan and probably couldn't step out her door without bumping into one of her in-laws.

"Still, you have plenty of family around."

"Since Pat died I don't see much of my in-laws. At least, socially." Then, as if someone might overhear her, she lowered her voice. "Thing is, I never did get along with them. Couldn't abide some of their silly notions, if you know what I mean."

Salome knew exactly what she meant.

Early in the twentieth century, Kevin O'Kelly and Salome's grandfather, Joshua Waterhouse, had been business partners, builders responsible for the village's distinct storybook character. But during the construction of the Perfume Mansion, they had turned on each other, the poison of their bitter hatred flowing into their respective bloodlines.

Petty quarrels and lawsuits continued into the next generation, escalating into an act of particular viciousness. At the end of World War II and shortly after Salome's birth, Brian O'Kelly, Kevin's oldest son, tried to pass a city ordinance forbidding residency to *anyone* of Japanese descent; allowing them admittance to Holyrood only as house servants or gardeners. Had it passed, Salome's parents, Reginald and Satomi Waterhouse, Satomi being Nisei, a second-generation Japanese-American, would have been forced to move. The ordinance received little support but served to refresh the animosity between the families, keeping the feud alive.

Salome had always tried to resist participation in the hos-
tilities with the O'Kellys, avid supporters of the internment
of Japanese-Americans from 1942 through 1945. Though she
had suffered certain indignities fostered by the O'Kellys, she
harbored no animosity toward Britta simply because of family ties. Besides, as a feng shui practitioner, her purpose was
to help anyone.

"Listen, why don't you make a copy of the Bagua I drew.
When you go home tonight, locate the children position in
your house. If a window is there, hang a small, faceted crystal on a nine-inch red ribbon or cord. If there's a wall, put
up pictures of your children and grandchildren. By doing so,
and thinking about how much you'd like to see them, you'll
be stimulating that area of your life."

"That doesn't seem like much. You think it will help?"

"I *know* it will. But keep me posted. It's a start. There's
more we can do if you'd like."

A moment later they parted company.

Salome located the public telephones in a breezeway and
used a prepaid phone card she kept in her wallet. Mandy
answered after the second ring. Salome had to stick a finger
in her ear so as to hear his voice over what sounded like a
steady stream of rocks hitting the pavement.

"What's going on? Why can't you come up?"

"Phyl wouldn't let me leave town which is why I canceled
earlier. But that's changed and I can come up now."

"What does Phyl have to do with it?"

"Mandy, there's been a murder. Unfortunately, I found the
body . . . can you hear me?"

"Me and everybody else in the neighborhood. No need to
shout, honey."

Salome glanced around. Had anyone overheard her? A few
people passed into the city offices but no one paid her any
mind.

"I'm calling from a public phone outside the cop shop and

can barely hear you for the rain," she said, lowering her voice.

"It's pissing here, too. So who's the victim?"

"Guy named Palmer Fordham. My tenant at the Perfume."

"Jeeze la bloody wheeze!" Mandy exclaimed. "Honey, I know him!" Then he amended his declaration. "Knew him. Look, you'll be risking your life driving up now. Besides, Jeremy's here and we broke out the champagne early since you canceled. There's a huge party at Murph's I was going to take you to later. Pre-Chinese New Year sort of thing. How about I call you mañana? We'll re*shedy*ule—as Jeremy would say."

Not until his midthirties, after two marriages, did Manderson Monroe finally accept his homosexuality. But when he did, it was with abundant enthusiasm, like someone suddenly discovering they'd been living in the wrong country, speaking the wrong language. Then, two years ago, he learned he had AIDS. Many times she offered to do a reading on his flat but he always found some excuse to put it off. Finally, last November, he agreed. Then last week he'd called to tell her his doctor wanted to do a biopsy to determine whether or not he had colon cancer. With the possibility of bad news on the horizon, she'd quickly offered her services to further enhance the health areas in his flat and so they'd set up today's appointment.

"Augmenting the health sectors is really important now, Mandy. Did you hang the wind chime in your hallway like I suggested?"

"I'm looking at it right now!"

Salome sighed. "Good."

"Jeremy's holding it."

The hallway in question was about twelve feet in height. "Mandy, unless Jeremy's a giant, you need to hang it!"

"So did Phyl tell you to stay in town before or after you told her we had an appointment?"

"She's conducting a murder investigation, Mandy. Her decision had nothing to do with you."

"Look, get your bod home. I'll hoist a few glasses in your name and we'll talk tommary. Love ya."

The line went dead. Salome hung up, disappointed that Mandy hadn't taken the November consultation seriously. Still, just because he hadn't hung the wind chime didn't mean he'd ignored all the other suggestions. She made a mental note to take the stepladder with her when they settled on a time for her to go up to see him. If necessary, she'd hang the wind chime herself.

She felt a little weak, and her head hurt. A bench was nearby. She sat down and looked out at the rain.

People came and went in and out of the city offices. No one even gave her a second look. Certainly the rain focused attention but still, she was a middle-aged woman and, even had the sun been shining, middle-aged women were, for the most part, invisible.

Whenever she went to a local convenience store to play the lottery, the clerk invariably ignored her, always chattered on to his cohort. Even when she stood right in front of him at the cash register, waving the Lotto ticket. Though she knew the color of his eyes, she was certain he didn't know the color of hers.

Maybe her ex-husband had been preparing her for this phase of her life during the last years of their marriage. After a day researching a part of his current mystery novel, she'd carry the printouts, pertinent points highlighted in green, from her home office to his. Rarely did his eyes leave the computer screen. She'd pull up a chair. He'd lean toward her then glance down at the notes, then back at the screen. Even when she pointed out certain areas, he never actually looked at her face. Sometimes while she talked, he would simply stare out the windows overlooking the lawn of vibrant green that gradually merged with a deep forest separating their property from that of a retired CIA agent in McLean, Virginia. But never at her.

But there was someone who broke the rule, who *studied* middle-aged women, and using his artistic gifts transformed them into sea goddesses. Palmer Fordham. A middle-aged woman had brought him to the attention of the world. And he had been having an affair with a middle-aged woman, Barbara Boatwright.

Oh dear, she thought, as a grim scene projected on her mind: Barbara and Palmer enjoying a glass of wine together. Her husband, Charles, suddenly charging through the French doors, dragging Palmer to the floor then battering him to death.

Opening her umbrella, Salome dashed through the rain to her car, leaving the vision behind. For one thing, the reasonably tidy crime scene didn't fit the imagined scenario. For another, Charles Boatwright was in South America and not expected back until March. Still, he might have returned early.

For a moment, she considered returning to the police station to add to her statement what she'd seen at Barbara's in December; what she'd heard from Barbara herself. But if the affair had nothing to do with Palmer's murder she'd be stirring up unnecessary trouble. No. It was for Barbara to come forward on her own, and not for Salome to force the issue. At least, not yet.

Turning on the engine, she was reminded of how murder complicated the lives of so many people, even those on the periphery of the crime. But she wasn't on the periphery, and had been rudely tossed center stage. Maybe the time had come to apply what she'd learned about criminal investigation as Gabe's researcher—and hoped she could make the transition from fiction to reality without getting anyone killed. Herself included.

Chapter 6

WE try on clothes and test drive cars before buying, so why not spend a night in an apartment or house before moving in? Since studying feng shui, that had been Salome's view, knowing that the place we call home has more influence on our lives than we suspect and that we should take great care before making a commitment. She'd said just that to Palmer Fordam the November day they'd met in the offices of Waterhouse Properties after he'd passed all the requisite checks and had only to sign the lease.

"My God, I've never heard of *that* before!" he'd exclaimed. "Bet that doesn't make you popular with real estate people."

"The Perfume's my property. Just thought you might want to acquaint yourself with the resident ghosts. See if you get along."

He'd laughed, displaying teeth as perfect as the rest of him. But no, a night on the premises would make no difference.

"I *have* to live there, Ms. Waterhouse. Just give me the lease and a pen then I'll take you out for a drink."

As Salome crested Holyrood Hill and began her descent into the less-trafficked village, her jaw unclenched as her thoughts turned from surviving traffic to Palmer Fordham.

Given his sudden and dramatic reappearance in her life, their meeting seemed like days rather than years ago. She felt heartened that she could so clearly bring to mind his handsome features, that seeing his brutally beaten corpse hadn't obliterated her memory of him. Still, the man himself remained a mystery. Which is why she now parked in the tiny lot beside Waterhouse Properties, the first step in remedying her ignorance. Though she felt an urgent need to clean her cottage and perform a blessing ritual to protect herself from whatever sha she might encounter in the days ahead, as she'd learned from working with Gabriel, the more one knew about a victim the sooner one came to finding their killer.

Color photographs of available properties, details printed beneath them on card stock, lined the street-side windows of Waterhouse Properties. Passersby could stop and study the houses and condos for lease or sale, many no doubt disbelieving the prices. If the American dream had its foundation in property ownership, then on the California coast the dream had transmogrified into a nightmare. Coming from a family rich in property—not only did they own a substantial portion of Holyrood, what they didn't they managed for others who lived elsewhere—Salome was lucky. She may not have a love life, but most likely she'd always have a roof.

A bell on the inside door jingled as Salome entered with a brisk, wet gust of wind that sent the top pages of a legal-sized document on Jason Twitchell's desk flying.

"God, I hate this weather," he moaned, scooting in his swivel chair to the side of the desk to collect the papers. In his early twenties, Jason was the son of Cass Twitchell, the hottest agent at Waterhouse Properties until her retirement and move to Maui last year. Like his mother, he usually dressed with taste and style. Today, though, he wore jeans and an Oxford cloth shirt that might have been plucked from a laundry hamper. In general, he appeared to be paying for the night before.

"Wouldn't happen to have coffee with you?"

"The coffeemaker busted?" Salome asked as she hung her coat on the rack just inside the door beside the black umbrella stand. There were two other desks, both cleared of all but a telephone on each.

"Uh, well, Beth was supposed to make it."

So, Salome thought, Jason hadn't figured out how to use the coffeemaker. Or, most likely, expected someone else to take care of the chore.

"She called and asked me to come in to cover for her. This was her day to open up. She left soon as I got here. At least I didn't have any appointments scheduled. But who cares about real estate in this weather—except to hope it doesn't wash away."

"I'll put a pot on."

"Hey, thanks."

She moved down a short hall to an alcove where the coffeemaker sat stop a small fridge. While making coffee, she helped herself to a container of yogurt, wondering why Beth McCormick had left the office. A highly competitive agent, Beth never missed an opportunity. Bad weather didn't factor in to her pursuit of a sale. Had a police officer come in to pick up keys to the Perfume, delivering the news of Palmer's death? Still, that wouldn't give her cause to leave work. Or would it?

Again she thought of Dora and her parents, those who also had keys to the Perfume. She felt a twinge at the thought of the police delivering the news to her parents while picking up her father's set.

Certainly, it was natural for the lead detective to maintain control of the crime scene by any means. However, she couldn't imagine anyone who had keys actually letting themselves in while the investigation was underway. Reminded of Phyl's obsession with the mansion, the skin on her neck and shoulders prickled.

While the coffee brewed, Salome slipped into the room across the hall, where the records were kept the old-fashioned way, in tall file cabinets. A short wide cabinet held the blueprints for various properties. It was from there she'd borrowed the blueprints for the Perfume after receiving the anonymous letter.

Extracting a manila folder with Palmer's name on it, she shuffled through copies of various repair and gardening bills and a rent increase notice sent a year and a half ago, before finding Palmer's five-year-old lease application and attached credit check.

She made copies of the two sheets and was about to put the file back when she had a thought. It might be a good idea to check the names on the waiting list, those people who'd been interested in buying or leasing the mansion when it became available five years ago, some of whom would still have applications on file. There might be others added to the list since then—Blair Farrell & Associates immediately came to mind. She'd have to start thinking about finding a new tenant since the Perfume provided a sizeable portion of her monthly income.

Money from her feng shui practice was sporadic and depended largely on new clients—that was one thing about being good at what she did. Once she'd helped a client they didn't require her services again for a while.

Twice she checked the file and still couldn't find the list or any additional applications. Unfamiliar with the firm's policy on such matters, she wondered if they'd been tossed or were in a separate file. She'd have to ask. But having lived so long with a writer always dreaming up new ways to do away with people had made her more suspicious. Gabriel would certainly agree that the possibility existed that someone wanted the Perfume badly enough to kill for it.

Salome replaced the file in the cabinet and returned to the

alcove. As the coffee finished brewing, she read the rental application Palmer had filled out five years ago.

Per politically correct standards, the form didn't have spaces for date of birth, gender, or race. If today really was his birthday, the proof would have to be found elsewhere.

At the time he filled out the application, he'd been living at 221B Creekside, the converted garage behind 221, a two-story house sporting a windmill located beside the Perfume Creek, his landlord a local art dealer, Rita Van Horn. Located several houses south of Dora Whalen's cottage, Palmer had resided for three years in the shadow of the Perfume mansion.

He'd listed his previous address as an apartment on Pine Street in San Francisco, and had lived there six years.

Under both present and prior occupation he had written "Self-artist," with the "present" showing an enviable gross income.

Credit references included an account with Wells Fargo bank, first opened nine years ago, and a Visa card he'd had for over a decade. His credit report gave him high marks indicating he'd never had money problems.

Of the two personal references, one was Rita Van Horn. The second, a William Renfro, "art school instructor," address and phone at the San Francisco Art Institute.

Finally, under "Nearest Relative" he'd written Babette Fordham, sister, address and phone number in Houston, Texas.

Salome folded the sheets and slipped them in her pocket.

"How do you take your coffee?" she called out to Jason. Though she didn't particularly like catering to him, especially after he'd so willingly provided Susan Truro with her address, Jason Twitchell was a source of information.

"Black, uh, thanks."

Carrying two steaming mugs, a pile of cookies on a saucer atop one, she entered the outer office and sat in the chair beside the desk.

He wolfed down a cookie then sipped his coffee.

"Don't you make coffee when it's your turn to open up?"

"I just pick up something from Billie Ruth's bakery. Uh, I'm not really good with machinery."

A coffee maker? Machinery?

"So why did Beth leave?"

Jason's hazel eyes widened and he suddenly sat far back in his chair as if moving away from danger. "Oh gosh! You don't know about the—the—" he stammered.

"The murder? I know."

Relief flooded out of him. After a beat, he took a deep breath and sat straighter. "From her babbling over the phone, I finally made out that the police had just been here to pick up keys to the Perfume because Palmer Fordham had been murdered.

"When I got here, she was slumped over the desk, crying her eyes out. She said something about this being like the day Kennedy was shot."

They were silent for a moment as Salome digested that bit of hyperbole.

"Did she say if she'd called my parents?"

"No."

"Did you?"

He gave her a horrified look. "Was I supposed to?"

"No, no. Don't worry about it. Remember Susan Truro from Blair & Associates?"

His expression segued into embarrassment, color rising from neck to hairline. "I told you I was sorry about that."

"Anything you remember about her?"

"It's Blair *Farrell* & Associates. Sure, I remember Susan. I've been trying to hook up with her. Even drove over to San Jose one afternoon to surprise her but she wasn't in."

"What do they do?"

"They're high-powered publicists. When I was there? Well, the receptionist asked if I was a client. I said a *potential* client—just joking, really. But she took me seriously. My clothes probably convinced her—I don't normally look so messy."

"I know. Go on."

"Now look, don't get pissed—I mean angry." He took a deep breath. "I said I'd come to see Susan about a property the company had expressed interest in buying in Holyrood."

He surprised her by suddenly raising both hands and looked resigned. "Fire me if you want. I just got my degree in marine biology and would rather be working with dolphins. Unfortunately so do about a million other people around here—"

Salome interrupted. "Jason, I'm just a client. Waterhouse Properties manages my property. I can come and go as I please but I neither hire nor fire agents."

Jason relaxed.

"You named the Perfume specifically, right?"

"Well, yeah. So, anyway, the receptionist called Blair Farrell herself. She was really vivacious and friendly and almost as good-looking as Susan but a lot older. I mean, there's nothing wrong with older women but—"

Salome intervened again before he dug a hole for himself. "Jason. Get on with it."

"Anyway, she gave me the tour of their offices. They handle big Silicon Valley computer companies, a few rock groups, and movie stars who live in the Bay Area, some up-and-coming game design companies—she shows me all these posters and packaging stuff and monitors all around that display TV ads. I figure she's into some sort of exclusivity thing—like those stores that have no price tags on things—know what I mean? If you have to ask what something costs, you shouldn't be there. Must be why they don't put what they do on their business cards. But, anyway, it was obvious she was showing off, letting me know she had the bucks to buy a property like the Perfume.

"Then we go to her office. I'm sitting in front of this huge glass desk. What do you think is on the wall behind it?"

She was beginning to lose patience. "The shrunken head of a competitor? I don't know."

Either he hadn't been listening or chose to ignore the comment. "Here's this gorgeous woman stepping out of a powder blue ocean onto a bridge. The waves were painted like pink begonias and the water dripping off her body was the begonia petals that made the waves. Know what I mean? Kind of like Escher's work only with turgid, red-rimmed flower petals. Totally awesome."

"A Palmer Fordham sea goddess."

"And the subject, the woman, was Blair Farrell! Anyway, she tells me she's his publicist, the one who got his career going.

"Ms. Farrell said San Jose was getting too much like L.A. for her taste and she wanted to move to Holyrood and work from a home office in the Perfume a few days a week. She said Palmer planned to leave California and *he* suggested that she contact Waterhouse Properties and talk to us. She didn't want to be on a waiting list and offered a hundred thousand over the top bid."

He lowered his eyes for a moment, seemingly mulling over something.

"When was this?" Salome asked impatiently.

"Couple weeks ago. Susan hadn't been returning my calls—that's why I decided to just go over there and surprise her. Anyway, after I got back to Holyrood, I called Mother and told her about it." He played with a pen for a moment then looked up. "Thing is Blair Farrell offered me an extra ten percent above the regular commission. Mother had a fit. She said it was nothing more than a bribe and besides, Beth McCormick handled the Perfume and if she found out I was making a deal behind her back, well, I'd be in deep poop.

"The next time I saw Beth I told her there'd been some inquiries about the Perfume. She got real haughty and said *she* was taking care of the sale, that any calls about the Perfume were to be directed to her and her alone. I thought it was kind of weird she didn't ask me *who* inquired."

Salome's annoyance morphed into anger. "The Perfume is not for sale! As the owner, I think I'd know."

"Yeah, sounds fishy."

Her head began to ache. She definitely needed something more substantial than yogurt and cookies.

"Do me a favor. Keep your eyes and ears open. And another thing," she said, going to the rack and putting on the Drizabone, "the waiting list and old applications aren't in the Perfume's file. I just looked. Would they be kept separately?"

"They should be in the file. Beth would know."

"Would you mind giving her a call and ask? Tell her I need them."

While snapping up her coat, she peered out the pane of glass in the door. She could barely make out the bikini shop across the street for the opaque sheets of rain. Something shiny, a gum wrapper maybe, caught her eye. Oddly, it seemed to move toward her. Then she realized it sailed on water spilling over the sidewalk.

"Look, I really don't feel like calling her now," Jason said. "I mean she was so—"

"Hell's bells!" Salome cried, cutting him off. "The street's flooding! See if you can find some towels and put them at the door." She jerked open the door. "Be back in a flash!"

With that, she ran to her truck, leaving a startled Jason Twitchell wishing he hadn't answered his phone that morning.

Chapter 7

THE fire station was just two blocks up the street. A Lincoln Town Car was backed up to one of the two bays, the trunk open. In the adjacent bay, a spotless fire truck stood at the ready, engine aimed at the street. Salome parked nearby and dashed into the cavernous interior.

An attractive young fireman in a short-sleeved dark blue uniform and a local restauranteur, Hector Gonzaga, loaded sandbags into the Lincoln's trunk while Rita Van Horn, owner of the Sand and Sea Gallery, stood nearby, her pointy nose and chin appearing to have been recently sharpened. Beads of water glittered on her heavily lacquered black hair. Her makeup would have been perfect but for the false eyelash coming unglued at the outer edge of her left eye, probably from all the moisture in the air. She wore a lightweight dollar green raincoat and matching boots, the color of money a good match for her eyes. Though not beautiful, possibly because she tried too hard to conceal her age, at sixty she was still a striking woman.

"What a horrid day!" Rita announced. "You hear about Palmer?"

Salome nodded, moving further into the bay.

"The esplanade's flooding. Everyone else closed up and

sandbagged this morning. Hector and I are the only ones who've stayed open. But with Palmer dead I expect a lot of business. His paintings'll be worth a fortune now. At least the phone's aren't down."

Salome was taken aback by Rita's lack of emotion. "Yes, but it's still early for the news to have gotten out. How did you hear?"

"Hector popped into the gallery around ten-thirty. Cops had just been to see him. Seems they found food cartons and a receipt from his restaurant at the Perfume, indicating a delivery last night. Hector thought I'd need to know since I still handle some of Palmer's business."

Her eyes hardened and she spoke with authority. "It was a large order. Too much for one person and Palmer wasn't a big eater. Clearly he had company last night."

Abruptly, she turned to Hector. "That's enough, Hector. I need to get back."

"Salome, *chica*," Hector said pleasantly, though winded from his exertions. He wiped his sweaty face and dirty hands on a towel pulled from the back pocket of his jeans. Beneath a damp windbreaker, he wore an apron tied at the neck, now gritty with sand. He must have come straight from the kitchen. "What happened to your head?"

"Just a bump," she said. At least he'd noticed, which was more than she could say for Rita—or Jason for that matter. But she patronized Hector's restaurant and rarely went into Rita's gallery. As for Jason, to him her age made her about as substantial as fog.

Rita trotted over to the driver's side. "Wipe off your pants before you get in."

Hector rolled his eyes and closed the trunk. He offered to bring cioppino to the fireman later. "Made fresh this morning. Hate to see it go to waste." The two men shook hands then he spoke to Salome. "If you're hungry, come on over. I'll feed you. On the house. I'll be camping out at the restaurant."

"Sounds wonderful, Hector. I was just thinking about food."

"Hector!" Rita snapped.

"The Boss Lady calls."

Once they left, Salome backed the pickup into the vacated space, glad to note the pile of sandbags hadn't been depleted altogether. She introduced herself to the fireman.

"Clay Bethune," he said.

"I need a small load for Waterhouse Properties."

As they began hoisting the heavy burlap bags into the bed of the pickup, she wondered if any were the ones she'd filled. Every year, in preparation for winter storms, the locals, many of them business owners, volunteered for the job though the bags were for anyone who might need them. Salome had been doing it since her teens.

Together they loaded nine into the truck.

When they finished, he asked, "Got someone to help you unload?"

She nodded and thanked him then drove back to the property management firm. Salome and Jason sandbagged the front and side doors. Having left the top half of the Dutch side door open, Jason was able to reenter the office by vaulting over the lower half. He said he'd try to reach Beth and if he had any news would call Salome.

Her estimation of him climbed a few notches when he didn't complain about sticking around when so many other businesses in the village had closed because of the foul weather.

By the time she was back behind the wheel, her stomach was squawking as loud as her head. She mentally reviewed the contents of her refrigerator but nothing drew her like the thought of Hector's cioppino, a hearty seafood soup. Besides, she and Palmer had had a celebratory drink at the Beach Bistro after he signed the lease. Maybe by returning to the restaurant, she could recall a few more details about the man.

All the shops, restaurants, and galleries on both sides of

the esplanade had sandbags piled at the entrances. She parked in front of the Beach Bistro beside Hector's rusting '76 Toyota. The only other car in sight was Rita Van Horn's sleek Lincoln, parked just across the street. Easy to see why they'd used Rita's car to collect sandbags; the Toyota itself would have fit in the Lincoln's trunk.

Water rushed down the narrow passageways between the one-story buildings and down onto the beach, the runoff bypassing the back entrances.

Sandbags were piled at the side kitchen door, so Salome sloshed with the flowing water to the back patio, where white metal tables and chairs were stacked against a long wall of glass. Most of the beach was under heavy surf but at least the water hadn't breached the seawall. She banged on the sliding glass door that opened onto the patio. A moment later Hector appeared.

"Come in, come in!"

"For the price of lunch I'll take cioppino to that cute fireman," she offered as he quickly shut the door behind her.

He laughed. "You got a deal! Cioppino okay for you, too?"

"Absolutely."

He spread out his arms. "Sit wherever you want, Salome. The restaurant's yours today." He then went off to the kitchen.

Salome slid onto a wooden stool at the end of the bar— the same seat she'd occupied five years ago when Palmer had bought her a glass of wine after signing the lease. She removed her coat and stared at the empty seat beside her, conjuring up Palmer's image. He'd been wearing a pale blue polo shirt, crisply pressed khaki trousers, and Docksiders without socks. His tan emphasized bright blue eyes and short champagne-colored hair. His hands and fingernails were clean and free of any trace of paint. She thought he looked more like a man who did a lot of business on the golf course, rather than an artist. Nor did he fit the stereotype of an artist suffering the "pain" in painting.

"What's a matter? That seat dirty?" Hector asked. He carried a tray with a large, steaming bowl of cioppino, a basket of bread, and a ramekin of butter.

Salome looked up, somewhat startled. "Nothing of the sort. I was just thinking."

He set down a paper placemat, napkin, and cutlery, then set the food in front of her.

"In fact, I was thinking of Palmer Fordham. We had a drink here, in this very spot the day he moved into the Perfume."

"Hate to think some crazy's loose, killing people. Bad for business." Then he added with a cynical expression, "But I gotta be honest with you, Salome, I wouldn't a cried if someone whacked him two years ago."

"Why? What happened?" Salome buttered a slice of sour dough while mentally saying her version of grace, thanking all the life forms that had gone into the creation of her aromatic meal.

Hector nodded at the painting behind the bar, in pride of place between mirror-backed shelves of liquor bottles and glasses. His wife, Dolores, partially in profile, seemed to be dancing on a dark angry sea in a red and black ruffled flamenco costume intricately painted to resemble foamy, crashing waves. Her black hair was pulled back severely in a bun at her neck and a small seahorse had been painted in front of her ear to resemble a spit curl. Her hands were high above her head with clamshell castanets in her curled fingers. The painting oozed passion and power and it was hard to tell if Dolores danced to the tune of the sea or if the sea moved to her beat.

Salome glanced at the painting. "It's stunning, Hector. Of the ones I've seen, it's always been a favorite."

Beneath his apron, his chest puffed out. "Yeah, stunning—made my life *stunning*."

Then he looked at Salome sweetly, his head cocked. 'Hector,' " he said in dulcet tones, mimicking his wife, " 'Hector, Palmer Fordham wants to paint me.' Fine I say. Just be sure it washes off. Dolores, she don't laugh. But, Dolores is a beautiful woman. So, I think, why not. But, I tell her, I have to hang it in the restaurant. Good for business, you know—"

Hector stopped abruptly. "Oh! You want some wine? How is it?" he asked, eyeing the bowl.

"Wonderful," Salome said. "No wine, thanks."

Hector then resumed his narrative. "So anyway, couple a weeks later Dolores and Palmer bring me the painting. Gorgeous, stunning. Then Dolores ruins my day. She says, 'Hector, you owe Palmer twenty thousand dollars.' "

Hector paused to pour himself a glass of the house Merlot, the product of a local vintner. After a lip-smacking, fortifying sip, he said, "So, after I pick myself up off the floor, wondering if I'm gonna have a heart attack, I grab the bat behind the bar and go after them both."

Salome didn't stop spoon-to-mouthing despite the vision of Palmer's beaten body that flashed before her eyes. A part of her wondered if a baseball bat had been the murder weapon, and of course, if Hector had been the slugger. Still, she doubted he'd be speaking to her so ingenuously if he were guilty.

"And," Salome prompted.

"Like a fool, I chase them out to the street. It's September, hot, lotsa tourists, lotsa *witnesses*. Dolores is screaming. Palmer, he stops. He asks Dolores why she didn't tell me the cost. She screams at him, she screams at me. Palmer, real calm, says his lawyer will be in touch then walks away real cocky-like. Dolores gets in her car and races off, nearly killing a couple a tourists. I get home that night, Dolores ain't there but a note is. She's gone to her mother's place up in Half Moon Bay. I call. We talk. She's gonna divorce me if I don't pay Palmer. I call my lawyer. He says, 'Hector, take out a loan.' It'll be cheaper than a divorce and a lawsuit and I'll get to keep my restaurant."

He drank more wine, his gaze now focused on the heavy surf behind her, possibly looking for a time when life was simpler, a day at the beach, a *sunny* day at the beach.

"Well, I'm certainly glad you're still cooking," Salome remarked.

"Hell, Salome. It's all I know. Hard to believe, but I been working here going on fifty years. Started out washing dishes and busing tables when Mom owned the place."

He pulled a pack of unfiltered cigarettes from the pocket of his shirt, shook one out, and stuck it in the corner of his mouth. With a click, he popped the top of an old Zippo.

"Not gonna turn me in, are you?" he asked with a sad, ironic smile. In California, a law forbidding smoking in all public buildings, including bars and restaurants, had been in effect for several years.

"Far as I'm concerned you should be able to do what you want within the confines of your own business."

"Big Brother, he don't just watch anymore, he moved in with us." Hector sighed, finished his wine, then refilled the glass. "Sure I can't interest you in a taste?"

She hesitated. A shared glass often resulted in a shared confidence. Not that he'd been reticent. But there might be more he could tell her. "Why not?"

He set down a glass of the dark red Merlot. She'd just have a few sips.

"Nothing's been the same between me and Dolores since."

"You mean, since the painting?"

He nodded. "Thank God our kids are grown."

"You still paying off the loan?"

His face filled with anger. "Probably for the resta my life. But I gotta say, that Palmer Fordham, he had some *cojones* on him.

"After I paid him—and he'd only take a cashier's check—he was in here at least once a week. Ordered takeout, what, three, four times a month. I catered his last two Halloween parties. We're talking big bucks for that. Still, like I said, me and Dolores don't have the same relationship. She shoulda told me how much a sitting cost. 'Course, he was famous and I guess his signature's ninety percent of the price."

"Rita told me the cops found takeout from here up at the Perfume."

"Man, did they give me a scare! Yeah! Delivered the food myself. I get a call about midnight, a little late, but it's the Perfume Mansion so I do my best to put together this meal and then delivered it."

"Did Palmer call in the order?"

"Some woman. Palmer, he knows when the restaurant closes but sometimes, he has a little too much to drink and forgets the time."

"You recognize the voice?"

"Didn't pay much attention except to the order—sixty bucks' worth."

"Did you call back to confirm?"

"Nah. Hell, it's the Perfume! Anyway, I drive up there. No light on. I'm fumbling around for the bell when I see this envelope propped by one a the double doors. 'Beach Bistro' written on it. I opened it and inside was the exact amount of money for the order plus a twenty percent tip. So, I rang the bell a few times, and when no one answered, left the order and came on back to the restaurant."

The food must have made its way from the front door downstairs because Salome hadn't seen any deliveries at the door when she arrived that morning.

Cops said they found the bag with the receipt stapled to it, along with the empty cartons in the kitchen."

Salome wondered if the food from the Beach Bistro would match Palmer's stomach contents. If so, that he'd eaten sometime after midnight, time of death would be more easily established.

"What time did you make the delivery?"

"Musta been about quarter to one."

"Did you give the envelope the money was in to the cops?" Salome asked.

He frowned. "Nobody asked for it. Huh. Now that I think about it, I just told them the money was at the door."

"Do you still have it? The envelope."

"Gee, don't know. Musta tossed it when I tallied the night's receipts. Hey, might help the investigation, huh? I'll just see if I can find it. You set here? Want a second helping?"

"I'm fine, Hector."

When he left, Salome resumed her musings about Palmer. After a moment she recalled that he'd given her a verbal resume of his unusual rise to fame.

Chapter 8

☯

LIKE many artists on the coast, he launched his career painting seascapes.

"You paint what you see, right?" he'd said.

But the competition was fierce and money spread too thinly. He turned to painting portraits on commission. It paid the rent but little more. He began doing nude studies and found he was quite good but now his money went to pay models. He looked for a gimmick, something to put him on the map. Finally he found it in Botticelli's "Venus on the Halfshell" and a serendipitous encounter with a Chinese-American woman by the name of Rose Tang.

A student at San Francisco State, Rose had skipped classes to spend a day swimming at Holyrood Beach. It being the off-season, no lifeguards were on duty. The sea was reasonably calm and Rose thought nothing of swimming out about a hundred yards from shore until her long hair became tangled in the thick kelp beds. She had to kick to stay afloat and the more she kicked the more entangled she became. Had Palmer not been surfing nearby, she might have succumbed to exhaustion and drowned. As it happened though, Palmer heard her cries for help, pulled her from the kelp and onto his board and paddled back to shore.

In gratitude, Rose offered him money. Instead, he asked if she'd model for him. She ended up staying three days, during which they became lovers. He painted her coming out of a jade green sea, her waist length black hair transformed into opaque ropes of kelp that entwined her arms and legs while her athletic body strained against the pull of the sea. But that wasn't enough. He turned the foam on the waves into delicately wrought rosebuds.

"It was the most powerful piece I'd ever done," Palmer had said. "Female beauty and strength and the will to survive in a sea both beautiful and dangerous. Didn't hurt that I was in love with her." Then he went on.

Rose went back to school, promising to come down when she could. Palmer showed the painting, which he now called *"Rose Rising"* to Rita Van Horn. She'd been showing his seascapes for about a year but not that many had sold. He also worked in the gallery, doing general labor and sales and filled in when she went on selling trips.

She showed little interest in the painting but at the time was busy packing for a week-long selling trip to New York. To his further disappointment, she hadn't included any of his work.

After she left, Palmer replaced the paintings in the storefront window with *"Rose Rising,"* even though he knew it might cost him his job.

Two days later a tall, middle-aged man entered the gallery, wanting to know how he could get in touch with the artist of the painting displayed in the window. Palmer eagerly declared himself to be the artist.

"I'm Arthur Rush," the man said.

Palmer instantly recognized the iconoclastic filmmaker's name. Just the previous year he'd been nominated for best director for *The Epiphany*, a quasi-supernatural sci-fi thriller about a nuclear scientist believed to be the Antichrist—another in a string of box office successes.

Instantly, Palmer envisioned himself working in the art department on Arthur Rush's next movie.

"Tell me, is your model real?"

Palmer's airy vision vanished as quickly as it had appeared. Rush wanted to contact Rose. Still he offered Palmer a thousand dollars for the painting—as long as it came with her phone number.

Palmer refused to simply hand over her number even if it did come with a thousand-dollar price tag. He told the filmmaker to come back later, that he'd have to talk to Rose himself. That was fine, Rush said. He was staying at the Otter Haven Resort, having come to the area to scout additional locations for a film he was shooting down the coast in Big Sur.

Palmer immediately took the painting to the print shop at another gallery, with a rush order for a print run of two hundred.

Then he called Rose with the news.

Rose and Arthur Rush met in the gallery the next day. He hired her on the spot in a supporting role, neither of them concerned in the least that she'd never acted before. To his credit, Arthur Rush gave Palmer a check for a thousand dollars plus shipping costs and an address in Los Angeles, where the painting was to be sent.

Rose was thrilled and before leaving with Rush pledged Palmer her undying love.

He never saw her again. In the flesh, anyway. When the film was released nine months later, Rose's picture was splashed all over the media, usually on the arm of Arthur Rush. Though he felt stung that she'd never contacted him again, Palmer did hope to cash in on her success by selling the prints of "Rose Rising" at the Sand and Sea Gallery. But Rita refused, calling them silly Botticelli rip-offs.

About the same time, Rush's wife Millie showed up at the gallery looking for Palmer. She brought two things: a desire to win her husband back from "that bitch Rose Tang," and her checkbook. She wanted Palmer to paint her own "Venus on the Halfshell" likeness.

At first, Palmer couldn't imagine painting this fifty-five-year old woman with overly dyed platinum blond hair worn in the short, fluffy style of Marilyn Monroe. Not to mention a body less than perfect.

But she offered ten times what her husband had paid for "Rose Rising." He asked for time to come up with ideas. She said he could contact her at the Otter Haven Resort when he was ready, and that she would not be leaving town until she had her painting.

Palmer racked his brain but couldn't seem to find the special groove for Millie. Then one morning while getting out of bed, he slipped on a sky blue silk robe Rita had worn the previous night—one of several items of lingerie she kept in his closet. He picked it up and after a brief examination, called Millie Rush, barely able to contain his excitement.

In the final painting, Millie Rush stood on the sea, wearing a silky hooded cape that trailed into and became part of the pale blue water. Her delicate feet stepped on perfect chrysanthemum white caps. Beneath the shimmering garment, her body seemed to move with an older woman's voluptuous grace and sexual mystique. And as if she'd just scooped it from the bottom of the sea, she looked upon a dripping piece of peach-colored coral held in her right hand. In the background, gray clouds were building, but the woman didn't seem bothered, suggesting that she'd already weathered many storms.

This was nothing like the life and death struggle in the kelp bed as expressed in "Rose Rising." No, this was a woman comfortable with her own wisdom of self and place, someone who could still find fascination with whatever she happened to find on the way.

Millie Rush's eyes filled with tears when she saw the completed work. She vowed to make Palmer famous.

Though he was somewhat astonished by what he'd fashioned from a middle-aged woman humiliated by her husband's interest in a younger woman, he doubted her claim. But he did ask if she'd tell her friends, believing he might be able to make a living doing these stylistic sea goddesses.

What he failed to realize was that Millie Rush wasn't just an extension of her famous husband. Having worked for years as a publicist, she had an extensive network of contacts.

Before leaving Holyrood, she had five hundred prints made, which he signed and numbered. She gave him the first twenty, had one framed, and insisted that Rita hang it in her gallery, saying that if Rita didn't handle Palmer she had friends who would. Rita hung the print.

Millie sent prints to her media contacts and friends and soon Palmer found himself flying back and forth to L.A. creating what were to become his trademark sea goddesses. While a couple were of young stars, most were of middle-aged women—former stars, wives of stars and studio executives. Within six months his Venusian portraits were "must haves." Then, as word spread, he started taking his services to other wealthy women in other parts of the country, staying in guesthouses or fancy hotel suites. That went on until *People* magazine did a spread on him, which sent his career into orbit.

Palmer wrapped up his story by saying he had simply tired of the travel and constant demands on his time and finally realized that whoever wanted his services could afford to come to him. Now, too, he could finally afford to live in the Perfume Mansion, the place he'd lusted after since he first saw "her."

She'd been so absorbed by her reverie, Salome jumped when Hector returned.

"You still willing to deliver lunch to that fireman?"

"Sure. And, Hector, I'd really rather pay for my meal."

"No, no!" He waved his hands and shook his head emphatically. "Thing is . . . since you'll be out anyway, would you mind dropping off food for Rita, too? I'd do it myself, but well, we don't get along so good. Only reason she asked me to help with sandbags is 'cause nobody else was around. And, I been thinking, Dolores's painting'll probably be worth some money what with Palmer dead and all. I might ask her to find a buyer, if she don't charge too much commission. Wanna kept her on my good side, know what I mean?"

"Sure. No problem. But what about Dolores?"

"I could have a print made or something. She wouldn't know the difference. She don't come in anymore, anyway. If I could come out ahead of the game, it might make up for the hell I been through."

"You find that envelope?"

He shook his head. "Musta gone out with this morning's trash. All I can think. Unless it's in Dolores's car. Had to use hers last night 'cause my battery was dead. Picked up a new one this morning first thing. She don't like me using her car. Says I ruin her upholstery." He looked down at his dirty apron and laughed.

A few minutes later, Salome left, carrying two insulated bags, re-energized by her own meal and certainly encouraged by the information she'd gleaned about Palmer both through memory and Hector's input. She wondered if he'd been involved in the artist's death—despite or because of his earnest confession of past events. Still, he *had* been at the Perfume around 1 A.M., and hence, had the opportunity. He also had a motive and the means—the baseball bat, though he might have stabbed Palmer first with any of the kitchen knives available to him. He *almost* fit as a suspect. But doubts stemmed from his character. High-strung and emotional, the crime scene would have resembled a war zone if Hector had had a go at Palmer.

LEAVING THE ENGINE RUNNING, SALOME dashed out of the pickup and handed over the bag containing bread and a large carton of Hector's cioppino to Clay Bethune. He accepted the offering with obvious surprise.

"Wow. I really didn't expect him to follow up," Clay said. "You know if it's any good?"

"Just had some. It's excellent."

"Super. I've been looking for a good Italian restaurant. Just moved down here from San Francisco."

"Well, I can honestly say, the Beach Bistro's comparable to any in North Beach. The same family has owned the place since the nineteen thirties. They were originally fisherman from Half Moon Bay and know their seafood."

He seemed anxious to be off so Salome cut short the history lesson, though she would have enjoyed a few extra minutes in the company of such a fine-looking man.

"Well, if it's authentic I'll certainly patronize his place. Thanks."

Walking away, he reminded her of someone but she couldn't make the connection. Maybe it was just the sight of a nicely formed backside. In any case, it was nice to see vital, new blood in Holyrood.

Returning to the esplanade, Salome parked alongside Rita's Lincoln. Lights were on inside the Sand and Sea Gallery in sharp contrast to the stormy skies and darkened shops, which she supposed was why the paintings never looked better.

A makeshift sign on the front door directed her to the back of the gallery. A moment later, she knocked on the gray metal door, the bag from Hector's in her free hand.

Rita pulled the door open and for an instant just stood staring at Salome in a most unnerving way.

Salome lifted the insulated bag. "Hector asked me to bring you something to eat."

"How strange. I was just thinking about you."

"Enough to invite me in out of the rain?"

Salome dripped on the linoleum floor in what was the gallery's office.

"Hang your coat on the rack in the bathroom." Rita nodded to a partially opened door where a toilet could be seen and plucked the bag from Salome's hand.

While Hector had been garrulous and open, Salome didn't expect Rita to be quite so forthcoming. Then she had an idea.

When she reentered the office, after closing the bathroom door, Rita was sitting at an old government-issue metal desk, the surface littered with files and stacks of paper, wolfing down the hot soup. Her attitude had altered considerably in just a few moments. Maybe it was the food.

"Sorry I was so abrupt just a minute ago. Pull up a chair. I'd forgotten just how good a cook Hector is," she remarked, then added, "Thing is I need to talk to you about something."

Rita wiped her mouth with a napkin and pushed the container aside. "I've been trying to track down all of Palmer's sea goddesses. My God, the list is *huge*."

Salome noticed her eyes were sparkling and that she hadn't repaired the false eyelash, which had curled up to the middle of her left eye. A vain woman, Rita probably never missed an opportunity to glance at herself in any reflective surface. She must be quite preoccupied not to have even glanced at herself in the bathroom mirror when she hung up her raincoat.

"Uh, Rita, your left eyelash is coming unglued," Salome said, then quickly remarked, "I don't know how I could help locate his work."

Absently, Rita peeled off the eyelash while saying, "No, no, that's not what I meant." She dropped the furry accessory in the top middle drawer of her desk.

"You must be anxious to find a tenant now that Palmer's gone."

"Well, I—"

Rita raised her hand. "Just hear me out. I want to host a show of Palmer's work. As many paintings as I can get my hands on. And I'll need a good-sized venue. The gallery is just too small for a show of this size. What better place than the Perfume! After all, he did live there."

"And died there," Salome reminded her.

Unfazed, Rita went on. "That, too, has its appeal, doesn't it? Look, aesthetics aside, art is a cutthroat business. Selling it relies on elements that someone not in the business may see as amoral. So let's don't get into that."

Rita cleared her throat. "Anyway, the show will attract sellers and buyers from all over. Maybe even national press coverage. We are talking big bucks here, Salome. I'm willing to give you a percentage of the take plus the costs for using the facility."

"It's a residence, Rita, not zoned for commercial—"

"Yes, of course. That's just it. *I* want to be the next tenant. Use part as a gallery—by invitation only—part as my residence. Naturally, all sales will take place here since the Perfume isn't zoned for commercial use. You have to admit the space, the mansion, would be perfect to showcase Palmer's work. I intend to have prints made of as many of his originals as I can. A percentage of profits could even go to some scholarship fund."

She paused then went on. "Frankly, I'd like to lease with an option to buy. What's it worth now? Eight, ten million? 'Course the market's so damn inflated what with all that money in Silicon Valley. To be honest, I don't have the kind of money it would take to buy straight out. At least not yet. I'm a partner in a gallery in New York and own another in La Jolla that my sister runs, the ladder a lovely beach community near San Diego.

"Come on, I know you've got to be tempted to sell! But think for minute—I'm established here. Everyone knows me. I can be counted on to maintain the dignity of such an important property." Rita took a breath and continued.

"Like everyone else, I know how your father feels about selling the Perfume and I understand him wanting to keep it in the family."

This seemed to be the time to move on to the subject Salome had thought of while hanging up her coat.

"Actually, Blair Farrell's made an offer."

Rita leaned back in her chair as if she'd been physically struck. "Jesus! The bitch!"

It was enough to tell Salome Rita was acquainted with Palmer's publicist.

"You know what she's doing, of course?"

"Not the particulars."

"Ever since Palmer fired her, she's been trying to get back at him. I'll bet the farm once she bought the Perfume, she'd turn around and sell the property for double or triple to developers who'd start passing money and promises around town and once they were in would tear it down and we'd end up with some cheesy cheek-to-jowl condos or hotel chain that would absolutely ruin Holyrood. Next thing to come in would be the cheap T-shirt and souvenir shops with those horrible rubber sharks and otters, just the sort of places we've all worked hard to keep out. Absolutely, do not sell to her!"

Rita's vehemence matched Salome's father's own arguments.

"Why did Palmer fire her? I heard she's the one who got him in *People* magazine." She hadn't heard anything of the sort but it seemed possible.

"Oh she'd like to take credit for his success. But it was me who put him on the map. But that's another story. Why did he fire her? She was taking too much control of his life—you could say she overhauled him. From hairstyle to underwear, she completely altered his image. However, she didn't have the control over his property she wanted. So, she asked him to marry her."

Suddenly Rita laughed. "In reply, he fired her. Best move he made in years."

Unless, Salome thought, it got him killed. "When was this?"

"Last summer."

"Maybe she was in love."

"You've got to be joking! Blair Farrell loves Blair Farrell and that's it. She wanted to take advantage of the community property laws in California. By marrying him, she'd own half of everything."

"How do you know?"

"Palmer, of course. And besides, she'd been trying to get him to drop me and let her control his work exclusively through bigger galleries. Palmer and I did have our ups and downs—he dropped me and I dropped him a few times—but that's par for the course in the art world.

"Palmer's confided in me for years. It's no secret he wanted to buy the Perfume. Look, I don't mean to besmirch his name but when your father had his heart attack at Christmas, Palmer really thought his chance had come, that it was just a matter of time before you'd finally agree to sell. Blair must have found out, too, and no doubt would outbid him—she knows what kind of money he makes. She'd own it then unload it, all out of spite. And then, of course, turn around and make herself a bundle. For her, revenge is a business tool."

"Do you think she might somehow be involved with his murder?"

"I wouldn't mind pointing the finger at her." She paused, looking thoughtful. "I just remembered something I heard. When was it?" She rubbed her temples.

"What did you hear?" Salome prompted.

She stared at her desk for a long moment, concentrating. "Something about seeing someone in town. God, why can't I remember the details . . . wait! I think it was Halloween! At his masquerade party. Was that a drunken brawl! Yes. Palmer said he'd seen an old friend, someone from his days in San Francisco. He wasn't too happy about it either."

"Did this person threaten him or something?"

"More an annoyance. God. Who—?"

The telephone trilled.

Both women started. Salome sighed, feeling sure Rita had

just about located the thread in her memory connecting to a possible suspect.

Rita instantly snapped into professional mode, no trace of the tension of a moment ago in her voice.

"Sand and Sea Gallery. Rita Van Horn speaking . . . Peter! Yes . . . terrible. Listen, would you hold for sec? I've got a client on another line—no, no, we've finished our business."

Rita hit a button on the phone console and looked at Salome imploringly.

"Would you mind terribly?" she asked. "It's a call back from my partner in New York. How about I call you later? We can have dinner or something."

"Fine."

"Just one more thing. Would you talk to Phyl for me? I really need to get into the Perfume. Palmer was working on something new and I need to find out what it is. And there's a stash of paintings somewhere that have to be inventoried."

"I doubt if I can help."

"Just try." Abruptly, she turned around and began talking to the caller.

Salome retrieved her coat from the bathroom. The toilet was in direct line with Rita's desk. If the woman wanted to maintain financial stability, she really should keep the bathroom door closed and the toilet lid down. She performed those two tasks before quietly letting herself out while Rita huddled over the phone.

During the drive back to her cottage she couldn't get the picture out of her mind of some shadowy stranger lurking around the Perfume, watching Palmer. In which case, if that person hadn't done the deed, maybe they'd seen who had. Of course, Rita could have made up the whole thing to shine the light of suspicion on some nebulous stranger—and away from herself.

Then, what she saw as she turned into Sea Horse Lane prompted her own murderous considerations and an uncharacteristic curse.

Chapter 9

☯

SALOME quickly shifted into reverse, hoping the hedge and heavy rain had shielded her slight penetration of Sea Horse Lane. She backed up a few yards, then drove straight up Dolphin Way to the Otter Haven Resort, her feelings toward Emily Harkin ranging far from the benevolent. Holding a red-and-white-striped golf umbrella, she'd been standing in Salome's driveway, talking to a local television news reporter.

Salome glanced at the rearview mirror, relieved to note the empty street. The TV people had missed sight of their quarry.

She pulled into a long carport just beyond the front gate, where only a handful of cars were sheltered. A large parking area was located on the north side of the property but she didn't feel like trekking from there to the lodge. Besides, this time of year there were few guests. At the moment, most business came from locals partaking of afternoon tea. But that would soon change.

Just next week the resort would be filled to capacity during the annual AT&T Pebble Beach National Pro-Am golf tournament. A shuttle would provide guests with transport down the coast to the world-famous golf courses in Carmel. The small shop in the lodge would do a brisk business selling foul weather gear. At tournament time, the resort always tripled its inventory of inexpensive umbrellas, raincoats, and lightweight boots. It was a given that Pacific storms, along with the rich and famous, would make an appearance. As she did every year, Salome would lend a hand wherever needed.

As she switched off the ignition, she wondered who had brought reporters to her doorstep. Had they heard she was a suspect? How long would they stay? Surely they'd gone to the Perfume first. Had Phyl, wanting to get them off her back sent them to Salome's?

She opened the door of the cab, grabbed her handbag and umbrella, and stepped outside, now confronted by a wall of water sluicing off the roof—and that she might be the messenger of death. What if the police hadn't yet come to the resort to pick up the Perfume's keys? She couldn't think of anyone, not even Emily, who'd relish the thought of telling Reggie Waterhouse a murder had been committed in the Perfume. Never mind who the real victim was, he'd react as if his own flesh and blood had been violated. She spent a few minutes rehearsing what she'd say, including an explanation for needing the spare keys to her house and why she now sported a bandage on her head.

Finally, with some courage mustered but no real script devised, she opened the umbrella and headed for confrontation.

Gatay, gatay . . .

SATOMI AND REGINALD WATERHOUSE LIVED IN the north wing of a sprawling yellow and white Queen Anne Victorian lodge overlooking the usually calm waters of the cove commonly known as Otter Bay and had done so during most of their fifty-four years of marriage. Cyprus trees older than Holyrood itself brooded over the twelve-acre resort, the extended branches hovering above the rooftops of the scattered guest cottages.

Salome and her four sisters had grown up here, each working every job inside and out.

In 1916, Joshua Waterhouse had purchased the grand old mansion, then on six acres from a wealthy San Francisco banker after his wife and son had drowned in a boating accident. The bereaved banker willingly sold out for well below the property's value and moved back East. While adding onto the mansion and refitting it to function as a twenty-bedroom lodge, Joshua began gobbling up adjacent property and building guest cottages in his signature storybook style. But there was one parcel he couldn't convince the owner to sell. With its weedy, overgrown garden and small clapboard house, Joshua considered it an eyesore, especially given that it was located right next to the front gate. Eventually, the owner did sell—but to Joshua's arch rival, Kevin O'Kelly, who gleefully maintained its slovenly appearance.

Salome mounted the wooden steps to the porch and peered through the oval glass in the door while shaking the rain off her umbrella. She could make out the red and black Oriental rug on the hardwood floor of the wide foyer, the mirror above the small Japanese *tansu* chest, and the door to the coat closet. The rooms beyond looked gloomy. She wondered if her parents were even home as their car hadn't been in the carport. Of course, they spent most of their time working in the lodge itself and an employee might have taken the car to run an errand. She tried the brass doorknob, slick with moisture, but the door was locked. Standing on tiptoe, she reached up and found the key above the door and let herself in, feeling uneasy. Since her father's heart attack, her parents' health had never been far from her mind. Though both were in their eighties, neither Satomi nor Reginald Waterhouse would of conceive of retirement. At Christmas, Salome and her sisters had urged them to at least take a vacation.

"Where would we go?" her mother had said. "This is the most beautiful place on earth."

She had a point. Then her father's heart attack pretty well put travel considerations to rest.

After unlocking the door, she returned the key to its place, entered the foyer, then locked the door from the inside.

"Mom? Dad?" she called out while pulling off her boots. "It's me!" She hung her coat on a rack beside the door; only dry outerwear was allowed in the coat closet.

On a low table were a dozen pairs of slippers. Shoes were not worn in the apartment. There were no other shoes or boots by the door.

"Mom? Dad?"

Still no response.

Her feet in the black scuffs, she went to the mirror and let out a groan. Tiny stitches poked through the thin gauze bandage now moist with her own perspiration and the damp air. But without it, the stitches would be exposed. The Bride of Frankenstein look would upset her parents even more. She'd just have to smile a lot.

The foyer opened on a large living room to the left, a hallway straight ahead, and stairs to the right that wound up to the bedrooms on three floors. Just past the stairs was a study that overlooked the grounds, the door closed. While approaching the lodge, she'd noticed that the heavy curtains were drawn, effectively containing any light within.

She padded into the living room, where a long couch faced a wall of windows low to the floor. The windows afforded a view of the wide porch that wrapped around the front of the lodge. Beyond, the lawn sloping down to the cliffside always reminded her of a rolling bolt of emerald velvet. At the furthest reaches, a sensual curve of white beach was nudged by water usually the color of pale green jade. Even as an energetic child, she'd never been able to enter this room without pausing for a moment to wonder at the sight of such elegant beauty.

"Mei!" Though named after her paternal grandmother, immediate family had always called her "Mei."

Salome spun around at the sound of her mother's voice. She beamed in toothy display. Then, feeling silly, edited her smile to more natural proportions.

"Mom! Hi!"

Satomi wore a pale pink cashmere twinset, a strand of baroque pearls, and gray wool slacks with a silk lining that rustled as she moved toward her oldest daughter.

They hugged each other, Salome bending slightly as her mother was barely five feet tall. But size made no difference when she was enveloped in her mother's unique and subtle scent, which, if bottled, would serve better than Prozac, sensimillia, Maui Wowie, or any other psychotropic. A combination of Ivory soap, white ginger perfume oil, and pine incense that lingered in her hair from her morning prayers, the scent never failed to invoke a feeling of security, protection, and absolute trust.

When they pulled apart, Salome imaged for an instant how she might look if she ever reached octogenarian status with the same grace as her mother. Satomi had a sprinkling of silver in her black hair, a high, smooth brow, and deep dimples on either side of a bow-like mouth. Their noses were similar but Salome's was longer in Waterhouse fashion and her hazel eyes were a compromise between the deep brown of her mother's and the sharp blue of her father's, the epicanthic fold of her mother's eyelids less pronounced in Salome.

Having spent too much time in the sun, Salome doubted she'd achieve the perfection of her mother's wrinkle-free, lustrous complexion at an advanced age. Besides having good genes, her mother used a costly cream made of crushed pearls and faithfully attended aerobic classes at the senior center in town. Since her divorce, Salome had neglected physical upkeep beyond the superficial. Clay Bethune, the fireman, suddenly sauntered across her internal screen and she wondered if maybe she should take a bit more interest in her physical self.

"Good heavens, what happened?" Satomi asked, squinting at Salome's forehead.

"Well, I, uh, fell in the study."

"Oh dear."

"It's just a little cut, Mother. Unfortunately, I demolished Kwan Yin," Salome said quickly, diverting attention from herself. "And feel terrible about it."

Satomi sucked in a breath. After a pause, she smiled as beatifically as the Kwan Yin herself. "Well, we can replace her, can't we?"

Years ago, Salome's grandmother brought a score of exquisite porcelain Kwan Yin goddesses, along with other goods, back from China.

Suddenly Salome thought her mother might be assuming she'd come over simply to pick up a replacement for the shattered statue.

"Mom, the reason I'm here has nothing to do with Kwan Yin. Uh, something a bit more dramatic has happened."

"Ah yes, Palmer Fordham's murder."

"You've heard, then."

"Phyl called," she replied calmly. "She told us you found the body. Then a policemen came to pick up keys."

Her mother had been tossed in and dug her way out of so much social compost during her life that little riled her.

"How's Dad taking it?"

"Seems to have done him some good. He's not quite so lethargic. For a moment there, I thought he was going to jail. You could say he was reluctant to give up the Perfume's keys."

Satomi grabbed her daughter's arm. "Come on, Mei. We've been trying to call you. He's in the study arguing with one of our least favorite people."

"Phyl's here?"

Satomi stopped. "We care deeply for your cousin! Her

problem is she's too much like your father. They both regard the Perfume as if it were human."

"Then who—?"

Satomi yanked on Salome's arm and pulled her toward the study.

Salome herself had rearranged the large, comfortable study/office according to feng shui principles. Her father sat at a mahogany desk auspiciously placed at an angle diagonally across from the door, in the room's power position. He wore an eggshell cable knit sweater and leaned back in a high-backed, swivel armchair, big bony hands grasped at his middle. When wife and daughter entered, he acknowledged them by shifting his ice blue eyes briefly, then returning them to the person seated in one of two red leather chairs in front of the desk. He had a craggy, weathered face that looked bored, though his eyes sparked with subdued anger. At least he wasn't charging around the room.

On the desk, a green-hooded banker's lamp was switched on and highlighted two small objects on either side of the brass stand which, only after close examination, revealed the otters coaxed from the wood by a couple of aspiring sculptors—Salome and her sister Willow, at ages seven and six respectively. The only other item on the desk was a telephone to her father's right.

Behind him and to his left, a tall floor lamp with a pleated peach-colored silk shade bathed his broad shoulders and shaggy sand-colored hair in soft light. He, too, had not succumbed to gray and at this point in his life, probably never would.

Until Salome feng shuied the room, he'd complained of neck and shoulder pain. The pain stopped after Salome moved the bookshelves that had been looming behind him from the middle of the wall to the ceiling, to a space across the room. She then placed the floor lamp in that corner. Almost immediately the bunched muscles in his neck and shoulders relaxed.

Behind the heavy forest green and gold brocade curtains, a bay window faced west. In front of the curtained window was a plush sofa flanked on either side by rosewood end tables and ginger jar lamps—tables and lamps originally among the booty brought back from China. In a shallow brown bowl on the coffee table was one of her mother's *ikebana* arrangements. Using just a few graceful sansevieria (mother-in-law's tongue) leaves and tiny red star lilies, the arrangement resembled a boat with a sail and scull—a reflection of her father's former passion for sailing.

Aside from a few seascapes painted by her mother, most of the remaining wall space contained floor-to-ceiling books, many on property and real estate law and management. In a locked cabinet were Salome's grandfather's meticulously and ponderously written journals. Her father's journals were there, too, though far less in number—not only an indication of his terse style, but he'd only begun keeping journals since his father's death, whereas Joshua's editions had accumulated over a lifetime.

At the opposite end of the room, just by the door, a fire crackled in the hearth, warming a cozy grouping of overstuffed chairs and a small sofa. That no one was sitting around the fire told her the conversation probably had to do with business.

Finally, she noticed her parents' guest.

Mavis Hicks-Dulane was a short, sturdy woman in her late seventies, her white hair a neat cap of tight curls around a lined face with a determined expression. Mavis glanced over at Salome as, at her mother's urging, she sat down in the other red leather chair. After depositing her daughter, Satomi took a seat on the couch.

"Just the person we need," Mavis chirruped brightly in an ersatz British accent. Perhaps thirty years ago she'd taken an extended trip to the British Isles and returned with altered speech patterns and a slightly superior attitude. She'd also brought back a husband—Dulane—who had vanished soon after their arrival in Holyrood. Maybe the quaint village and Mavis's storybook cottage and rose garden were all just a bit too much like home and he took off for America's glitzier environs. Satomi had suspected something more sinister, especially since Mavis never displayed even a tic of disappointment or hurt and liked to boast that as a dual-national she was in line for the throne, not the least bit bothered by the millions ahead of her. No, Satomi figured he hadn't left at all, that, purpose served—Dulane had become one with Mavis's prize roses.

Mavis was head of the Historical Society's Preservation Program and Salome knew what was coming next. Whenever the Perfume came on the market, Mavis showed up. This had been going on for years.

"We've just been discussing the donation of the Perfume to the Historical Society."

Out of politeness, Salome acted surprised. "Oh really?"

Her father frowned as if to say for God's sake, don't encourage her!

"We simply can't have things like grisly murders happening in such a venerable landmark. That's what happens when outsiders are allowed to live there."

"Didn't the city council just vote to hand over the old police station for your offices?"

Mavis's pale complexion reddened slightly. "Well yes, but we need something permanent and more in keeping with our status.

"Surely you're well off, Salome—being married to a bestselling author and all."

"Divorced."

Mavis hadn't done her homework. While the divorce hadn't been more than a blip on the radar everywhere else, in Holyrood it made headlines, thanks to Emily Harkin. Maybe Mavis had been in London that week, drooling outside Buckingham Palace, or had simply forgotten.

"Going on five years."

Unruffled, Mavis plunged on. "Alimony, then must keep you—"

"I think you're getting a little too personal, Mavis, but for the record, I don't receive alimony."

"Your business, then. The feng thing."

The room went dead quiet. Then from the couch came a tinkle of laughter. Salome bit her lip. Her father swiveled around in his chair.

"Mavis, while Dad and I would both agree that the Historical Society would be a fine tenant, I find it remarkably presumptuous that you actually believe we'd simply turn over a multimillion dollar property"—*to a bunch of dotty old women*, she nearly added but didn't—"so your society has a nice place to host teas."

"Our work is essential! Not just to the community but the state of California! And we don't just host teas as you say." In a huff, she leaned down to pick up her handbag.

"And how did you find out about the murder so quickly?"

For an instant, Mavis actually appeared guilty. "Dora called me! Dora's a member of the society, even if she is just a servant. Anyway, she's been coming in a few days a week to clean my house. She was supposed to come this morning but, uh, under the circumstances, couldn't make it."

"The Perfume's not big enough for her?"

"I think she's planning a vacation and needs the extra income."

Mavis stood up, prim as a starched napkin, handbag gripped tightly. "And, Reggie, it's time you turned over your father's journals to the society. Such a source of local history shouldn't be kept from researchers."

Reggie slowly rose from his chair but made no move to escort Mavis to the door. "Snoops, you mean. Good day to you, Mavis."

Satomi smiled her farewell as Salome did the honors, walking Mavis out of the study. She automatically moved toward the foyer, wanting to rush Mavis through the closest exit.

"No, no, not that way," Mavis said. "I'm meeting some ladies for afternoon tea in the lodge. Since I was already here, I decided to pop in and see your parents."

"Fine." Salome turned into the long hallway to the door that connected to the lodge itself. A wind chime hung midway to counter the rush of energy from the front door to the lodge-side door.

"And, Salome, you really should reconsider. Only through our efforts can you be certain . . ."

Salome opened the door, tuning out the familiar pitch. Mavis stepped out of her slippers and into a pair of black pumps that were on another low table near the door.

"Enjoy your tea and crumpets, Mavis."

Salome locked the door and returned to the study. She hoped her father wouldn't start berating her for leasing the Perfume to a man who'd ended up a murder victim.

Chapter 10

"WHAT happened to your head?" her father asked when Salome and her mother were seated in the red leather armchairs.

Salome related her "adventure" breaking into the cottage with Ralph Blue, trying to keep it light. After she asked to borrow the extra keys to her cottage, her father pulled out a drawer and put a set on the desk. Then he shoved them across the slick surface. Salome reached out and caught them as they flew off the end. With barely a glance, she dropped them in her handbag.

"Thanks, Dad. Uh, how are you feeling?"

"I feel all right." His hands began to shake a little as he mumbled something incoherent.

"I beg your pardon?"

He hesitated, then said gruffly, "What are your plans for the Perfume?"

"Haven't made any."

"Good. You'll be going back to Washington in a few weeks anyway, so just let me take care of it. A family should live there. It was a mistake renting to a single man. Yes, I know, we were all impressed by his excellent credit rating.

But you weren't in the right state of mind, having just gotten divorced."

"Reggie!" Satomi scolded.

Her father glanced briefly at her mother then, softening slightly, said to Salome, "If you need money, I'll advance you the rent. And given the inflated price of real estate, we can certainly get away with a fair-sized increase."

"Too bad it wasn't reduced to rubble in the last earthquake," Satomi added, leaving no doubt as to her opinion of the Perfume.

For decades the Perfume Mansion had proved its relentless tenacity by surviving such elemental events as temblors, floods, and vicious winter storms, sustaining little or no damage, proving a unique marriage between Waterhouse construction standards and the ground on which it was built.

"Money's no problem," Salome said.

"Didn't kill him, did you?" Reggie asked. "The way the damn laws are written these days, it's hard as hell to get rid of an undesirable tenant."

His dry humor and wry delivery often confused people, making it difficult to determine if he was serious or not.

She chose to ignore the remark and mentioned what she'd learned at Waterhouse Properties.

"And, I checked the Perfume's file but couldn't find the waiting list or other applications."

"That damn Beth McCormick! I've a good mind to fire her. You know she's been bugging me to sell the Perfume. Disappointed the hell out of her when that heart attack didn't put me six feet under. Rumor has it she's been carrying on with Palmer Fordham. Only reason I know she didn't kill him is she wants that damn commission too much. She probably got rid of the waiting list. Still, I doubt we'll have any problem finding a tenant. I'll give her a call."

"And now a TV van and Emily are parked in my drive."

"Stay here," Satomi offered. "They'll give up if you don't go home."

"I was thinking of changing into my maid's uniform and going in through the patio. That way, if someone happens to be at the back I can just say I'm there to clean the house. Emily'll be expecting me to arrive at the front."

Reggie reached for the telephone. Salome and her mother rose and started toward the door.

". . . you want to keep your job, Ms. McCormick, you'll be in my home office in thirty minutes," Reggie said into the phone. "And bring that damn waiting list!"

Salome trooped upstairs to the third floor bedroom she'd once shared with her sister Willow while her mother went off to find a replacement for the Kwan Yin.

Because she often helped out at the resort, Salome kept a freshly laundered maid's uniform in the closet. She changed into the pale yellow dress and starched white apron, and threw on a lightweight raincoat. She left her street clothes on the bed; she would pick them up at another time. Finally, she plucked the comfortable but unattractive white maid's shoes from their box and went downstairs.

"You're welcome to come for dinner," Satomi said while Salome slipped on the shoes then a cheap pair of clear plastic overshoes found among a collection in the closet.

"Thanks, Mom, but I've got a lot to do. I'll just leave the Drizabone, if you don't mind. Doesn't fit the image."

Satomi handed over a large sturdy plastic bag. Inside, swathed in bubble wrap, was a new Kwan Yin. Salome added her walking shoes and purse to the bag.

"Well, don't forget to eat. And be careful, especially of the police. Phyl sounded just a bit too pleased when she said you'd found the body."

"How do I look?"

Satomi cocked her head. She frowned then pulled out a small drawer in the Japanese chest. She shook out a pleated pink plastic rain bonnet and tied it under Salome's chin. Then she pulled it down over Salome's forehead.

"There. That's better. Need an umbrella?"

"Mine's just outside the door."

The two women kissed good-bye. Salome inhaled deeply of her mother's wonderful scent.

"I'll pick up my car and clothes later. And, Mom"—she lifted the bag conveying the statue—"thanks for replacing Kwan Yin."

Huddled under the umbrella and gripping the bag with her other hand, Salome hurried across the sodden grass to the south side of the resort. There she turned and followed a narrow trail that ran beside a cliff-side fence of tall black spikes. It was dark now and the dirt path slick. Up ahead she could just make out the pale yellow glow of streetlights at the end of the lanes. The rain had decreased but she knew it was only a brief interval before the next line of squalls hit the coast. Just a few feet beyond the fence, the sea crashed against the cliff, loudly claiming more of the land.

She stopped at the edge of her property. Seeing no one lurking around the back of the cottage, she stepped over the low wooden fence. Though she felt like running, she kept a steady pace all the way to the patio, in case someone unseen might be watching.

All day she'd kept her composure. But now, when she spotted a movement to her left, her jangled nerves leaped into action. She dropped the keys.

"Who's there?" she called out.

"Someone's at the back door!" A male voice yelled. A light switched on, pinning her to the spot.

Salome scrambled to pick up the keys and insert them in the lock. She frantically tried one, then the other. Her shoulders sagged as she realized her father had not given her the proper set. From inside she could hear the insistent ringing of the telephone, the sound scouring her nerves even more.

There was only one thing to do.

Holding her head down, and tipping the umbrella forward, she headed for the light.

Keeping the umbrella between her and the man, she scurried around the side of the house. Someone else joined him but she could only see the bottom of a raincoat and boots.

"Who are you?" a woman asked, the voice familiar as that of a local newscaster.

"The maid."

"Where's Salome Waterhouse? We need to talk to her."

Without answering, Salome hurried toward the front door.

"If she's inside, would you please ask her to come out?"

The persistent reporter followed her to the door. "Look, may I come in? I'd really like to get out of this rain."

The audacity! Salome thought and didn't answer.

"It's very important I talk to her. I'll put her on TV."

Hardly an enticement. Salome turned the knob.

Then she heard someone running across the street.

"Salome!" Emily shouted.

She must have taken a bathroom break. Emily called out her name again.

Still using the umbrella as a barrier, Salome slipped through the door, slammed and locked it. Outside she could hear Emily. "That was her! That was Salome."

"It was the maid."

"The maid? She doesn't have a maid!"

Then the pounding began. Without stopping to remove her footwear, she ran to the wall of glass overlooking the patio and quickly closed the curtains.

The phone stopped ringing as the answering machine picked up. Going from room to room, she closed all the curtains. In the study, she lowered the volume of the phone's ringer. A glance at the display told her she had fifteen messages. Definitely a record.

She went into the kitchen and poured herself a glass of Kirin beer.

After a few moments, she returned to the foyer. While removing the raingear and sipping her beer, she listening to Emily and the reporter arguing on the porch.

"How many times do I have to tell you! I'm a friend. She'll talk to me. You people spooked her."

"I'm here for a statement and won't leave until I get it."

"Go get in your van. Let me talk to her alone." After a pause, Emily resumed her pleading. "Salome! I know you're in there. Talk to me, please. It's for your own good—to stop the rumors."

Rumors? What rumors?

"Look, the O'Kellys are planning to sell off the paper. Michael O'Kelly's in town to take care of it. This story could keep us alive, Salome. What would Holyrood be without *The Echo*? Talk to me now, your version, and I'll see it's in tomorrow's edition. But the paper goes to bed at ten. There's not much time."

Now Salome realized that Emily was *competing* with the TV people.

She might have simply grabbed her beer and gone off to soak in a hot bath, leaving them all to rot in her driveway had Emily not spoken the magic words. No, much more than magic. *Traumagic*—if there was such a word.

Michael O'Kelly had been her first love and a forbidden one at that. They'd dated in high school, surreptitiously of course, until his older brother found out and reported to their father, who had actually followed them to a favorite parking area near one of the local beaches one December night in their senior year. He waited until she and Michael were in an embrace, then roughly dragged them out of the car.

The older brother drove Michael home while his father, Brian, who had once tried to make it illegal for anyone of Japanese descent to live in Holyrood, chauffeured Salome back to Otter Haven, where her parents were hosting a Christmas party. Holding her arm, he took her into the lodge and while she stood sobbing, used a vocabulary of lurid invectives and racial slurs in front of the stunned partygoers. Two men, one of them a young Hector Gonzaga, had the presence of mind to hustle O'Kelly back to his car before any blood was spilled.

The next day Michael was shipped off to a private school in Massachusetts and Salome never saw him again.

Time is supposed to dilute the intense emotions of youth. But just imagining him somewhere nearby, just *hearing his name* made her face flush and her mouth go dry. She took a drink of the cold beer.

"If you don't talk about it, it'll look like you have something to hide. Everyone who's ever known Palmer or been involved with the Perfume is going to be interviewed. Give me an exclusive. I'll do the stories on behalf of you and your family. You don't want your father to have to go through this, surely not after his heart attack."

She resented Emily for exploiting her father's health and, at the same time, felt grateful to her for providing the information that Michael O'Kelly was actually in town, apparently for the first time in nearly thirty-five years. She'd heard he didn't even show up for his father's funeral.

But Emily was right about her father. Someone needed to be a buffer; the media would only exhaust him.

Despite her trepidation, in one swift movement Salome opened the door and jerked Emily inside.

Chapter 11

EMILY stood wide-eyed and momentarily speechless. Salome locked the front door.

"Kindly remove your shoes. You'll find slippers in the closet." She grabbed the glass of beer and headed for the study. Then changing her mind, she closed the door, deciding she didn't want Emily in her sanctum.

"Would you like a beer or coffee?" she asked.

"Uh, coffee would be fine."

The foyer opened into the wide, airy living room. The curtains at the south now formed a wall of heavy eggshell linen, shutting out the magnificent view. Nine linked tassels hung at one-foot intervals across the top, Salome's addition when she moved in five years ago. This was the fame/reputation gua of the house and red was the color attributed to fame. She might have replaced the curtains with red ones but considered that too much and instead hung the tassels.

On the north wall was a fireplace surrounded by local river rock imbedded in the masonry. A favorite painting hung above the mantel, an Andrew Annenberg original of a fantasy underwater scene in which dolphins swam through the sunlight-pierced water of an Atlantean world complete with a pyramid in the background.

Two sofas upholstered in sea green watered silk flanked the fireplace on a thick Berber rug. Small Japanese *tansu* chests with polished brass fittings served as end tables upon which were porcelain lamps glazed in pale green and gold with matching silk shades.

Between the sofas stretched a low teakwood coffee table with inward curving legs. On the highly polished surface was another of Satomi's *ikebana* arrangements, this of a sprouting stalk of bamboo and two water lilies in a clear oval bowl. On the bottom were opaque white stones.

In the family gua on the east wall and positioned above a pair of comfortable overstuffed chairs and a long sideboard covered with framed family photos was a six-foot-long three-paneled screen featuring the Japanese Dragon Horse, Kirin, symbol of great good fortune, painted vibrant red on gold silk.

Salome glanced at the dragon while envisioning protection for her family that, at the moment, would be the best manifestation of good fortune for all, then went in the kitchen. Almost immediately she had an inspiration.

A moment later Salome returned to the living room carrying a tray with a fresh glass of beer, a mug of last night's coffee, and two linen napkins. Her mother would never have approved of serving stale coffee to anyone, even Emily. But to Salome's way of thinking, Emily was lucky to get anything at all, including entry to her house. Though it meant she continued to carry old baggage, Salome hadn't yet forgiven Emily for another irritation—headlining her divorce in *The Echo*.

Emily stood in front of the mantel, gazing up at the Annenberg painting. "Where on earth did you find this? I've never seen the likes in any local galleries."

"San Francisco. Please, sit down," she offered, not wanting to talk about art though artists were certainly at the forefront here.

"This is quite a beautiful room." The remark a reminder

that Emily hadn't been inside the house since Salome took up residence, after buying it from her parents.

"Thank you."

"I remember when your grandmother had phones all over the house, even in the bathrooms."

"One of her idiosyncrasies," Salome replied with a slight smile. With anyone else and at another time she would have invited talk about her namesake. Not now, though.

Emily held up a small tape recorder. "Do you mind?"

Salome sighed. "I'd prefer that you take notes . . . but all right. I suppose this way I won't be misquoted." And would have to be more cautious about what she said.

"You've got your exclusive, Emily, but only if you agree to my terms. If you don't, well, you can maybe enjoy the coffee and we'll talk about the weather for a couple minutes."

Having actually been invited—no, pulled—into the house, Emily would not be likely to give up now. But, you never knew.

"What terms?"

"I want you to write a feature about my mother's artwork, her *ikebana* and watercolors. You will mention that not one gallery in Holyrood or our single florist has ever displayed her art. You get my drift?"

Emily rubbed her face then pressed her fingers to her lips. She shook her head, clearly confronted with a dilemma.

"The O'Kellys own the properties leased by the galleries and O'Kelly's Florist! Need I mention *The Echo*! I write a story like that and I'm history."

"Didn't I hear you say something about *The Echo* being on its way out, that Michael O'Kelly's in town—"

Before Salome could even savor the sound of saying his name out loud, Emily interrupted.

"I've got till the end of February and then we'll be shut down. Not counting this one, that's two more issues. They control the content, always have."

"Maybe it's time *you* did. Stir your readership out of complacency by writing a really strong journalistic piece about this murder—along with some hard-hitting reporting about things that have been going on too long beneath the surface. Come on, Emily, you've been laying down long enough. Get up! You've got an opportunity to show your stuff. A month you say? You can turn this paper from a biweekly into a weekly if you want."

Emily took a sip of the coffee, grimaced, then put the mug down on the napkin. Salome could see ambition suddenly coming from behind—years of behind.

"Oh man," Emily said, "you bring back the awesome days of my youth at the *Berkeley Barb*."

She stared at Salome for a long moment. "You know what I feel like? Right at this moment? Like Jerry Garcia if he'd chucked the Dead for an exec position at some oil company. A tie for tie-dye."

She shook her gray head as if to dislodge her original ideals and integrity from a dusty shelf. Suddenly she blurted, "You want photographs with that story about your mother?"

In about fifteen minutes, Emily had the first installment of her story and a new best friend.

Salome cleared up the "rumor" Emily mentioned—that she'd been *leaving* the Perfume at 7:30 A.M. rather than arriving. (A rumor, Salome thought, Emily herself might have started.) However, she refused to say anything about the state of the body or crime scene. "That I can't talk about until Phyl gives the thumbs up."

"Any ideas who might have sent you to feng shui the house?" Emily said. She'd already asked the question and now only worded it differently.

"I really don't have a clue."

"Who are your local clients?"

Certainly a good question but not one Salome was likely to answer. Phyl might try to force her to produce a list but she hoped not. Such a thing had never happened before. On the spot, she decided that she'd go to jail before relinquishing a client list. Phyl would have to get a court order and physically take her files herself. No way would Salome willingly lend a hand.

"Unless my clients say otherwise, their identities remain confidential."

"Really, Salome, aren't you carrying this a little too far? After all, you're not much more than a glorified interior decorator."

It took some self-restraint, but too much was at stake here for Salome to let her ego take over and did not take the bait. Instead, she laughed, something of a feng shui "cure" in itself which worked to deflect the aspersion to her profession.

"What's so funny?" Emily asked.

"While there are practitioners with backgrounds in interior design, mine, I'm afraid, ranged far from that civilized endeavor. Maybe you've forgotten but, in the past, my concerns focused on bodies and blood splatter rather than furnishings and wallpaper."

Emily appeared momentarily surprised then said, "Do you think the murder was drug-related?"

Salome shrugged. "Like I said, I'm completely in the dark as to Palmer's private life."

"Palmer's been keeping company with some real low-lifes."

"How do you know?"

"I talked to Dora, of course. And the Perfume does have something of a history in that regard."

"Well, that's the first I've heard of it."

"Oh, come on, Salome! Maybe I've only been here fifteen years but I've heard the stories. Your grandfather smuggled booze during Prohibition. A ship would anchor in the Bay and they'd transport the liquor by boat up the creek and unload in the lower rooms. Same thing in the sixties and seventies with marijuana from Mexico."

"You're talking about rumors, not fact."

"Now, I'm not saying your grandfather knew about *that*. It would be easy enough, though, if someone had a key to the creek-side door, to stash the dope and do their deals at night while ole Joshua was asleep upstairs. Anyone who worked there could have gotten hold of a key."

"Well that implicates Dora's parents, even Dora herself."

"Dora's straight as an arrow. But there used to be a lot of day laborers tending the grounds. Mainly Mexicans, illegals. The Whalens took care of the mansion itself; Mrs. Whalen doing all the cooking and cleaning, Mr. Whalen doing all the handyman jobs. 'Course they both spoke fluent Spanish. It was Mr. Whalen who carted the gardening crews back and forth. But you probably know all that. Hmmm—could be a drug dealer joined the crew and worked something out with Mr. Whalen."

"If that were the case then why stay on as house servants? He would have made a bundle in the dope business."

"The lure of the Perfume itself? Then, too, if they left they'd be giving up the goose that laid the golden egg . . . besides the free rent. Still, it would be interesting to look into."

"And the O'Kellys would love any story that put my family in a bad light."

"You're the one who suggested some hard-hitting reporting." Emily checked her watch then slipped the tape recorder in her jacket pocket. "I'd better get over to the office and file the story. At least I've got time before the paper goes to bed."

While escorting Emily to the door Salome said as nonchalantly as possibly, hoping Emily wouldn't pick up on any subtext, "Is Michael's wife with him?"

"Michael?"

"Michael O'Kelly."

"Oh! Not that I know of. I only just met him. At least he seems more than your basic bean counter. Has a Harvard MBA."

The question was out before Salome could stop herself. "Any idea where he's staying?"

"Well it wouldn't be Otter Haven, would it?" Emily laughed. Then she gave Salome a suspicious look. "Why do you want to know, Salome?"

"I remember him as being a decent sort of guy. Not like the rest of the O'Kellys."

"Oh. I thought you might be gunning for him or something."

"Just curious. I've tried to stay out of the feuds."

"Well, he's at his aunt's B and B. The competition if you could even call it that. The place looks like a haunted house. Assuredly, the O'Kellys don't have the Waterhouse touch where residential property is concerned." She shook her head. "What a waste. Such a great view, too, overlooking the village and all. Funny isn't it how your two families bookend the bluff, as it were." Suddenly her eyes widened. "Hey, they can see clear across to the Perfume! Someone might have seen something. Could be a good lead."

While Emily put on her raincoat Salome said, "Please, Emily, just keep it general when you talk to the TV reporter. Unless they've left."

"Oh they'll be there. But no problem—you didn't socialize with your tenant and hardly knew him. Of course, they'll want to know why it took so long to get one relevant sentence. I'll just say we discussed your future plans for the Perfume, information not really newsworthy or related to the crime. Then she added proudly, "They can get the finer points from tomorrow morning's *Echo*. This is *my* story now!"

Now geared up for the weather—and more—Emily gave Salome a long look. Finally, she said, "Thank you, Salome. You just might have saved the paper and my job."

"Just don't forget our deal."

"I won't. And I promise you, they won't go near your father."

As the official spokesperson for the owner of the Perfume Mansion, Emily spoke to the TV reporter camped on the driveway and, later, would be seen on the 10 o'clock local news. Salome needn't have worried about Emily. Unwilling to share the story, her story, she offered up only a few sound bytes.

Back in the study, Salome heard the van pull away. She sighed, feeling as if a block of negative energy had disappeared, allowing more positive energy to resume its flow around the property.

However, she knew it was just a matter of time before the big guns arrived to milk the story from every teat. Aside from the weather, this was a slow news time of year and Palmer had been something of a celebrity. Holyrood would have to endure a few days of disruption until other bad behavior drew the attention of the media.

Sitting at her desk and playing her phone messages, Salome jotted down the names and numbers of those to call back: Janelle, Barbara Boatwright, and two clients in San Francisco. Of the remaining eleven, two were from her mother, two were hang-ups, and seven were from Bay Area TV and print journalists.

She rang the clients first though both had canceled appointments and said nothing about rescheduling or wanting a call back.

"Hi, Alice, this is Salome Waterhouse," she said, bringing forth good cheer. "I got your message."

"Yes, uh, I'm real busy now and think I'll just wait on this feng shui thing."

"Well, just so you know, I also conduct consultations on the phone. You fax me the layout of your apartment and—"

"Look, I'm sorry, Salome but I've changed my mind."

Salome put a fake smile in her voice. "Okay. Well, do call me if you change your mind again."

Salome hung up and rang the second client, a young gay

banker named Bill Foley she'd met through Mandy. After two rings his tape kicked in. Salome had just begun to explain that she could provide a reading over the phone, when he picked up.

"Look, Ms. Waterhouse, I heard you own that mansion where the gay artist was murdered. You expect me to believe this feng shui really works when a murder happens on your own property? Give me a break." He hung up.

She felt stung. But her own discomfort dissolved when she realized what he'd said. Gay artist? Palmer Fordham? But then Mandy had said he'd known him. But Mandy knew a lot of straight people, too. So what was the deal here?

For a while she fretted at her desk, in too much of a funk to make any more calls. The cancellations were a strong reminder that this murder could ruin her business. Her head began to throb. On the verge of tears, even the thought of Michael O'Kelly's sudden proximity had no power to lift her spirits.

Chapter 12

A few blocks away, Michael O'Kelly also sat at a desk, this in the turret room on the third floor of his Aunt Livia's decaying bed and breakfast inn. He sipped a scotch while staring at the rain slide down the bay windows facing the village. Earlier his aunt had entered carrying a tray with an ice bucket, a bottle of Glenlivet, and a highball glass. She set the tray on a table by the bed then closed the curtains. Rather stiffly, she'd invited him to watch TV in the lounge, treating him like any other paying customer. He said he had too much work to do and thanked her. Once she'd left, he opened the curtains.

He could hardly believe he was actually in Holyrood again, his thoughts and emotions right where he'd left them thirty-five years ago, centered on Salome Waterhouse.

On the off chance she might still be in Holyrood, the previous night he'd called directory assistance only to discover no Salome Waterhouse was listed. Today, he'd casually asked Emily Harkin if she knew Salome.

"Lives across the street from me," Emily had replied.

Using the reverse directory at the office, he'd found her phone number.

Finally building up the courage to call, he found himself

unable to speak upon hearing her voice invite him to leave a message, his hand on the receiver shaking. He hated himself for plunging into such adolescent behavior and wondered if the magnificent façade he'd so carefully constructed over three decades might be on the verge of collapse—and if it did, would there be anything behind it?

Annoyed with himself, he got up from the desk and walked across the creaking floor with its faded patch of worn carpet and stood at the windows rattling in the storm. He ran a hand through his shaggy gray hair. *Christ*, he thought, *two phone calls and you're questioning your whole life*.

At one time, he'd loved the view from his aunt's old Victorian. Then Holyrood village had appeared enchanting to him. Now, through the rain, the yellow street lights, the faint glow at the curtained cottage windows, BEACH BISTRO glaring in pink neon, gaping darkness on either side of it, all came together reminding him of the poorly painted watercolors he'd reluctantly bought in Paris on his honeymoon. Though he hadn't known it at the time, his wife had been more attracted to the painters and their aura of seedy romanticism. Barely a year later, she returned to Paris, thanks to Daddy's deep pockets, and he'd never seen her or the ghastly pictures again.

He drained his glass then added more ice and scotch from the bedside table. He glanced at the worn chenille bedspread and the two tiny pillows that looked like they'd been stolen from the overhead rack of an airplane. If his aunt hadn't owned the property outright, she would have been out of business years ago.

Soon after his arrival the day before yesterday, he'd walked around the Bluff and village, half fearing, half hoping he'd run into Salome. Though he hadn't seen her, the pristine elegance of Otter Haven in contrast to the state of Aunt Livia's B and B and his Uncle Damon's cottage located just outside the lovely resort made him acutely aware of the differences between the two families, and left him feeling embarrassed to be an O'Kelly.

The last time he'd seen the nine-bedroom Victorian, it sported bold red paint with crisp white and gold trim, a sturdy front porch, garlands of holly and berries wrapped around the pillars. A twelve-foot blue spruce stood in the front window, covered in silver balls that reflected the multicolored lights and brightly wrapped presents stacked so high they peeked over the sill.

That memory made his first sight of the house all the more shocking. The peeling, faded paint gave the exterior a diseased look. Dusty, yellowed mini-blinds now hung in the unwashed window. A couple of aluminum and plastic chairs had blown off the sagging porch into the weedy yard. The fanlight above the front door needed attention. More than window cleaner and a rag, someone would have to use a chisel to remove the crusted dirt and soot from the corners.

Just inside, knobby plastic runners branched into the lounge on the right, up the stairs to the left, and down the hall straight ahead. A flat round plastic fixture housing a low-watt bulb and dead insects had replaced the chandelier that he used to swat to create the tinkling sound of the many crystals. The house smelled of mildew and must and gave off an essence of chronic depression that his aunt didn't seem to notice when she greeted him, though "greeted" wasn't the right word given the chilly reception.

"Hello, Michael," she'd said. "You're looking well."

"Aunt Livie!" He started forward to give her a hug. She took a step back and he stopped himself, noticing the look in her ball-bearing eyes and knew she'd never forgiven him for consorting with a Waterhouse—or for staying away from her brother's, his father's, funeral. She moved behind a small reception desk.

"Mary said you're not sure how long you'll be staying. She reserved the room on *her* credit card."

Setting down his hanging bag and briefcase, Michael

reached into the pocket of his navy cashmere coat and brought out a long wallet. Her eyes were on it as he pulled out a Platinum credit card. She may not have kind feelings toward him but she was eager enough to take his money.

"Use this. And I want the form from the transaction Mother called in."

When returning his credit card, Livia gave him a hard candy smile then pulled a folder from the desk drawer. She handed him a Visa form with hand-printed numbers and his mother's name, Mary Jane O'Kelly on it. He tore it in two and slipped the pieces into his coat pocket.

From a small cabinet she lifted a set of keys from a hook.

He followed her up the creaking stairs to the third floor, averting his eyes from her large bottom under the gray wool skirt but was less successful avoiding the sound of the cilice. A Catholic contraption of spiky barbs that poked one's thighs whenever they walked, it was meant to keep the wearer's mind on Jesus instead of lust.

It must work, he thought ruefully. His aunt showed no signs of lust for anything, including life.

"Per your mother's instructions, I've laid in some bottles of scotch. The price, plus cost of delivery, will be charged to your room. All phone calls are on long distance rates so don't act surprised when you get the bill."

They reached the first landing and she turned to the right, creating a disturbance in the air that smelled of urine. Michael set his gaze firmly on the old flower-patterned carpet beneath the glaze of the runner.

"Mary booked the bridal suite for you. It's an extra twenty-five dollars a day and has its own bath. A continental breakfast is served between seven and nine. Not a minute after."

"I'll be eating out."

"The bed won't be changed and you won't get fresh towels unless you call down and make a request."

"Will that be at the long-distance rate?"

Livia finally laughed, more a cackle really.

First thing, after he'd entered the room and Livia left, with a promise to bring up his libation in an hour (at extra charge), he opened his briefcase and removed his cell phone. He punched in the numbers for the rambling house in the highlands across the highway where his mother lived.

"Tell me, Mother. What did I do to deserve this?"

MICHAEL FINISHED HIS SECOND SCOTCH, PUT on his coat, and grabbed the umbrella he'd bought earlier in the day. He needed to grab a bite. Though pink neon didn't whet his appetite, the Beach Bistro looked to be the only restaurant open. Afterward he'd take a long walk. The rain didn't deter him—he'd experienced plenty of nor'easters in New England.

Maybe he'd even stop by Emily Harkin's. *To discuss business*, he told himself.

TO SALOME, HOUSE CLEANING AND MAINTEnance was a form of honoring one's space that, in turn, honored oneself. Results were quick and never failed to produce a feeling of well-being. Once cleaned and tidied, the ch'i flowed smoothly, creating a harmonious atmosphere. If more people—men especially—understood the principle, they wouldn't regard cleaning as an unpleasant chore.

And so, she lit some pine incense, put on a tape of taiko drumming, and set to work redirecting the ch'i flow in the study.

While depositing the pieces of the broken Kwan Yin in a garbage bag, she thanked the spirit of the Chinese goddess of compassion and serenity for her years of service, apologizing for bringing them to such an abrupt end.

She picked up the polished stones from the fountain, deciding to set it up in the helpful people gua on the other side of the study. Though she certainly needed to enhance her fame/reputation sector, she decided that, this time, she'd place a large red candle on the windowsill.

The base of the fountain, being made of resin, hadn't been damaged, just overturned. As she reached for it, she noticed the oval red sticker on the bottom of the pedestal. The printed words seemed to leap out at her: "MADAME WU'S HOUSE OF WISDOM."

Instantly she experienced an "Ah Ha!" moment, a synchronistic event that physically caused her skin to prickle.

Since Madame Wu had sent the fountain, a gift to honor her completion of feng shui studies, she'd cleaned it periodically but hadn't had any reason to turn it over to look at the base.

Once she reestablished the fountain and new Kwan Yin on the small table in the helpful people gua, she switched off the music and blessed the space.

At the conclusion of the ritual, she went to the desk and looked up the phone number of her mentor.

She'd met Madame Wu almost a decade ago in Arlington, Virginia, where she was giving a talk on feng shui at a conference on eastern philosophy. After the talk, Salome had introduced herself, sensing a kindred spirit. They went out for tea and talked for nearly three hours. Salome told her that since an early age she'd been listening to houses, taking their pulse, as it were, and somehow understanding the difference between bad spaces and good spaces; that both her father and grandfather had been builders. That though her father's houses were built during the postwar boom and not unique like her grandfather's, she'd loved to go with him to the sites and run through the wooden frames, believing herself to be inside the skeleton of some mystical entity, loving the heady aroma of the fresh-cut pine.

Madame Wu had said, "When you are ready for the teacher, the teacher will find you," and proceeded to offer herself, explaining that her practice was bicoastal and that she maintained two home offices, one in Washington, D.C., the other in San Diego.

Salome studied with Madame Wu for four years, meeting at her house near Dupont Circle and accompanying her on consultations whenever she was in town. Salome read everything available and practiced on the homes of friends in the D.C. area and New Orleans, where Gabriel researched his books. Madame Wu considered Salome a natural and after the lengthy apprenticeship declared her ready to hang out her shingle. About that time, Madame Wu opened a shop selling feng shui enhancements and a school in San Diego, limiting her time in the D.C. area. But she trusted Salome enough to turn over a portion of her client list, most of whom had already met the budding practitioner.

Salome punched in the San Diego number, hoping her former mentor was home. If anyone could give her good advice, it was Grace Wu.

Chapter 13

MADAME Wu's decision to open a school and feng shui store in San Diego instead of the Washington, D.C. area had nothing to do with the weather and everything to do with the Bagua and feng shui. Because of its long-held position as gateway to the United States, practitioners considered New York as the door or "mouth of ch'i." Since New York occupied the helpful people/travel gua, that put San Diego in the wealth sector—a good place for business.

Salome could hear soft Chinese music in the background when Madame Wu answered the phone.

For the next fifteen minutes Salome poured out her story—finding the body, the sensation of evil emanating from the Perfume, breaking the Kwan Yin, the canceled appointments in San Francisco, and her concerns about performing an exorcism.

After listening patiently, Madame Wu said, her accent still slightly British from years spent in Hong Kong, "Indeed, my dear, you couldn't possibly sell or rent the property until an exorcism has been performed. You haven't done one have you?"

"Not yet. I'll need guidance."

"Let me know when the police release the property. Next

week I'm off to a conference in New Zealand but will leave numbers where you can reach me.

"In the meantime, there's much you need to do to prepare. First, I can tell you're keen to track down this killer—leave that to the police. Oh I know you probably consider yourself quite capable, having worked on so many fiction books with your former husband, but please, stay away from the murder investigation. I sense you're already in danger."

"I don't see how."

"On one level, when you found the body, you put yourself in an area of tremendous sha which manifested to your detriment when you fell and hurt your head and destroyed the Kwan Yin. On another level, maybe you saw something the killer overlooked. If this person doesn't already know about your discovery of the body, they soon will.

"There are things we can do to protect you, but I'll get to that in a minute. Learn everything you can about the house including the day it was ready for occupancy. That will be the birth date."

"Hold on a sec."

Salome moved over to the drafting table and checked the blueprints. At the bottom right hand corner of the top sheet she found her grandfather's name and a date.

"Now I don't know if the date I found coincides with final construction or not but the date on the blueprints is September nine, nineteen-nineteen. That's a lot of nines."

Madame Wu sucked in a breath. "Very auspicious."

There was a pause then she continued. "Find out all you can about who has lived there, particularly the first occupants. The impressions they left on the house will be the foundation of all that has subsequently occurred there. Also look for anything that has happened in the immediate vicinity. Because of what you said about sensing malignant energy, could be some terrible event occurred if not on the property then near it at some time."

At this point, Salome mentioned her experience in the subterranean chambers at age seven and her belief in the existence of a secret room despite evidence to the contrary in the blueprints.

"Now that's interesting. Such a space would contain stagnant sha and being at the foundation, adversely affect the residents. In which gua is the kitchen?"

"Wealth."

"Hmm. Very auspicious for financial security. And the position of the stove?"

"Thing is, I haven't been in the house in five years, Grace. I don't know what's been moved and what hasn't. But I'll talk to the housekeeper. She'll be the best source of information about the interior. Her family has worked there since the house was built. And she can tell me in which room the victim slept, the position of his bed and so on."

"Just remember, the history is especially important—vital to preparation for an exorcism and blessing. You don't want surprises. However, if there is a secret room, by tearing down the walls the negative energy would be released. Depending on other factors, simply *sealing the door* might be all that's needed."

The feng shui cure or enhancement known as "sealing the door" involved preparing a mixture of realgar and a certain number of drops of alcohol. This preparation was then dotted at specific points on the inside of the bedroom door, front door, and all other doors leading into the house, followed by a transcendental blessing. The remainder was then flicked around the center of each room while reinforcing the effort with further blessings.

"Now, to you. First, clean your house completely and make any small repairs. Eliminate clutter, being especially mindful of the helpful people, career, and fame/reputation guas on the property as a whole, then the house then in each room."

Though Salome had already thought of these things, it would have been impolite to mention the fact.

"Do you have a garage?"

"Detached."

"Good. Do the garage, too. Once you've completed the tasks do your transcendental work. Though I don't really need to be telling you this, my purpose is to *reinforce your intentions* by speaking aloud."

They discussed various enhancements—crystals, wind chimes, plants, colors.

"I'm sorry about what's happened to you, dear. Fallout from this terrible incident. But your concerns now are self-protection, rescuing your reputation, and putting together a history of the mansion."

"I'll take care of it."

"Keep in mind that good chi is available every day of our lives."

"Grace, thanks for taking time to talk to me."

"You have my blessings."

Salome put the phone back in the cradle and took a deep breath.

For a moment, she considered Madame Wu's advice regarding the criminal investigation. While she appreciated her mentor's concern, she couldn't just back off. This just happened to be the first time in twenty years she had the opportunity to use all she'd learned as Gabe's researcher. Well, she'd keep a low profile. While compiling a history of the mansion it wouldn't be the least bit unusual for her to slip in questions about the present.

Though spiritually buoyed by her conversation with Madam Wu, the events of the day had left her physically exhausted. Tomorrow would be soon enough to return the remaining calls. Still, she thought she'd better inform Phyl about Palmer's sister, in case her cousin hadn't found that information, as she'd need to notify next of kin.

When the answering machine kicked in she felt some relief, as she didn't think she had the energy to explain how or why she had the number in her possession.

"Phyl, Salome. Palmer has a sister in Houston, Babette Fordham." After reading the phone number from Palmer's rental application she started to hang up then remembered something. "Oh, and thanks for permission to head up to Mandy's. I'll let you know when I leave and return."

She shut off the lights in the study and padded down the hall to her bedroom. When she arrived at the entrance, in knowledge/spirituality, and switched on the overhead, she suddenly stopped as if physically hitting a wall. Maybe it was Michael O'Kelly's presence in town, but for the first time in five years, she regarded the bedroom with a professional eye. Despite having a bedroom in the relationship gua of the house, it was pretty clear why she didn't have a love life.

Tatami mats covered the floor and other than the one-person futon tightly rolled in the top right-hand corner, nothing else but old white curtains occupied the colorless, uninteresting space. Though the futon was positioned in the room's relationship gua, the far side of it was flush against the wall, providing no path for another person.

If she encountered this bedroom in a client's house, she'd know instantly that the client's love life was either suffering or nonexistent and she would get to work. Obviously, a larger futon was needed and with space on *both* sides to accommodate two people. She'd further suggest a bed frame and round nightstands on either side with matching lamps. Decorative items should be in pairs, say two pictures, two figurines, and no mirrors or TV. The bedroom, in which we spend a third of our lives, should be reserved for two activities only: sleeping and making love. And though some consider mirrors sexual enhancements, when a person wakes up in the night and encounters their reflection in a mirror, it startles personal ch'i. Like seeing a ghost. Over time this leads to spiritual and internal physical problems.

She was also an advocate of keeping the TV out of the bedroom. However, to those who enjoyed watching TV in bed, she always suggested covering the set when it wasn't in use.

As to color, she'd tell the client to use pastels. *A nice peach tone on the walls would be better than the stark white you've got here . . .*

A hard rain suddenly pelting the windows brought her back. She pulled out a pillow and comforter from the closet, then unrolled the futon, laughing at herself for even thinking of Michael O'Kelly in terms of her bedroom. That she slept well in this room was all that mattered. Besides, he was probably happily married and hadn't even given her a thought.

ACROSS THE STREET, EMILY HARKIN BUSTLED around, checking her liquor cabinet, fluffing the pillows on the sofa, and putting together a plate of assorted cheeses and crackers, another form of ch'i on her mind. Michael O'Kelly had tracked her down at *The Echo*, saying he wanted to meet at her house. She wondered why he didn't just come over to the office. At least she'd finished the story and left it with the assistant editor to copyedit. He'd have to put the paper to bed by himself but when the owner's representative called, she couldn't very well protest. Not that she wanted to. He'd be arriving shortly to work out some "kinks," as he'd said.

Of course he meant newspaper business but she couldn't help imagining some subliminal message. Why else would he want to meet in a more intimate setting? They were both healthy adults and, as she'd learned today, divorced. Further, unlike most of his rat-faced kin, those she'd been dealing with for years, he was quite the hunk. Christ, he even had his own teeth!

Emily went into the bathroom of her bedroom and stripped. For a moment she stood commiserating with the mirror above the sink framing her torso.

How strange, she thought. Wasn't it just days ago that I was a beautiful woman with a fine figure. What happened?

How did my breasts get so far away from my collarbone?

She stepped up on the toilet seat and turned around and looked over her shoulder at her backside. Not so bad. Butt and thighs Betty Grable firm, legs always her best feature, muscle tone maintained by running back and forth from her house to the offices of *The Echo* in the village.

Stepping down off the toilet, she tucked her hair in a neon pink shower cap and entered the shower stall. For the moment dismissing the effects of time on her body, she thought about the Historical Society now housed in the former police station and just around the corner from the newspaper's offices. Definitely a source of material for the series she planned. *The Echo*'s morgue contained nothing that reflected badly on the O'Kellys. But Mavis Hicks-Dulane at the Historical Society would know where the bodies were buried and probably had the records to prove it.

Like Salome suggested, she'd do some hard-hitting investigative journalism. Not that she'd print anything while the O'Kellys still owned the paper. That would be career suicide and she'd have to be careful, keep her own files hidden in her home computer. Among others, Michael had mentioned a *real* paper down the coast interested in *The Echo*. Maybe she'd do a one-eighty and instead of whining about the sale, suggest he sell to them. Then, of course, she'd have to scramble to convince the new owners to keep her on and to maintain the paper's integrity and not turn it into one of those all-classified rags.

And who knew? Her investigation just might reveal Palmer Fordham's killer. In fact, she wouldn't put it past someone in the O'Kelly clan to have concocted the sensational murder. . . .

Suddenly her body went rigid. Good God! What if Michael O'Kelly had come to Holyrood as the family hit man and this business of selling *The Echo* was just a cover? But while not a particularly warm person, he didn't have that edge and lack of conscience needed to whack people.

She relaxed a bit and began lathering her body with heavily scented lavender soap. Then she considered Damon O'Kelly who lived just by the gate to the Otter Haven Resort. He definitely had an edge and likely no conscience took up space in his addled brain—but neither did much of anything else.

Now taking a more benign form, her speculations returned to Michael O'Kelly and where the seduction would take place. The couch? The sheepskin rug in front of the fireplace? Oddly, the thought of him as a killer heightened her excitement.

She shut off the water and grabbed a towel. She started for the bedroom and then stopped and regarded herself in the mirror again.

"Eat your hearts out Woodward and Bernstein. Harkin's on the story."

As to the "sudden" decline of her breasts, she quickly decided what action to take.

Raise the mirror.

Chapter 14

I *have every right to be here, every right, every right.* Like the mantra Salome chanted after finding Palmer's body, Phyl's repeated itself in her head but without the calming result. Quite the opposite. An internal debate was going on, one side accusing her of trespassing despite the fact that as lead detective, she *did* have every right to be inside the Perfume. Even alone and past midnight.

The department didn't have the manpower to post a guard outside which gave her another reason to be here—to check on things; make sure no one else had taken a nocturnal interest in the place.

She stood in the Perfume's foyer, bathed in the blazing light of the chandelier, a yawning cavern of darkness ahead of her. Still wearing the same clothes she'd worn all day, she carried a small evidence kit and a flashlight and wore latex gloves.

Around eleven-fifteen she'd left her office in the new police station, actually believing she'd be able to sleep after a martini and a bite. But somehow all the small brown envelopes containing keys to the Perfume had ended up in her briefcase and after a sip of the chilled Bombay gin she just couldn't keep from testing them.

Certainly she needed to know that Dora Whalen, Waterhouse Properties, and Reggie Waterhouse had given her the right keys, and until now she had not had the opportunity to test them. Sure enough, one set didn't work; those keys from the envelope marked "Otter Haven." She'd have to talk to her Uncle Reggie and suspected he'd handed over the wrong keys on purpose. But at his age, he could get away with claiming absent-mindedness.

The victim's keys were yet to be found, providing yet another excuse for her to be here. And, too, she told herself, she'd have a better chance of uncovering some overlooked clue without all the SOC (scene of crime) techs and ancillary personnel in the way.

Fordham's wallet hadn't been found either, creating a convenient pointer toward robbery/homicide, a possible break-in by a stranger or strangers. The DMV had provided his birth date, confirming Salome's reason for the early morning consultation as did the letter her cousin so quickly provided. But convenience always raised red flags.

As the internal accusation was overridden, she began to enjoy standing in the foyer, convincing herself that the Perfume itself welcomed her home. She'd always believed the property should have been hers. Unlike her cousin, the mansion provoked no silly fears. Her grandfather had certainly known how much she loved the place and how much Salome disliked it. Yet, he'd left it to Salome. Perverse bastard!

But now that it was a crime scene, the Perfume belonged to her and her alone. From her years as a homicide detective with the SFPD, she well knew the dangers of emotionally connecting with a murder victim and also knew she was doing just that on a primitive, territorial level, regarding the property itself as a victim. At the same time, wouldn't this intense feeling she had for the Perfume help her do some really inspired investigating?

Unless, the unwelcome little voice interjected, she prolonged the investigation so she could come and go as she pleased, for as long as she pleased.

Suddenly, she heard a soft, muffled sound. A door closing? The creak of a stair under a light footfall? Or was the house itself sighing under the burden of death? Couldn't blame the weather, as outside it was dead calm. After a final, violent squall, the rain had ceased about the time she left the station.

She reached behind her and switched off the light, then pulled out her gun, realizing how foolish she'd been to stand in the rich glow, making a target of herself. For, just as she had every right to be here, killers often felt the same.

For a long moment she didn't move, and just listened, angry at herself for allowing guilt, probably a companion to her deep-rooted desires, to overshadow common sense.

After a while, she was satisfied that the sound had been natural. Maybe a rodent in the walls.

Still, with the Glock in one hand and a flashlight and an evidence kit in the other, she crept silently down the carpeted stairs to the living room.

At the bottom, she set the evidence kit on the floor and swung the light around while holding the gun out, deep shadows forming on the boundaries of the beam. Then, she gave a start as she caught a pair of eyes staring in from the veranda.

Her skin prickled and felt burned. Then she realized the light had caught a raccoon staring in the room. Unconcerned, it waddled off into the trees at the edge of the veranda.

Phyllis laughed nervously then abruptly stopped. If Salome had been telling the truth and one of the French doors was open when she arrived, most likely it hadn't been open all night. Otherwise they'd have seen evidence of nocturnal creatures.

She'd learn more about the time of death at the autopsy scheduled for 8 A.M. The medical examiner had given her a rough estimate determined by livor mortis—the blood collection on Palmer's backside where the body had touched the floor—the degree of rigor mortis, and the body's temperature. But with environmental conditions to consider, particularly the body being so close to an open door, it was far from accurate and he'd covered his bases by guessing the time of death as sometime between midnight and maybe three to 4 A.M.

She swung her flashlight over to the fireplace. Oddly, Palmer hadn't built a fire last night even though there were other indications that he'd entertained—empty food cartons in the kitchen, the half bottle of wine and two glasses on the coffee table. And the night had been cold. She'd checked the thermostat and it was set at fifty-five, indicating he conserved heat. Palmer himself had worn only a pair of thigh-length Billabong shorts and no other bits of clothing were in the room. Having worn only a pair of shorts on a winter's night suggested he'd gotten heat from another person.

Yet, given his reputation as a ladies' man, wouldn't he have had a fire going, if not for heat then for atmosphere? She sighed. *What do I know about the mating habits of the latest crop of males?*

A couple of other details, on the surface somewhat innocuous, bothered her. But sometimes the innocuous revealed more than the obvious.

He'd used a small room just off the living room for an office. Unlike his studio upstairs, the little office was neat and minimally furnished with an oak desk and chair and a two-drawer matching file cabinet. Behind the leather desk chair a digital phone/answering machine hung on the wall but without the cordless handset. All messages had been erased. The volume had been turned down completely, suggesting that he didn't want to be disturbed. So, what was the handset doing under the sofa? Because of the placement, instead of being say *beside* the sofa or on the coffee table, it appeared to have been kicked there. And why bring it to the living room at all?

Phyllis moved over to the L-shaped sectional sofa, which

had been vacuumed for hair and fiber and again checked around and under the cushions for his keys and wallet, her thoughts on the phone again.

She knew a woman had called in the order to the Beach Bistro. The redial feature on the phone had confirmed that the last call made had been to the restaurant. But wouldn't the woman have simply gone in the office and used the phone? After all, the menu was right there in the top drawer of the desk. If she'd picked up the menu and taken it in the living room for Palmer to look over and after calling in the order didn't feel like returning to the office, the *menu* would, like the phone, be in the living room. But since the menu was in the drawer, why not return the phone at the same time? Or simply stay in the office and make the call.

Then there was the file on the desk—a million-dollar life insurance policy he'd taken out at Christmas, leaving one Babette Fordham, sister, as his sole benefactor. Was it coincidence this file just happened to be on his desk after his body was found? Had he gone over it recently, neglected to return it to the cabinet, then met his killer?

In her mind, she replayed the call she'd made to Ms. Babette Fordham, resident of Houston, Texas, her date of birth on the insurance policy indicating that she was his older sister.

After the initial shock of hearing that her brother was dead, (under questionable circumstances, Phyllis said) Babette had refused to discuss him. In fact, she didn't believe it.

"Look, I don't know who you are! You might be some tabloid geek or someone with a perverted sense of humor."

"Let me give you the number of our local police station. You can call and confirm."

"Bull. That doesn't mean anything. This could still be a setup."

"Tell me then, do you have a copy of a life insurance policy issued by"—she named the company and the policy number—"and dated December seventeen of last year?"

Quiet enveloped the other end of the phone.

"Ms. Fordham?"

Phyllis listened to a sob, then quickly went on. "When was the last time you saw your brother?"

"Christmas. I, uh, was out there at Christmas." She inhaled another sob. "How did he die?"

Without answering, Phyllis presented her own question. "Are you aware of any enemies he may have had?"

"No."

"How long were you in town?"

Phyllis listened to more snuffling and choked sounds. "A couple weeks, I guess. Look I can't talk anymore."

"What about other relatives—"

Abruptly, she'd hung up.

Throughout the day, Phyllis called back, only to connect with busy signals, not even an answering machine. She then tried to get someone from the Houston PD to go over and talk to Babette but they had plenty of big-city problems and neither the time, personnel, nor the inclination to help out and Phyl didn't have any personal contacts in Houston to call on for a favor.

Further, the beneficiary of a million-dollar life insurance policy couldn't be dismissed as a suspect just because she answered a phone in Houston, Texas—if, indeed, Babette herself really answered the phone.

Phyllis had called Britta and asked her to find information on early morning flights to Houston out of San Jose International and the Monterey Airport. She hadn't placed the call to Babette until around noon, making it two hours later in Texas. She'd have had enough time to leave the scene and fly to Houston.

"And check on private planes as well. They're supposed to file flight plans."

Earlier that morning she'd called Britta to amend her edict that Salome stay in town. Talking to one of the deputy sheriffs instantly reminded her that the head honcho was on vacation. Knowing him to be a stickler for detail, she hadn't wanted him accusing her of using a light touch with her own kin, especially if he wanted to question her and Salome wasn't available.

Phyllis left the living room and climbed the stairs to the studio at the top of the mansion, stopping in the doorway to survey the strange scene.

In what could have been a marvelous room in which to watch sunrises and sunsets were odd bits of second-hand furniture now sporting a light dusting of fingerprint powder. An old ottoman upholstered in faded pink velvet, something one could imagine thirties actress Jean Harlow posed on, her platinum head propped on the bolster, her mouth formed in a crimson smirk, seemed to have been carelessly shoved into the middle of the room. Nineteen coffee tables, in varied shapes and sizes, some taken apart, were scattered everywhere along with half a dozen sheets of Plexiglas in varying sizes. And then there was the twin mattress about ten feet from the doorway.

Earlier in the day, she'd gone through the five expensively furnished bedrooms with their king-sized romper beds neatly made with gorgeous coverlets and thick pillows. Despite the elegant and comfortable accommodations, he'd chosen to sleep on this stained mattress under a filthy comforter that might have been plucked from a homeless person's grocery cart.

The smell of stale body odor and turpentine still prevailed as she moved toward the rough-hewn table along the back wall littered with boxes and nubs of charcoal, crumpled tubes of acrylic and oil paints, mayonnaise jars crammed with brushes, and stacks of sketch pads.

An easel leaned against the wall, a sketchpad propped open on the lip. All the pages were filled with drawings of mermaids in various positions: swimming, at rest, reclining with the head propped on a hand.

To the right of the table had been a strange sculpture—

the lower body and fin of a fish, five feet in length and carefully painted in a mixture of iridescent pink, green, blue, and gold. It had been carted off to the lab. Upon first seeing it, she'd been attracted by the sparkling colors used to intricately define hundreds of scales. The interior had been constructed so a real person of a certain height could fit both legs and lower body inside. For the moment, anyway, she'd instructed the techs to simply dust the surface for prints and, as best they could, remove hair and fiber from the interior without sawing it in half. Someone might have fit inside, but she couldn't bring herself to allow the beautiful construction to be mutilated. Not just yet, anyway. She figured the fingerprints on the wineglass and food containers would provide the best lead to whomever Fordham had spent his last night with.

Beneath the table were the discarded remains of inexpensive newsprint tablets, just the front and heavy cardboard backing. She imagined him sketching then discarding whatever didn't appeal to him.

She further surveyed the room. Beside the door had been a pile of dirty laundry, about five days' worth—not that much by your average man's standards—now bagged and in the lab. Possibly someone else's clothes would be among Palmer's. He'd been using a bathroom on the second floor close to the stairs. In it was a towel smelling of mildew tossed over the top of the shower stall, where black mold crept up from the bottom tiles. The medicine chest above the sink had been empty. On the sink itself she'd found a worn, paint-stained cake of Ivory soap and a disposable razor.

As yet, they'd not found evidence of any drugs. Not even in the warren of rooms at the sublevel, where they did discover bags of plaster of Paris and assorted plaster casts of fish—none quite so appealing as the one in his studio.

Dora had told her Palmer had been living in the studio for a couple of weeks, said she'd brought dinner to him and per his instruction, knocked on the door to let him know food had arrived and left the tray on the landing. In the morning, she'd find the tray on the kitchen counter. Laundry he put out for her to collect maybe twice. All she knew was that he was working on a new project and didn't want to be disturbed.

"And the phone?" Phyl had asked. "Did he take it up to the studio with him?"

"It was always in the office off the living room. He fixed it so it only rang once then the machine picked up. He told me not to bother answering it."

Phyllis spent a few more minutes again shifting through the mess on the table, checking the coffee tables, ottoman, and bed, looking for his wallet and keys and evidence of drugs, irked that such a potentially beautiful space had been so abused, the hardwood floor dirty and splattered with paint, the fabulous views shut out by ratty old sheets tacked above the windows but which he'd moved to the side to admit light during certain hours.

She thought of his refrigerator, packed with food, and yet he'd ordered takeout. No, she reminded herself, *someone else*, had ordered the takeout. A woman.

She experienced the old familiar buzz at the back of her brain that told her something didn't make sense.

A few moments later, Phyllis trotted downstairs, let herself out of the house, and after stowing the kit and flashlight in the trunk, plopped into the driver's seat of her vintage Mercedes 190SL. With resounding *snaps*, she pulled off both latex gloves and threw them on the floor in front of the passenger seat. Palmer's body and the crime scene screamed of staging—insulting to cops perceived by the perp as too stupid to recognize the signs. But staging often worked in the cops' favor by revealing more about the killer than he or she realized.

Phyllis reached over and popped open the glove compartment. From beneath the maps, she fished out the stash of taboo cigarettes and the old Zippo Mandy had given her decades ago on which was engraved, PHYL THE PILL.

She lit a smoke and leaned back, trying to both relax and recall everything Dora had said during the interview in the small cottage by the Perfume Creek at about 9:15 A.M.

DORA HADN'T BEEN PARTICULARLY FORTH-coming, especially about certain guests.

"A couple of times I saw a young woman come out of the bathroom on the second floor after I took dinner to him. He didn't want me spending time in that part of the house. And the mold in the bathroom—"

"When was this?"

"I said. A couple of weeks ago."

"Who was she?"

"I don't know."

"What did she look like?"

Dora had fidgeted, obviously uncomfortable. Finally she said, "Oh, I don't know . . . *unsavory.*"

"Can you be more specific?"

"Well, she looked like a, well, a floozy."

"You mean a prostitute?"

Dora immediately seemed to shrivel into herself, clearly repulsed by the word, the suggestion of impropriety, or God knew what. A long time had passed since Phyl experienced such a reaction to straight definitions. She looked at Dora, who huddled over her darning, concentrating on every stitch.

Darning, she thought. Didn't that go out with the Civil War?

"Dora, I don't mean to upset you, but we are dealing with a murder investigation here. Any information you have about any sorts of people going into and out of the Perfume is of utmost importance. You understand?"

Dora pursed her lips, then dropping her darning egg and sock into her lap, she nodded. "She was short and had short blond hair. She came on certain evenings. A man came with her. Big and mean-looking. He was blond, too, and sometimes while she was upstairs, he'd go out on the veranda. But she was just the recent one."

"What do you mean?"

"First, you have to assure me that anything I say will be in strictest confidence."

"Of course."

"No, I mean it, Phyllis. This is my home and while Waterhouse Properties always supports me as the housekeeper to the new tenant, I have my reputation to consider. Though it's never happened, I could be fired by the tenant. If I tell secrets what would happen to me?"

Dora picked up her darning egg and sock and resumed stitching.

"Whatever you have to say goes no further than me." Which wasn't exactly the truth. She always confided in Ralph but nothing went past him.

Dora heaved a sigh. "Well, that Barbara Boatwright's been a regular since December. Her husband's out of town, you know."

Dora continued darning. Phyl found herself momentarily fascinated by the old-fashioned activity then looked away, not wanting to distract herself.

"Barbara Boatwright? Was Palmer painting her?"

"I wouldn't call it *painting*. Imagine! A woman of her age. She made a complete fool of herself, dropping by at all hours. One night when that Beth McCormick from Waterhouse Properties was over, I answered the door. Beth and Mr. Fordham were having dinner. I told Barbara he was busy. Then what does she do? Waltzes around to the back of the house and charges in through the patio right into the dining room. He told her if she didn't leave him alone he'd get a restraining order. Boy, did that make her mad! She said something about her investment and talking to her attorney, then stormed off."

"And when was that?"

"Just after New Year's, I guess."

"Have you seen her since?"

Now seeming to warm to the subject, Dora looked up, her black eyes shining. For a moment Phyllis was struck by her magnificent bone structure, inherited from her parents who'd both been of Hispanic descent. As a young woman Dora had been quite a dark-haired beauty but for some reason had never married. Even now in her sixties and completely gray, she was still an admirable-looking woman, though she dressed like a frump.

"Several times. And, well, someone else has been around."

"Oh really? Who?"

"Can't say. A couple times I've seen someone moving around the trees at the back after dark. I couldn't say for sure if it was Barbara Boatwright but I wouldn't put it past her."

"When did this start?"

Dora concentrated on her darning. After about a minute, Phyl repeated the question.

"I'm thinking!" Dora snapped.

The darning worked as a convenient prop, keeping Dora from making eye contact.

Finally, she said, "Must've been after his Halloween party."

"And you didn't call the police," Phyl remarked, her irritation evident. Quite possibly he'd been stalked for the past months and Dora hadn't bothered calling. People complained about crime and lack of police protection but didn't want to get involved. That always set her teeth on edge.

"Well, I told *him*, didn't I! If he wanted to, he'd of called. Who knows. He might have been playing some silly love game. He'd also been carrying on with Billie Ruth. That's gone on a couple years. He used to chase her around the trees. In their underwear. And other women. Beth McCormick was gaga for him. They liked to go at it on the lawn by the cliff."

"In broad daylight?"

"Of course not!"

"Any idea who visited him last night?"

"I don't know."

"How did you spend the evening?"

She jerked up, seemingly startled by the question. "Me?"

"It's a simple question, Dora. What did you do last night?"

"Well, I worked on an afghan and Mr. Boelkerke's socks. Then I went to bed."

"What time?"

"Ten. That's when I usually go to bed."

"And you didn't see anyone or anything unusual at the Perfume?"

"Well, I didn't look, did I."

"But sometimes you do. Were you sleeping with him?"

Dora's initial reaction bordered on murderous but she quickly contained herself. "That suggestion is disgusting."

Dora set down her darning egg and sock then stood up. "Please leave now, Phyllis."

"If you happen to remember anything—anything at all— call me any time." Phyllis handed over a card with various phone numbers printed on it. "And you'll need to go into the station and give a statement. And we'll need your finger-prints and hair and blood samples."

"I'm sure my fingerprints and hair are all over the house. But certainly not my blood!"

"I know that, Dora. It's simply to eliminate you as a sus-pect. You can refuse, of course. If you'd like, I'll send a squad car to pick you up and bring you back home."

"I'm sure that's very nice but I can walk."

Dora hustled Phyllis out to her creek-side garden. Just be-fore she closed the door, Phyllis actually darted back up the path. "Oh, Dora! One more thing!"

Dora regarded Phyllis with a mixture of annoyance and amusement. "Is this the Columbo treatment?"

Phyllis ignored the comment. "Did you see Salome on the back patio this morning—leaving the Perfume?"

Dora looked surprised. "Salome? What would she be doing there?"

"Did you see her?"

"She never comes to the Perfume. No I didn't see her."

"What time did you get up this morning?"

"I told you before, around eight."

Dora then slammed the door.

WHILE ENJOYING HER CIGARETTE, PHYLLIS CONsidered that Dora might be protecting Salome. She made a mental note to prep Britta for taking Dora's statement. Not that she needed to. Dear Britta could make a stone talk. And she felt certain Dora kept a closer eye on Palmer's doings than she let on.

Phyllis stubbed out the butt in the ashtray then started the car and pulled out of the drive, satisfied her memory for detail was still intact.

But something else made her uneasy. She'd found a sort of diary/address book earlier in the day and sincerely hoped the media wouldn't soon discover some of the names therein. Over the years, Palmer had created individual sea goddesses for many well-known, well-heeled women, privately of course. But she'd come across a name that gave her the shivers. According to the date, Palmer had painted her when her husband was a mere governor. Now she was the First Lady.

Chapter 15

EVERY village must have an idiot. Damon O'Kelly was Holyrood's. He'd been installed in the rundown cottage beside the gate to Otter Haven for forty years. During that time he'd done his best to scare away tourists with his crazy behavior and weird "lawn art." But, of course, that had been his family's intention. However, as often happens with a negative purpose, the result backfired. Like the beach, the wharf, and the architectural delights, he'd become another seaside attraction.

Early in the morning, under a low ceiling of dark clouds, Salome approached Damon's on her way to pick up her truck and the clothing she'd left at Otter Haven. She carried the items borrowed yesterday and the keys her father had shot across his desk.

Displayed on the oxalis-choked yard, used as both an outdoor studio and gallery, were Damon's wood carvings. Among the forest of oddities were a dog with a fanged cherub's face, a Pinocchio-faced Madonna cradling a snarling punk baby, a squat troll bearing the heads of the last three presidents, and a headless donkey with its tail arced high and the head of the current mayor poking out of its behind.

Suddenly, Damon himself shot out of his front door. A short, stocky man who appeared to have been carved from a stump, he had wispy, red-gray hair and skin that looked stained by the very redwood he used to create his art. Given the sort of images that must fill his mind, Salome was always surprised he hadn't gone completely white.

"Whaddya want?" he snarled and picked up a carving tool from a cluttered table on the porch. He wore stained gray sweatpants, a thin T-shirt latticed beneath the neck by years of wear and washing, and a woman's peach-colored leather jacket of 1980s vintage with excessively padded shoulders, one side faded pale pink by sunlight.

He dashed down the steps toward her.

"Not a thing, Damon. Not a thing."

Damon had been taunting Salome and her sisters since they were children. Over the years, he'd become no more than a familiar landmark that made noise.

He stopped at the rickety picket fence at the border of his property and Dolphin Street and glared at Salome, the carving tool gripped in his hand. Abruptly, his expression softened. He cocked his head then farted loudly.

"The Salome operrr-a! *Tutti con tutti!*" he sang out, his voice a rich baritone. He might have enjoyed a singing career had early drug use not addled his brain.

"Damon!" a woman called out. Livia O'Kelly stood at the door. "Get back in here and finish your breakfast. And you, Miss Waterhouse, go on about your business."

Though Damon was considered harmless, Salome momentarily questioned that assessment. She wouldn't put it past the O'Kellys to sic poor old Damon on any tenant in the Perfume Mansion. One of the hateful brothers could have tossed him into the Perfume's living room with instructions to use Palmer Fordham as he did a piece of wood.

"You have a good day now, Damon," Salome said and passed beneath the arc above the open gates. Of the two, Livia was the more terrifying and, like her brother, seemed to have special radar that alerted her whenever a Waterhouse was in range. She always fixed his breakfast and in the evenings, brought over his dinner on a foil-covered plate. Salome wondered if she would mention to Michael that she'd seen Salome this morning. Probably not, unless to say she'd seen *that ugly Salome Waterhouse. You wouldn't believe how she's aged. . . .*

Once in her parents' quarters, she gathered her clothes and put away the items she'd borrowed. Neither Satomi nor Reggie was around. Both early-risers, they were most likely in the lodge, having breakfast or seeing to the myriad details required to run the resort, especially now, preparing for the upcoming golf tournament.

Finally, she entered the study. The curtains were still drawn and the heat hadn't been turned on. It was cold and dark and she felt like an interloper. She hurried over to her father's desk and switched on the banker's lamp. Immediately she had a thought.

Besides talking to Dora Whalen, what better source of history than her grandfather's personal journals, the very books Mavis Hicks-Dulane had been pestering Reggie to donate to the Historical Society. Salome had looked at them a few times but had been put off by the cramped, antiquated handwriting.

In the top drawer of her father's desk she found the key to the cabinet. Her father kept the journals in chronological order.

Knowing the Perfume had been built around 1919 for actors Connor and Lily Sebastian, she pulled out volumes that bracketed and included that date. That at least provided a start. She didn't relish the idea of reading them all but would if she had to.

She locked the cabinet and returned the cabinet's key to the desk. Then she exchanged the keys he'd given her for a set that upon examination looked like those to her cottage. On a pad of paper she wrote a note to her father.

"Studying history of the Perfume. Borrowed journals 1918 to 1922.

Love, Mei"

After parking the truck in the garage, she tested the house keys, relieved to find that they worked. She put away her clothes and took the journals into the study, planning to read them later.

For the next few hours, while the latest line of squalls hit the coast, she cleaned her house, blessing the helpful people/ travel, fame/reputation, and career guas of the cottage and in each room. Once the house was cleaned and "cleared," she went outside.

In the garage, she put away scattered gardening tools and using a broom, swept away cobwebs high in the corners and cleaned the only window that happened to be in the fame gua. She hung a twenty-millimeter faceted crystal on a nine-inch red cord in front of the pane. This would raise the ch'i in the otherwise gloomy interior and stimulate the fame/reputation gua.

During a break in the weather, she went outside and mended a loose wooden slat on her fence, pulled oxalis, and skimmed debris from the surface of the pond in the Japanese garden while the wind chime in the arbor sang loudly.

Satisfied with her efforts, she finally settled in the study. Before tackling her grandfather's journals, she switched on the telephone's ringer, then returned the remaining telephone messages from yesterday.

Barbara Boatwright answered on the first ring. Salome couldn't help picturing her at the top of her house, eye to the lens of the telescope, staring into Palmer's studio.

"Jesus, Salome! Why didn't you return my call yesterday?"

Salome replied with her own interrogatory. "Did you send me money for a feng shui reading of the Perfume?"

"Oh God. I heard about that. Of course, I didn't."

"When's Palmer's birthday?"

"The guy's been murdered and you want to know his birthday! What kind of idiocy is this? Are you trying to remind me of our age differences?"

"Do you know his birth date?" Salome insisted.

A sigh strong as the wind outside her study *whooshed* over the phone line. "No!"

"Did you kill him, Barbara?" Though she felt strange asking, this is exactly what fictional P.I. Antoinette de Beauharnais would have done, knowing the suddenness of the question just might spur the truth, or at least, an honest reaction. She wished she and Barbara were face-to-face.

"How could you even ask such a question?" Barbara accused. "But believe me, I sure as hell want to know who did. I've been set up."

"How do you mean?"

"Your cousin came over yesterday. Wanted to know about my affair with Palmer. She wouldn't tell me who told her—I figured you had. How could you do that to me? I'm a suspect! My God, Charles finds out about this . . ." she trailed off.

"I didn't tell Phyl. Someone else must have. Did anyone ever see you together?"

"Dora—I . . . one night I went over when he was having dinner with that real estate agent who works for your father. Beth something."

"Beth McCormick."

"I suppose I made a fool of myself. I guess maybe Dora or Beth told your cousin."

"When was the last time you saw Palmer? In person."

"Not since we broke it off. A couple weeks ago."

"Have you continued watching him?"

"No," her voice wavered. "Well, not often."

"So, you didn't see him or anyone with him the night of the murder?"

"I was at the store until ten. Came straight home and went to bed. Believe me, I wish I had looked. Still, I can only see into the studio. The trees block the rest of the house."

"Well, don't feel like the Lone Ranger. Phyl considers me a suspect, too, since I stumbled on the body."

"Our numbers are growing. Maybe we should start a club," Barbara said sardonically. "Cops questioned Billie Ruth yesterday, too. She called last night. My God, she's been carrying on with Palmer for years. Like me, she went through the indignity of being fingerprinted and having samples taken of hair and blood. At first I refused but then realized that would make them even more suspicious of me."

"Did you tell Billie Ruth about your affair?"

"Of course not! At least she doesn't have a husband to worry about. God. There's going to be a lot of shit coming out of the woodwork."

A moment later, Salome telephoned the next person on her list, Janelle Phillips. When the answering machine kicked in, Salome started to leave a message. Then Janelle herself picked up.

"Salome," she said, her voice high-pitched and nervous, "uh, do you have a list of schools?"

After a second or two, Salome understood what Janelle was talking about: a reference to yesterday morning's conversation.

"Ah. Of course. Feng shui schools are worldwide. You want a complete list or just those in the U.S.?"

"U.S." Then Janelle said, "Terrible about that murder. What's the guy's name?"

"Palmer Fordham."

"Oh yeah. He was an artist or something. Right?"

"A very well-known artist."

"Oh, really?"

"Haven't the police talked to you?"

"Why should they?"

"Janelle, you're my alibi witness for yesterday morning.

You see, I found the body. I'd appreciate it if you'd go into the station. All you have to do is tell them the time you saw me."

"Uh huh."

"Want me to drop the list by your—?" But the line was dead.

Salome stared out the window, for a moment doubting Janelle's interest in studying feng shui. Ignorance of Palmer Fordham seemed unlikely. This was a small town after all, and even those who didn't live in Holyrood year-round would be curious about whomever lived in the Perfume Mansion—hardly an obscure residence. When she'd feng shuied Janelle's new home on Bayview, she'd not seen one of Fordham's sea goddesses but if ever anyone would want one and have the money for such a painting, that person was Janelle Phillips. Palmer himself couldn't have failed to notice the woman. She had a strong feeling Janelle's likeness was *somewhere* maybe wearing a cowboy hat and spurs riding a horse-shaped wave.

At that moment, the phone interrupted her musings.

"Salome Waterhouse, feng shui consultations."

"Yellow, darling."

"Mandy! Hi!"

"Think Phyl the Pill will give you permission to come up and do me this weekend? Bring some wind chimes. I'm thinking of hanging one from my dick. Will it improve my sex life? Of course, it'll have to be a big one."

"You're sounding cheery."

"I feel like shit. Jeremy and I tried to hang that wind chime about five this morning. Thank God for pharmaceuticals, otherwise he'd have broken his neck when he fell off my shoulders. Anyway, we totaled the chime."

"Let's make this definite. You really shouldn't be putting off the consultation. How about tomorrow afternoon?"

"Super! We'll do something special when you're finished so plan on staying over."

"Phyl might not—"

Mandy broke in. "Tell Phyl we'll be sleuthing for her! Palmer Fordham wasn't exactly unknown in certain circles."

"What time's good for you?"

After a pause he said, "Around four?"

"Fine. And I'll bring my stepladder."

Mandy barked a loud gleeful laugh. "For a sleepover? I swear, you feng shui people kill me!"

"Honestly, I'm sure I won't be able to stay—"

"*Ciao*, darling," he interrupted and the line went dead.

From her files, she took out a folder containing a current list of feng shui schools, separating those in the U.S. from the rest, and slipped the pages into the bin of her fax/copy machine, unable to shake the feeling that this was a waste of time and paper.

Chapter 16

ʘ

WHILE the machine chugged out copies, Salome glanced at the number of new phone messages. Double digits again, up in the twenties now. She sighed, not wanting to spend more time on the phone, figuring most of the calls were from journalists pursuing a story.

Certainly the phone was useful but not her favorite means of communication. She didn't even like phone consultations, definitely preferring to be on site with a client. But when the client lived far away, the phone was cheaper than travel expenses.

And she was anxious to talk to Dora. In person. Definitely in person. And she wanted to stop in at the Historical Society.

The phone messages could wait.

The weather wasn't doing anyone any favors, though she was snug and dry enough in her Ugg boots, oilskin coat and matching wide-brimmed hat. In the sporadic, light rain she felt no need to open the umbrella. She enjoyed Holyrood's wet winters, preferring walks in the rain to trudging through the snow in D.C.

On Bayview, she stopped at Janelle's two-story Monterey-style house with a red-tiled roof, the structure consuming most of the lot. French doors opened onto a balcony that ran across the entire second story. Two wide windows with false shutters were on either side of the front door. Salome passed between the short hedges and walked up the slick flagstone path to the front door. Though modest in size and appearance, the house had cost a bundle; the price of a bay view.

She used a brass knocker in the shape of an oil rig to announce herself.

When no one answered, she stepped back and examined the front of the house. All the curtains were drawn. The Adirondack chairs usually on the balcony were nowhere in sight. She placed the sheaf of papers, protected in plastic, in the mailbox, then walked around to the single-car garage in the back. Through the window she saw that Janelle's BMW was gone.

Retracing her steps and continuing down Bayview, she hoped Janelle had driven to the police station to confirm that she'd seen Salome yesterday morning while out jogging.

She hurried down the concrete steps on the west side of the Bluff. Passing the Sebastian Theater, she walked along the beachfront, watching the surfers. Her eyes were drawn to a guy with gray hair riding the top of an eight-foot swell then expertly cutting down across the wave. He rode it in to shore then dragged his board—and himself—onto the beach. Even from this distance, she could tell he was exhausted. Then she came to the row of restaurants and her thoughts moved elsewhere.

She noticed the lights on at the Sand and Sea Gallery and Rita's Town Car out front, flanked by a couple of media vans. A few more businesses were open, but not many, and damp sandbags remained piled in front of most doors. Inside the Beach Bistro a number of bar stools were occupied.

Crossing the street, she glanced at Waterhouse Properties and wondered which agent was in today. Maybe she'd stop by after visiting Dora.

She moved down a slight slope to the Perfume Creek. The

creek-side homes were quaint, colorful wooden structures, mainly summer rentals with absentee landlords, a good number managed by Waterhouse Properties. Though all were well-maintained, they looked dreary in the rain—as did any empty house, to Salome's way of thinking.

She passed Rita Van Horn's red cottage with a small windmill built on the right side in the helpful people gua, which, when moving, would activate good ch'i. At the back, she could just make out the tiny garage apartment where Palmer had once lived. A welcome mat also sporting a windmill lay before the front door located in the career gua. This cottage had no back entrance, though there was a kitchen door at the side of the house in the wealth gua.

To the left of the footpath was a patch of lawn about twelve feet by twelve feet on which Rita had white wrought-iron lawn furniture, a few rosebushes, and a lovely Japanese maple.

Up ahead she could see the narrow footbridge that connected Dora Whalen's little house to the creek-side entrance to the Perfume Mansion. Even before she saw the house, she heard Dora's bamboo wind chimes *thunking* in the breeze.

A moment later, she spied Dora sitting in front of a wide window that took up both the fame and relationship guas. The configuration of this house was opposite to Rita's. The front door to this house was on the street side. Certainly Dora would use the creek-side door to go to work, but the front door still represented the "mouth of ch'i." The creek-side door was in wealth where the wind chimes hung from the eave.

Dora glanced out the window. Salome waved and moved up the path toward the house. Just as at Damon O'Kelly's, the small garden sported more yellow oxalis than any other vegetation.

Dora opened the door. "Hello, Salome."

"Hi, Dora."

For a moment both women hesitated. Dora eyed Salome suspiciously.

"Sorry to bother you, Dora, but I'd like a word."

Appearing reluctant, Dora invited her in. But then, in a sense, Salome was her employer. This was the caretaker's house and those who lived here did so rent-free, though their salary was paid by the Perfume's tenant. That had been the arrangement since the Perfume was built and when Dora's grandparents became the first house servants. Dora represented the third generation to work at the mansion. However, if the Waterhouses, Salome in particular, decided to sell the cottage, Dora would have to look for another place to live. Because of the price of local properties, most likely she'd simply have to leave Holyrood.

Further, the Perfume's tenant always had the option to hire someone else. That, of course, had never been done. In fact, it seemed unimaginable. Past and present, the Whalen family considered working at the Perfume a sacred duty.

"Would you like coffee?"

"If it's made, thank you."

Salome removed her notebook and pen from an inside pocket while Dora went off to the kitchen on the other side of the room. There being no place to hang a coat, Salome propped her stiff Drizabone against the door and set her hat and umbrella alongside.

The room was small, excessively clean, and furnished with hand-me-downs from the Perfume. One blue velvet armchair, a sofa, and cherry wood end tables sporting porcelain lamps were clustered in front of the small fireplace. An antique hutch too large for the space, featured a silver service that Salome's grandmother had left to the Whalens along with a set of cut crystal. Salome figured her grandmother left such impractical items to the Whalens for their resale value. And for sentimental reasons they hadn't been sold.

Dora set the steaming cup of coffee on a table beside the overstuffed chair in which she'd been sitting. As there wasn't another chair close to Dora's, Salome moved the blue velvet armchair over.

"I imagine you're pretty upset by Palmer's murder so I won't take up too much of your time."

"Thank you. I appreciate it." She then reached into a basket nearby and pulled out a sock with a threaded needle in the toe.

Deciding it best not to mention the word "exorcism" Salome said, "Thing is, after the police release the Perfume I'm going to feng shui the property. Before I do, I need some information, some history."

"Like what?" Dora pulled a darning egg with a three-inch handle from the basket.

"That's quite beautiful," Salome commented, noticing the intricate inlay on the oval of wood. "May I see it?"

Dora held it up for a moment then fitted the sock over it.

Salome let it pass. "Is the stove in the same place it was five years ago? Anything in the kitchen been changed?"

Dora appeared surprised by the questions.

"There's a new refrigerator. Big two-door affair Palmer bought. Stove's in the same place it's always been. Can't just move a gas stove around, now can you?"

"Did you cook for him?"

"Of course. Served, too, especially when he entertained."

"Did he entertain a lot?"

"Oh yes."

"So you often had to stay late?"

"Rarely later than ten. And the next day I wouldn't have to come in until late morning."

"How about night before last?"

"You mean the night he was killed?"

"Yes."

"What does that have to do with, whachacallit—fung . . ."

"Feng shui."

She set down the darning momentarily. "Look I've already

talked to Phyllis. You want to talk about the Perfume, talk about the Perfume."

In this situation, Antoinette de Beauharnais wouldn't back off. Salome didn't either, though she was feeling a little strain from applying fictional tactics to real-life situations.

"Let me put it this way, Dora, I own the Perfume. What goes on there is of interest to me."

"Wasn't before."

"Well it is now. And further, ownership of the Perfume includes this cottage."

Dora's cheeks reddened. "I see." She resumed darning. "No I didn't serve him or any of his lady friends that night. I left at five—and haven't been back since."

"Where did he sleep?"

"Anywhere he pleased."

"Any particular room on a regular basis?"

"Lately he slept in the studio. I never went in to clean because he wouldn't allow me to. You'd have better luck talking to one of his lady friends about where he slept."

"Who for instance?"

Dora stiffened and pressed her lips together tightly.

Salome changed the subject. "Did you like working for him?"

She shrugged. "He was easy to work for. Not demanding but I preferred the people who lived there before. You wouldn't remember them. The Flemings. They really loved and respected the Perfume."

Salome took the dig in stride. Dora had regarded Salome with disapproval since she'd inherited the property, obviously because Salome never showed the proper "respect" for the place.

"Why did they leave?"

"Divorce."

"Oh. Anything out of the ordinary happen while they lived there?"

"No."

"And before the Flemings, who lived there?"

"That would have been the group of lawyers from San Francisco. A time-share kind of thing. Sometimes they entertained clients. Sometimes couples would come for the weekend. All very well behaved. Always a full house during the golf tournaments."

"Before that?" Salome asked while scribbling notes.

"Before the lawyers," Dora said to tweak her memory. Then she rattled off a few names, affluent couples, empty nesters or childless. Salome found it interesting that no families with children had moved in. Further, they all left because of divorce.

Half jokingly Salome said, "I wonder if those lawyers specialized in divorce."

"As a matter of fact, that's exactly what they did."

Weird.

"Who else?"

"Mr. Waterhouse. But you'd know about your own family history."

"Refresh my memory, Dora." She sipped the strong coffee.

Dora heaved a sigh as if underlining her annoyance. "He lived there from the time he bought it from Connor Sebastian in 1924 till the day he died. Your own father lived there until he married your mother after the war. That's also when your grandmother moved into the house you have now."

Though they'd never divorced, Salome's grandparents had spent a large part of their marriage separated—Joshua on one side of town, his wife, Salome, on the other.

"And what about Uncle Charles?"

"Oh, Charles. Lived there until he went into the service in forty-one. He married Margie Andretti just a few months after your parents got married. They lived in the Perfume with your grandparents until Phyllis was about a year old. But Holyrood was too dull for him—having been in the war and all, I suppose. So they moved to San Francisco. Then, of course, Margie died, leaving him to take care of Phyllis.

So, he moved back to the Perfume. But Phyllis was too rambunctious for Mr. Waterhouse, always getting underfoot and there was too much to do to keep an eye on her. So Mr. Waterhouse gave Charles the cottage across from Holyrood church. Can't say Charles liked the Perfume all that much anyway."

Not like his daughter, Salome thought. "How do you mean?"

"Always complained that it was too drafty and full of ghosts. But he drank, you know. Frankly, he was somewhat common."

Salome was startled by the snobbery behind the remark.

"And Palmer? Was he common, too?"

"More trashy than common."

"What about the secret room?"

Taken by surprise, Dora jerked her head up. Her eyes flickered. "That's a fantasy."

"I saw it."

"Whatever you *think* you saw, wasn't a secret room," Dora spat.

But Salome had seen it in Dora's eyes. Confirmation.

"What about the first tenants, the Sebastians?"

"Well before my time."

Sensing that she wouldn't learn much more from the frosty woman, Salome closed her notebook. "Thank you, Dora. I appreciate the background you've given me."

She nodded. "And what do you plan to do with the Perfume now?"

"I haven't made any plans. But I'll let you as soon as I do."

Wanting to depart on a pleasant note, Salome said while putting on her coat, "And don't worry about having to clean up when the police are finished. There are special cleaning crews who handle crime scenes."

"Fine."

Though heartened by Dora's reaction to her question about

the secret room, she felt oppressed by the housekeeper and the cramped living room.

Just outside the door she took a deep breath of the fresh air, raising her hands and flicking her fingers to throw off the sha. As she did so, her left hand hit the bamboo wind chime. She felt a jolt. Fearing that she'd damaged the old, weathered chime, she jerked her head upward. It was silly; the chime was meant to be jostled and she put her reaction down to nerves.

SHE WAS SURPRISED TO SEE JASON TWITCHELL behind the desk at Waterhouse Properties again but, as he told her, it was his day to open. Unlike yesterday, he wore gray slacks, a starched white shirt, a green and gold rep tie, and a gray cashmere sweater vest. His clear blue eyes indicated he'd gotten a good night's sleep. On his desk was a nearly empty container of coffee from Billie Ruth's bakery.

As she took a seat, he sat back and regarded her proudly. "Guess what I found out?"

"Susan Truro has agreed to marry you."

He laughed. "I may be persistent but I don't move *that* fast. No, Blair Farrell flew to Tokyo on business day before Palmer Fordham was murdered."

If this was true, her absence certainly struck her from the list of suspects. Still, she could have hired someone to do the deed.

"And," he went on, "I dropped in on Beth McCormick last night after I left here. She lives in one of those apartments behind the mall. No furniture to speak of. A kitchen table, a couple chairs, and a mattress on the floor. I think she's having money problems. Got divorced last year.

"Anyway, I asked her about that list of people interested in the Perfume. She said there wasn't one. But I got the impression she was lying. I told her she needed to talk to you about the Perfume.

"She looked terrible. When I asked if there was anything I could do for her she broke down and told me to go away."

"Thanks for doing that, Jason."

"Sure."

"Any calls about the Perfume?"

"So far, just a couple. Locally, Rita Van Horn. I saw her earlier talking to TV people inside her gallery. Guess she's going to get a lot of free press out of this."

"Anyone else we know?"

"Some guy said he's with *Dead Artists*."

"Sounds like a prank."

"Oh no. It's a band out of San Francisco. Real popular. I've got a couple of their CDs."

"Well, just keep a list. My father'll be taking care of finding new tenants."

"Yeah, I know. He called."

THE SANDBAGS HAD BEEN REMOVED AND AN OPEN sign displayed on the front door of the Sand and Sea Gallery. Salome entered. As she closed the door, Rita shot out of the back. She was dressed in a red suit with matching red heels, carrying a cell phone. Hair and makeup were perfect, each eyelash and a big smile firmly in place. Indeed, she looked ready for her close-up.

"Salome. What can I do for you?"

"Just thought I'd stop in for a moment. You look like you're expecting someone so I won't be long."

"Some people are bringing in their sea goddesses—and I've got a photographer lined up to start the catalogue."

"You wanted to have dinner—to discuss the show?"

Her eyes brightened. "Of course! I'm sorry. My mind is so scattered." She paused as if flipping the pages of a mental appointment book. "Let's see. How about tomorrow night? Sevenish? Scott's? Unless you have some other place in mind."

Since she didn't know how late she'd be returning from San Francisco, she decided it best not to make plans for tomorrow night and said so. "How about Saturday night?"

Rita hesitated, then said, "All right. But I won't be available until around nine."

"Scott's at nine on Saturday. And I wanted to ask you, did Palmer mention that he was planning to leave California?"

"Good heavens no. He loved it here. He was from Houston, you know. Not exactly paradise. Who told you that?"

"Actually, my source heard it from Blair Farrell."

"God. Not her again. She'd say anything to spite him."

"Well, I'll see you Saturday night, then."

As Salome turned to leave, Rita moved up to the door. "Oh, and, Salome, please ask Phyllis to let me in the Perfume. Surely they're about finished with the crime scene. Thing is, I know he's got a bunch of paintings stashed somewhere. Mostly early work. And there's his collection of prints of sea goddesses. It all needs to be included in the catalogue."

"Rita. Just because we're cousins doesn't mean—"

"Please!"

"Have you talked to her about it?"

"Of course. When she interviewed me this morning. I even volunteered to be fingerprinted and took care of that right after we talked. I've been cooperative with her. Now she should be cooperative with me!"

Rita opened the door and Salome stepped outside, thinking Rita naive in her assessment of police-citizen relations. But then, she was a headstrong person who wouldn't stop until she got what she wanted.

Salome set off toward the Historical Society's "new" offices in the former police station. Without warning, the light rain turned into a downpour. Salome increased her pace.

* * *

MAVIS HICKS–DULANE GREETED HER COOLLY, obviously still miffed by Salome's refusal to simply turn over the Perfume to the society so they could get out of jail, as it were.

"You've done a marvelous job in here, Mavis," Salome commented. Indeed, they'd transformed the once brutally sterile interior into an old-fashioned parlor with lots of framed photographs of Holyrood's early days, turn-of-the-century paintings, antiques, and strategically placed vintage lamps. A vase full of fragrant roses cut through the lingering jailhouse smells.

"How may I help you, Miss Waterhouse?"

"I'm putting together a history of the Perfume Mansion and would like to look at any materials you have."

The declaration seemed to thaw her a bit. Mavis rose from her chair and pulled out a drawer in a filing cabinet.

"Your father has far more information than we do. Your grandfather's journals really belong in our archive."

"How about before the mansion was built?"

Mavis indicated an old library table across the room. "Why don't you have a seat? I'll see what I can dig up."

Salome spent about an hour reading copies of old newspaper clippings and jotted down a few notes. About the only item of significance—in so far as its effect on the area around the promontory on which the Perfume had been built—was a fire that destroyed the cannery in January of 1908. Twenty-five souls had perished, mostly indigent workers and local Indians who'd been pushed off the land when the wealthy took notice of the area and began building their grand seaside estates. The land had been pretty much left alone, indeed, deemed haunted, until Lily and Connor Sebastian purchased the property in 1919 and commissioned Joshua Waterhouse and his partner, Kevin O'Kelly, to build them a grand mansion.

After finishing the pre-Perfume days, she opened an accordion file, disappointingly slender. She flipped through old sepia tone photographs of various stages of construction and men standing around in post-WWI attire. A woman was in but one photograph, taken outside the open double doors beneath the porte cochere. She stood facing the camera, wearing a calf-length summer chemise and a long rope of pearls, holding a large bouquet. On either side were two men who both regarded her with open adoration. Salome thought the tall man on the left, in his black suit and hat, while recognizable as her grandfather, looked like an undertaker. The shorter man wore a boater and light-colored suit and had an impish quality. To one side stood another man looking at the house, an arm extended toward the large double doors in a dramatic welcoming gesture, the other arm anchored by a fist on his hip.

She flipped the photo over. In faded brown ink she read, "Joshua Waterhouse, Lily Sebastian, Kevin O'Kelly. At right, Connor Sebastian, proud homeowner."

At the bottom right: "September 9, 1920."

A year to the day of the date on the blueprints.

She set the photographs aside and pulled out some Xeroxed clippings. Headlining the first:

LOCAL THESPIANS PLAY NIGHTLY TO PACKED HOUSE.

The story reported the success of *A Christmas Carol* as staged by Lily and Connor Sebastian at the newly built Sebastian Theater in December of 1920. The bulk of the article concentrated on Holyrood's growing prominence as a winter destination, thanks largely to the Otter Haven Resort and, of course, the presence of the nationally known acting couple, the Sebastians.

There were a few gossipy features about various celebrities who came to town at all seasons, staying either at Otter Haven or the Perfume.

Then she read a grimmer headline from June of 1922:

LOCAL ACTRESS MISSING

The story contained little detail, just that Connor reported his wife missing the morning after a party at the Perfume. The police "were investigating."

The follow-ups, written over the next few weeks were mostly speculative. Among them:

POLICE BAFFLED BY ACTRESS'S DISAPPEARANCE

KIDNAP NOT RULED OUT AS POSSIBILITY

STILL NO CLUE IN DISAPPEARANCE

Salome noted the change in tone as the story progressed, revealing more about Lily Sebastian's private life and less about the investigation. Any sympathy or concern vanished as surely as the actress when reporters began referring to Lily as a "party girl," a "good-time girl," an actress more interested in the attentions of "other men" than in her marriage. References were made to her use of cocaine and opium while an ingenue in silent films and that her husband had brought her north to rescue her from Hollywood's "evil influences" despite her "fantastic earnings."

Gradually, popular opinion held that she'd simply taken off with another man, "a mysterious stranger," leaving her devoted husband behind to worry and fret.

PERFUME MANSION SOLD TO LOCAL BUILDER headed a story about her grandfather's purchase of the Perfume in 1924, two years after Lily Sebastion's mysterious disappearance. Though the price wasn't disclosed, her grandfather's "beneficence" colored the report. Connor Sebastian, it seems, had fallen on hard times and couldn't afford the Perfume's upkeep. Joshua installed him in one of the small cottages at Otter Haven and paid off Connor's mounting debts.

FORMER OWNER OF PERFUME IN DEATH PLUNGE—SUICIDE OR ACCIDENT?

In the last article, Salome read that Connor Sebastian's penultimate resting place had been the narrow roadway beneath the Perfume's jutting promontory. Apparently, he'd wandered over to the Perfume after a performance as Scrooge in *A Christmas Carol*, during which theatergoers reported that he'd seemed drunk. In the final scene, instead of embracing the boy, he'd flung Tiny Tim into the wings like a Christmas goose. The boy was all right but Connor had stalked off the stage and disappeared into the cold, blustery night and was not seen again until his broken body was found the next morning by a tourist out for an early bicycle ride.

Salome's grandparents and their two young sons had been sound asleep in the Perfume and had heard nothing.

Salome sat back for a moment, considering what she'd read. The cannery fire, Lily Sebastian's disappearance, and Connor Sebastion's death certainly contributed to the lingering sha affecting the Perfume. Then she went over what Dora had told her about the Perfume's former tenants; divorce a major theme in the Perfume's history.

Mentally, she conjured a bird's-eye view of the mansion. Of course, she thought. The house had been built in a modified "boot" shape, leaving a void in the relationship gua. The hearty old palm tree was too far away to square off the missing corner.

She gathered the materials in a neat stack and set them on Mavis's desk.

Mavis looked up. "You know there is another source, though I wouldn't call him reliable."

"Oh really?"

"Herman Boelkerke."

"Hadn't even thought of him." Herman was close to her father's age and a longtime local fisherman.

"Do you remember, back in the sixties, when he staged a protest about the lack of nude bathing in Holyrood? Went to the beach one day wearing trunks made out of plastic wrap."

"Oh yes!" Salome laughed, now remembering. She'd been in high school at the time. "Looked like he'd stuffed meatloaf and a couple new potatoes down the front."

"Not exactly titillating," Mavis remarked. "Well, he wrote a book. Not long after your grandfather died."

Salome asked for a local directory.

"Herman doesn't have a phone. You'll just have to drop in. No matter what the weather, he enjoys having a drink on his patio of an evening."

"You have a copy of the book?"

"Oh no . . ." Her eyes twinkled mischievously. "Best that he tell you that story."

He lived but a few blocks away on Creekside. However, she thought it best to read her grandfather's journals first and would pay the eccentric Mr. Boelkerke a visit later.

Chapter 17

Ⓢ

MICHAEL O'Kelly stood at the window of the so-called honeymoon suite, drinking from a freshly poured glass of scotch, regretting his stay at Aunt Livia's B and B. She'd pounced, as if waiting for him, when he returned from *The Echo's* offices just about twenty minutes ago.

Earlier in the day, he'd rented a board and wetsuit, believing some wave riding would improve his mood. Though his mind may have existed within the skin of a teenager, his body hadn't so effortlessly responded and the exercise only served to remind him of his true age.

"I saw that horrible Salome Waterhouse this morning," Livia had announced, saliva spraying in a most disgusting fashion. "She was actually taunting our Damon this morning."

He'd not given her the satisfaction of acknowledging that he'd heard, and had simply taken the bottle of scotch from the lounge and climbed the stairs as if she weren't there.

In the gloom of late afternoon, a movement below caught his eye. He watched as a figure in a long oilskin coat and broad-brimmed hat ascended the steep concrete stairs. Just a short time ago, he'd done the same, but having to stop every few steps. It was a real workout and he had to admire the person for their fluid movement, not stopping once to take a breath. Whoever it was disappeared around the corner onto Bayview. Michael's thoughts immediately returned to his problem.

He had to stop this silliness but didn't know how. He plopped down on the cheap chenille bedspread. Aunt Livia had actually suggested he call Billie Ruth, said her bakery was quite successful and she was single after three tries at the marriage game. He'd dated Billie Ruth in high school but only to deflect his real interest in Salome. But he knew something about Billie Ruth that made her far from desirable.

He went over to the desk, where he'd left his cell phone. He reached for it then hesitated. He was supposed to meet Emily for dinner at six. Business, of course, since he'd left *The Echo's* offices early. His thoughts traveled back to last night when he'd gone to her house, most of his attention across the street. Emily had acted very strange, almost like their meeting was some sort of assignation. She'd looked very nice, very attractive, in some sort of slinky pants outfit that sent clouds of Chanel Number 5 into the air whenever she moved. But the scent reminded him of his first wife, the Francophile. Still, he'd managed to penetrate the miasma and found himself agreeing with Emily's sudden about-face regarding *The Echo*. He wondered if the silk and scent had been meant to seduce him into agreeing to sell *The Echo* to a paper in Monterey County.

He rubbed his chin, feeling the rough stubble. Still, Emily's suggestion made good business sense while at the same time preserving the tradition of the paper as a source of local news.

Personally, he found her enthusiasm for the recent murder disturbing but had to admit death had injected life into *The Echo*, and agreed to put out a special edition. Having spent most of his adult life as an investment banker, he didn't have the same sensibilities as Emily.

And the sooner he agreed to the sale, the sooner he could

get the hell out of Dodge and away from the demons of the past. As owner of the paper, his mother just wanted the money.

When his father died, Michael's mother inherited the house in the highlands, the newspaper, and the florist shop. The remaining commercial businesses had been dispersed among Michael's uncles and brothers. Missing from the will, of course, had been Michael.

And his relatives weren't particularly prone to sharing. In fact, his three brothers hadn't done much to help their mother during recent tight times. Of course, they were all married with children. Michael, being single and well-off, provided financial support when needed. He never asked what the money was for, but figured a portion went to *The Echo*.

And though they knew he was in town for the first time in years, none of his brothers had tried to contact him. At the same time, he didn't call them either.

Without punching in the familiar numbers, he put the phone down. No, he thought. He wouldn't call Salome again. He'd concentrate on selling the paper then catch the first flight back to Boston.

Chapter 18

AROUND eight o'clock Phyllis Waterhouse unlocked the rounded black door of her storybook cottage near the top of Holyrood Hill just across from the church. Originally named *Elven Home* by her grandfather, the cozy cottage was listed in the historical record. Any improvements she wanted to make had to first be approved by the local Historical Preservation Society. She could have used a new door with enough height so she didn't have to stoop when entering. But that would mean cutting into the original stone and her request had been denied.

The foyer was dark and narrow and just to the right were cramped stairs leading to the second floor. She'd wanted skylights, one above the door, one above the second-floor landing but that would have required a new roof which had to fit certain standards to maintain its appearance of faux thatch. Fine. Then she'd gotten the estimate from a local roofer. Hell, with what it would cost to replace the entire roof and add skylights, she could have bought a new house—though certainly not here. Maybe in Death Valley.

At least she didn't have to worry about a mortgage. Her father had left her the house—not only named for elves but built for them as well. At nearly six feet tall, she often felt like Alice in Wonderland, half expecting to wake up one day with her head jammed into the ceiling and her arms and legs poking out the windows and front door.

She set her keys on a small table then made a quick left into the living room. She switched on a lamp, then set down her briefcase. Still wearing her trench coat, she entered the kitchen and took a can of goldfish food from the door in the refrigerator.

Back in the living room, she sprinkled flakes on the surface of the twenty-gallon tank in front of the bay window. The nine orandas wiggled cheerfully, their wedding veil tails swaying gracefully while they gulped down dinner.

"If you'd seen what I saw today, you guys would be screaming for martinis," she said to her pets. She enjoyed the fish immensely, though she'd never told Salome. They were the happiest beings she knew and never had an unkind word. Did the location of the tank matter? Maybe.

A few minutes later, comfortably ensconced in her leather recliner, feet up to relieve the pressure on ankles swollen from a day which had begun by standing on the cold tiles in the autopsy room, she sipped a dirty martini. The concoction of gin and olive juice relieved the pressure on her nerves and soothed her annoyance with the mayor, who'd called to demand that she make an arrest ASAP. He wanted someone behind bars before the upcoming golf tournament. When she suggested he volunteer, he abruptly hung up.

She'd replaced her shoes with the thick sheepskin slippers she'd come to depend on like a drug. "Chocolate for the feet," had been written on the Christmas gift tag. "From Mei." Too many years with the San Francisco PD inclined her to think of heroin instead of chocolate.

She heaved a sigh, and put her cousin on the sidelines. For the moment, anyway. Then she checked her watch. Ralph would be over in just a few minutes and she wanted a moment to relax.

She hated autopsies and never could figure out why. She'd

certainly experienced unspeakable crime scenes but her mind at those times always jumped to investigative mode and the search for clues. In an autopsy room, focus was centered entirely on the corpse and the story it told from the inside. Perhaps it was the vulnerability of the corpse juxtaposed with such a cold, sterile, and isolated environment. And there was something grotesquely clownish about the paper bags on the hands and feet of the naked corpse that, of course, were necessary to preserve possible evidence. Perhaps, too, it was the heartless precision with which the medical examiner worked, removing and weighting organs like a butcher filling an order.

At the same time she did appreciate Tom Gordon's professional attention to detail. So as not to contaminate possible evidence beneath the finger-and toenails, he'd used twenty different sets of sterilized clippers. He couldn't be accused of doing sloppy work.

The doorbell rang. She shuddered, spilling the martini on herself. So much for relaxation.

She peered through the peephole to be certain a reporter hadn't learned of her whereabouts.

"Hey," Ralph said as she opened the door.

"Hey yourself. Got a fresh batch in the fridge."

About a year ago while discussing a local robbery over drinks after work, she'd discovered that, like her, Ralph favored dirty martinis made with Bombay gin. Certainly far more than his preference in libation led to their close relationship, but the drink had more or less opened the door.

She resumed her place on the recliner while he went off to the kitchen to help himself to the contents of the stainless steel shaker in the refrigerator. She stared past the aquarium down to the village, lights muted in the drizzle, to the choppy sea.

Earlier in the day surfers in their wetsuits had been out, looking to her like so many squiggly black sperm struggling against the swell of the sea's massive gray womb.

Palmer Fordham had once counted himself among their numbers. Ralph Blue, being a surfer, had been questioning the local wave cult.

Then, unwelcome and sudden, memory rudely intruded and she and Mandy were racing down the beach, each carrying long boards under their arms—back in the days before wetsuits. They'd met at the beach when his family had moved down from San Francisco. They'd been fifteen. Then *smack!* She even felt the board hit the water as she threw herself onto it, paddling frantically to get past the surf close to shore, her head turned to look at him, determined to outdistance him, to be the first to catch a wave—

"Hey, Phyl. You okay?"

Christ. Her eyes had started to water.

She turned away but Ralph moved right in front of her and extended a handkerchief.

She was mortified.

"What's up?"

"Surf's up," she barked, ignoring the offering.

"Ah," he said as if he understood and returning the handkerchief to his pocket, took a seat on the couch.

"I'll just freshen my drink," she said and went to the kitchen. For some reason, unwelcome emotions were being stirred up—like the feeling at the Perfume that she was trespassing. She wiped her eyes, added a dollop to her glass, then returned to the living room.

"How about your day? Any good leads?" she asked, her demeanor once again crisp and frosty.

Ralph shrugged. "Fordham hasn't surfed for months. Beth McCormick was pretty much a basket case. Seemed more devastated than guilty. Janelle Phillips wasn't home. House looked closed up. How'd the autopsy go?"

Outside the autopsy room they walked through the corridor of the county morgue until Tom Gordon opened a door leading to a quiet office. They'd both worked big city homicides, Gordon in the Los Angeles County Coroner's Office, and he wasn't reticent about talking to her, a former homicide detective with the San Francisco Police Department, about his speculations.

He looked away for a moment, then back at her, raising his hands palms outward. "Look, we've both seen some weirdness in our careers but this isn't something I'd expect to occur around here. However, I have seen this before. Right now, this is just between you and me. Okay? I need confirmation from toxicology before I make a statement."

"Phyl?"

Tom Gordon certainly didn't want her discussing his speculations with anyone. But, Ralph wasn't just anyone and so she told him.

Ralph nearly came out of his seat. "Fordham suffocated? Jesus. What about the battering?"

"Fordham *relaxed* to death. His lungs ceased functioning and he suffocated. In all that mess, Gordon found a puncture wound behind Fordham's right ear. We'll have to wait for the toxicology report but he thinks Fordham might have been killed by a poison, curare or something like it, administered by a dart."

"Maybe the wine was poisoned."

"Ingesting—eating or drinking—curare won't kill anyone but when it's injected into the bloodstream it's lethal."

"You're saying someone blew a poison dart into Fordham's neck?"

"But only to you. I'm serious, Ralph, this goes no further than you and me."

"Curare—isn't it South American?"

In the middle of a sip, Phyllis nodded.

"And Charles Boatwright travels to South America a lot, doesn't he?"

"I already wrote out a search warrant for the Boatwrights' place. We should have it by the A.M."

"You interviewed her. How'd she act?"

"Indignant. Pissed off. Though she did admit to having

had an affair with Fordham, she was hiding something." She took another sip of her martini.

Ralph sighed. "So, if he was poisoned, the battering was to cover up the actual means. Any defensive wounds?"

"None. Gordon suggested we look for a hoe-fork with a long handle. Found just such a tool in the gardener's shed. It's over at the lab now."

"Apparently our perp didn't know that once the heart stops there ain't gonna be no fountaining blood. Simple splatter from the battering wasn't enough. Otherwise, the curtains would have been drenched. For that matter, the perp, too. But no bloody footprints near the scene. Except Salome's."

Both sat silently for a moment.

"How about stomach contents?" Ralph asked.

"His last meal was fruit, not on the menu at Beach Bistro, but he did drink plenty of wine."

Ralph frowned.

"He didn't eat the takeout. Probably died about the time it arrived, when his stomach stopped digesting the fruit he'd consumed about eleven."

"Which puts Hector on the scene at the right time."

"And whoever ordered the meal. Hopefully, we'll have a match on food containers, the wineglasses, and bottle by morning."

"Maybe Hector fabricated the phone call and used the food as a pretense to go up there."

"Except that when I tried the phone's redial, I got the Beach Bistro."

"He might have called his restaurant after killing Fordham."

"There is that," she mused. After a pause, she said, "Oh yeah, there was bruising on the heels and ankles."

Ralph blinked then regarded her with a puzzled look. "The perp had a thing against his feet? What do you think?"

"That Palmer was dragged out of bed and down the stairs."

She took another drink, thanking whoever made the first

introductions of Bombay to olive juice. She would have liked to sit around and drink all night but she had to get back to the station after the "dinner" break. No rest for those in pursuit of the wicked.

Though she wouldn't even tell Ralph, on occasion she'd privately entertained the idea of Palmer Fordham in her own bed. Who wouldn't? Wasn't he the mirror image of Val Kilmer, one of her favorite big screen hunks? Now she was certainly glad she'd never gone past the fantasy.

"There's more."

Their eyes met.

"Gordon found thrush in the mouth and esophagus—yeast infection—and a mass in the abdomen. For some reason, Fordham's outward appearance didn't reflect what was going on inside. Happens that way with some people. They look great one day and they're dead the next."

"He had cancer?"

"Looks that way. We'll just have to wait for the test results."

"Whether or not he had cancer shouldn't have any bearing on the case."

"Maybe, maybe not. But he also had enlarged lymph nodes in the groin, neck, and armpits. After the autopsy, I went back to the Perfume to look for medical records. His last doctor's appointment was two years ago. However, he did have a certain test recently."

"For cancer?"

"No. For HIV. One of those do-it-yourself home kits."

"And?" Ralph asked breathlessly.

"I couldn't find the results."

Chapter 19

EYES blurring, Salome closed the last journal and dropped it on the table atop the others, wondering if she wouldn't be doing everyone a favor by burning them. Not only because of the scandal her grandfather had self-servingly and criminally averted but the writing itself; the rambling style of a self-absorbed egotist who had one reader in mind—himself.

If her father had read them, she could well understand why he'd kept the journals in a locked cabinet, ironically in the family gua of his study.

She was curled in the big leather poet's chair in the small TV/reading room off the study. She hoped her vision had not suffered permanent damage. A walk and a chance to gaze at a far horizon would probably do her good. And as Mavis had said, Herman Boelkerke might be on his patio enjoying a libation.

She pulled on her Drizabone and hat, grabbed her umbrella, and left the cottage.

The ubiquitous rain had reduced to a cold drizzle but she hardly noted the weather, her thoughts consumed by what she'd been reading for the past few hours, condensing the wordy narrative to its basic storyline.

Joshua Waterhouse had had an affair with Lily Sebastian, even going so far as to ask his wife for a divorce, believing Lily would marry him. Salome's grandmother., a Catholic and mother of two babies, refused. And, there was a secret room! He'd constructed it himself during a three-month period while Connor Sebastian was in Hollywood making movies to perk the family finances.

More absorbed by Lily's charms, Joshua did not reveal the exact location of the room, simply that he had cleverly concealed it for the lovers' assignations on the lowest level. He came and went through the creek-side door, with, he'd written, no one the wiser, more interested in tediously detailing every garment she wore and subsequently removed, along with descriptions of the texture of every square inch of her flesh.

Then one night he'd entered the room to find her dead, apparently of natural causes, as there was not a scratch on her perfect body. After numerous pages of lamentations and pondering "what might have been," he revealed her final resting place.

Before she knew it, Salome had arrived at Herman Boelkerke's creek-side bungalow, cigar smoke hanging heavy in the still, damp air. Herman himself sat outside on a deck overlooking the Perfume Creek, silhouetted against the warm glow of his front room. On a table beside his plastic chair was a bottle of whiskey and an ashtray.

"Who goes there?" he called out.

'Tis I, she considered answering. Instead, she said, "Mr. Boelkerke? It's Salome Waterhouse. I'd like to talk to you if you have a moment."

"Ah! The good Reggie's eldest. Permission to come aboard," he hailed and rose from his chair.

Tall and bony, he reminded her of a skeleton kids had been given the go-ahead to put together and didn't quite link up in the proper way. One shoulder was higher than the other. One foot angled out sharply and he was missing the fourth and fifth fingers on the hand that didn't hold the drink. When he moved, he creaked like an old wooden ship, appropriate, she supposed, for an old fisherman.

"Guess you must be looking for a murderer like everybody else. Certainly has put some life in this sleepy burg. I tell you what, I see a lot goes on around here!"

He regarded her for a long time, squinting in the darkness. She doubted he could see much past his nose, but at least he seemed willing to talk. She heard a *click* and saw that he'd opened the tiny gate to his yard.

"Please, make yourself comfortable," he said, indicating the empty chair on the other side of the table. "If nothing else, we can watch the fun."

She couldn't see anything "fun," just the cold water slinking by.

He then turned on an outdoor heater, a tall cylindrical contraption with a hood like those used at beachfront restaurants and Salome wondered if that's where he'd requisitioned his.

"Actually, I'm putting together a history of the Perfume, Mr. Boelkerke, and heard you once wrote a book."

Suddenly he laughed, the sound carrying across the water. "Want something to drink?"

"Soda or coffee, if you have it."

"Nothing stronger?"

"I might add a dollop of what you've got here."

"You hold the fort. Be back in a sec."

A moment later he returned with a steaming mug—but no book. He added whiskey to her coffee and to his glass which he raised.

By way of a toast he declared, "To tragedy, the great exploiter of human emotion." He took a long pull.

Salome took a sip, cringing slightly. She didn't care for spirits but a shared drink . . .

"Shakespeare knew just that! You ever want to write, by God, study Shakespeare."

"What about your book?"

He started chuckling then took a drag on his cigar.

"Because I was always going on about books and writing, people assumed I was a writer!

"One day, Brian O'Kelley offered me five hundred dollars if I'd write the definitive history of Holyrood. Fine by me.

"Brian directed me to the files of *The Echo*, which I found distinctly one-sided. After some checking around, I learned that your grandfather's journals were kept in a locked cabinet in your father's study. Though he knew I was compiling a history, he never offered the journals. So. Got myself a room at Otter Haven, checked myself in for a couple of days. Told everyone I just needed a change of venue. Every night I snuck into your father's sanctum and after locating the key, opened the locked cabinet and helped myself to the journals. Ruined my eyesight, I can tell you that."

"What did you learn?"

"What I'd always known! Your grandfather was a ghastly old geezer and dull as a post. Even so, I read as many as I could. I started with the latest then jumped back briefly to the first ones written after the nineteen aught six earthquake when he first arrived in Holyrood."

"You didn't read those written in the early twenties?"

He shrugged. "Frankly, I was most interested in his take on local life in the forties and early fifties when O'Kelly tried to chase your parents out of town with that ridiculous ordinance."

Herman suddenly went very still and quiet.

"Mr. Boelkerke?"

"Sure you want to hear this?"

"Of course!"

He sat forward, elbows on his knees, and looked out at the dark water swirling down the creek to the sea. In the distance, she could hear waves hitting the beach, oddly sounding like skateboards on pavement.

"Ole Joshua, he wasn't altogether against it, though in public he appeared outraged—probably because Kevin

O'Kelly's son was the instigator. You may not want to hear this, but your grandfather wanted to disinherit your father for marrying your mother after she and what was left of her family were released from that concentration camp."

In April 1942, her mother and family had been forced from their home in Salinas to a compound constructed almost overnight on the nearby Rodeo grounds. Then, the end of June, they'd been herded onto a train and shipped to the desert in Poston, Arizona. For three years they had endured internment. The detention camps were closed after Japan surrendered and the United States Supreme Court effectively closed the camps with a special ruling.

"One night, Reggie dragged me out of bed and we drove down to Salinas in a car full of blankets. There were no toilets, just ditches running under the privies. *Oosh!* The smell! He'd heard green lumber had been used to construct the barracks. He knew the wood would shrink and everyone freeze at night. We moved all around the compound and at places between guard towers tossed blankets over the barbed wire. I made those blankets into bullets so they wouldn't catch. I figured Reggie picked me 'cause I was so tall. After that night, I coulda pitched for the majors."

During those three years, Salome's father wrote Satomi daily, as her mother had told her. In the beginning, he tried to protect the Yamamotos' house in Salinas from vandals. When that didn't work, he managed to haul off many of their belongings—while posing as a vandal himself—and storing them. But he couldn't save the house itself that, after so much pilfering, was finally reduced to a pile of roof shingles.

Satomi's parents died in the camp; her father's pride destroyed, he spiraled down into insanity and death. The heat and a broken heart after her father's death killed her mother.

Herman shook his head. "You'd think the old bastard would have had more compassion. Reason I didn't put that in the book was because of your father. Reggie took his licks stoically. Always stood by your mother while at the same time he showed great respect for his parents."

Herman then creaked back into an upright position. "But, how could I write about Holyrood without including Joshua Waterhouse?

"Then, a course, I handed over the manuscript to Brian. The fool didn't bother to read it until the five hundred copies were printed. And once he did, each and every one went directly into the incinerator. Then he dropped dead. Good thing for me. Otherwise I mighta had to pay back the advance."

"So what didn't he like about the book?"

"Mainly that I gave your grandfather credit for Holyrood's unique character. Only fair. He was a visionary and Kevin O'Kelly hardly more than a construction worker Joshua brought down from San Francisco. Scrappy, though. And he finagled his way into people's pocketbooks and started buying up commercial property while your grandfather concentrated on residential real estate. Neither were particularly likeable fellows."

Both were silent for a moment. Salome pretended to sip her whiskey-laced java.

"Why did my grandfather change his mind about disinheriting Dad?"

"Well, I did speak to your grandmother, too. She more or less hinted that she knew some things about Joshua that would tarnish his image as the local patriarch and community leader. My opinion? She put the screws to him. As far as their living apart went, she said the Perfume was just too big for her. Ask me though, she left him but not far enough away so's he'd forget her. And she was a Catholic; didn't cotton to divorce."

"Makes me wonder why Granddad left me the Perfume," Salome commented.

"Well, he wanted it kept in the family, didn't he? But he didn't want Reggie to have it and Charles was dead. Being a traditionalist, he left it to his first-born grandchild. Even if you were—are—part Japanese.

"So, now you're writing a history of the Perfume."

"Just putting a history together, Herman," she mumbled, excavating the past making her a little nauseated.

"You talk to Dora?"

"Well, yes. She gave me a rundown on former residents."

"She talk about her personal life?"

"I didn't know she had one."

"Know why she never married?"

Salome shook her head.

"Dora was your grandfather's lover. Started when her parents retired and she took over control of the house. At about the same time your grandmother moved."

"Was that in Granddad's journals?"

"Not the ones I read. Besides, Dora wouldn't be a great love would she? Just someone to warm the sheets. Like a hot water bottle.

"I look and listen and have done for years. She darns my socks, you know. Tells me things, though in not so many words. Just the way she talked about him, too intimate for just someone who dusts."

Salome stared at him for a moment. Finally she asked, "And what about Palmer? How'd she feel about him?"

"*Oosh!* Did she hate him!"

"Enough to kill him?"

"Ask me, I wouldn't put it past her."

"I guess you've talked to the police."

"All us creek-side rats been questioned."

"You mention Dora's feelings about Palmer?"

"Hell no! That's for her to say."

"Did you see anything that night?"

"Damn sure wish I had. But can't rightly say I did. On the other hand, he hadn't been entertaining like he used to. Lights out early. At least early for him. Up on that top floor."

"Like what time?"

"Oh, I'd say around ten, eleven. He'd been drinking a lot lately. He took the bottles to the trash himself after Dora went home."

"How do you know?"

"Bottles make a lotta noise when you dump 'em in the trash. And sound carries here on the creek."

They chatted for a few more minutes about her father's health and the upcoming golf tournament.

"Mr. Boelkerke, thank you for talking to me."

"Glad to be of service, Miss Waterhouse. You come by anytime you want."

She hurried back down the path toward the village, wondering if she should stop at Phyl's and tell her about Mr. Boelkerke's remarks about Dora. Sure, why not? And she needed to walk off the angst resurrected by mention of the detention camps, thoughts of the maternal grandparents she'd never known, and Joshua's journals.

She headed up the narrow twisting streets to the top of Holyrood Hill.

Phyl's cottage was dark but for the glow of the fish tank behind the curtain liner in the front window. The curtains hadn't been drawn, a good indication Phyl wasn't home yet.

She knocked anyway, just in case. When no one answered she stood looking around.

The old stone church loomed across the street.

A moment later, Salome wove among the gravestones in the neatly kept cemetery, until she came to her grandfather's. If he'd requested some elaborate tombstone before he died, he hadn't gotten it. Her father had taken care of the arrangements for both his parents. Joshua's grave was marked with an ordinary slab, while nearby her grandmother's grave sported a fine marble angel on a pedestal.

She wondered if her father *had* read the journals and if he knew about Lily Sebastian. That her grandfather had actually recorded his actions amounted to either stupidity or extraordinary arrogance—believing that even if anyone had discovered the truth, he'd never suffer the consequences. Maybe he'd gotten a thrill knowing where the actress's body had ended up while the rest of the world believed her to have run off with another man.

In any case, in the dead of night, he'd removed her body from the secret room and carried it aboard one of his boats. Then sailing out to the deep waters off Monterey, he'd weighted her down and dropped the body overboard.

Did her father know that Joshua wanted to divorce his mother and marry Lily? Further, she couldn't imagine what her father must have felt when (and if) he read about Joshua's true sentiments concerning the proposed exclusion of those of Japanese descent from Holyrood. Though her mother had told her of life in the concentration camp, her father did not talk about that time, nor had he ever mentioned that his father considered disinheriting him for marrying Satomi.

She almost wished she'd done what Herman Boelkerke had done—read the journals surreptitiously without informing her father.

Though "Holyrood" referred to a piece of the true cross, at the moment nothing about the place seemed particularly holy or Christian.

Then oddly, she felt a presence. But maybe it was just imagination induced by the graveyard itself. Maybe her grandfather had rolled over in his grave. Or maybe it was simply the wind stirring leaves in the surrounding trees. But there was no wind.

At a brisk pace, she hurried out of the graveyard and made her way through the dimly lit streets to her cottage.

Chapter 20

MANDERSON "Mandy" Monroe lived on the top floor of a stodgy three-story Victorian row house in San Francisco's Hayes Valley. A parking space opened up in front of his building just as Salome approached. Not unusual, as she had good parking karma.

Once he buzzed her in, she kept the front door ajar. Making several trips in the light drizzle, she unloaded the stepladder, a tool kit, and assorted items purchased days before to enhance Mandy's health guas. After carting everything up to the third-floor landing, she paused to quietly chant the heart-calming mantra nine times, her hands just above her waist in the proper mudra.

Having performed a reading on the apartment in November, she knew what she'd see but still closed her eyes before entering. His disease was one that changed radically and she wanted to feel the current state of energy.

She pushed the door open and upon entering, experienced a charged, kinetic burst which she recognized as Mandy himself, followed by a surge from behind that rushed down the hall—that would be the ch'i entering from the open door.

Eyes still closed, she shut the door. Now she felt a heavy drag on her lower body. This she partly interpreted as the grip of his disease. It also suggested that he'd done little to change the energy in the flat. Well, she'd remedy that and brought in the tool kit, the packages and stepladder.

THE APARTMENT WAS IN THE "SHOTGUN" style: a long hallway on the left, the rooms lined up, one after the other, on the right. She'd never liked this layout, common to old Victorian houses converted into flats. Good ch'i raced down the hall, bombarding whatever was at the end, or in the case of a door being there, passing right out of the dwelling.

She had half a dozen clients in New Orleans living in homes with the shotgun configuration, a style also common there.

A quick glance in each room confirmed that he'd not implemented feng shui changes. The front room was still a jumble of boxes and meager furnishing, all inherited when a friend died. He continued to use the floor of the cluttered dressing room as a collection point for bills and receipts. She did give him points for maintaining a spotless bath. And he kept the door closed to the tiny room housing the toilet. She peeked inside, glad to note the seat and lid were down. A healthy fern hung above the tank and the casement window was open for ventilation. More points.

Then she came to the living/sleeping room. He hadn't moved the futon couch from its position against the wall in the hallway facing the two sash windows. No doubt he still didn't make it into a bed at night and continued to stretch out and sleep with his feet toward the front door. This was bad feng shui, a position symbolic of death (the dead being carried out of a house feet first).

She walked around the wobbly coffee table, dirty glasses littering the surface. Indeed, she had more work to do than simply enhancing the health guas.

The last room was the kitchen and straight ahead the door

to the outside stairs leading up to the roof and down to the garbage cans in the alley.

The stove was positioned beside the door, a bad placement for health and wealth since while cooking his back was to the kitchen's entrance. But she'd brought the cure for that.

For a moment she watched Mandy dashing around from a saucepan on the stove, to the microwave, to the sink. He'd always been a bundle of energy. AIDS had reduced his speed but, as yet, not by much.

As she entered the room, he greeted her but didn't stop moving. "Hello, sweets!"

He wore a pleated blue silk skirt that matched the blouse discarded on the couch and a Princess Diana wig with a large rhinestone tiara and dangly rhinestone earrings. Glittery blue eye shadow clung to his eyelids along with thick eyeliner and false eyelashes. The rouge on his cheeks only emphasized his general pallor. He'd chewed off the lipstick but there were still traces of red at the corners of his mouth. His beard was growing back, which led her to believe he'd dressed up earlier in the day.

"What're you all dolled up for?" Salome asked.

In the middle of the kitchen, Mandy paused momentarily and struck a pose. With a flourish of the fork in his hand, he indicated his thin, naked chest. "You mean, wearing this old thing?"

Salome laughed. "No, Mandy, the headgear and makeup."

"Auditioned for a part in a movie. Documentary, actually. 'Drag Queens—Dying Royalty?' That sort of thing. Jeremy, Frank, Poller . . ."

He had a habit of dropping names of people she didn't know, assuming because they'd been longtime friends, she knew everyone he did.

He came over and gave her a hug. Then he pulled back and frowned. "Who attacked you?"

"Had an encounter with a window screen. It's nothing."

"Did you really bring a stepladder?"

"And various items you told me last week you hadn't bought."

Looking a little guilty, he hurried to the stove and changed the subject.

"Honey, we were so *hot*. And I mean that both ways. Lady Die—with an 'e'—never looked better." He shrugged. "Sure it's tasteless but tasteless is my current job description. Anyway, the lights, this cold I'm getting—and of course, Marty—turned up the heat. Plus I ran to get home in time. Didn't want to leave a lady waiting in the street. Tore off my blouse when I got home. What? Just minutes before you rang. And they didn't feed us."

"Look, it's not good for you to be running around half naked. Let me get you a robe or something. Better yet, go finish changing. I'll look after the food."

"God, you are an angel. Brown rice in the micro, something green on the stove."

He darted past her.

She checked the rice then turned down the heat on "something green," a sauce that a sea creature might have regurgitated. Naturally, she noticed that the stovetop needed a good cleaning. She grabbed a sponge and started in.

"Oh, there's bubbly in the fridge," Mandy called out from the living room. "Would you open it? There's a good lass. And how about some early Beach Boys?"

A moment later, "Don't Worry Baby" slinked from his speakers, tweaking memories she'd rather were left undisturbed.

Not until his midthirties did Mandy openly recognize his homosexuality, after years of laboring under the false impression that he simply had weird tendencies. Mandy had been married twice, first to Phyl. While she started her career with the San Francisco PD, he worked in local theater. Love that blossomed in high school, flagged in the real world when work and social circles clashed. They divorced after five years. He was Phyl's first love and she still felt great affection for him. If only he'd told her that *his* first love was really James Dean.

In his late twenties he was briefly married to a stage actress who inadvertently became his shepherd into the gay community. She loved to dress up Mandy as the character she was currently playing. Then using him as a mirror, she'd study her role while he spouted her lines. He never protested, in fact, enjoyed it. They began going out socially with Mandy dolled up. They had a great, trippy time until Mandy started attracting more attention than his wife. As her hostility grew, he studied her bitchiness. He practiced doing impressions of famous women. She moved to New York. He got a gig at a Polk Street club featuring drag artists. They divorced. Eventually, he was invited to join a touring revue.

"Dennis Wilson, such an imp!" Mandy exclaimed from the doorway, referring to the late drummer for the Beach Boys. "Sagittarians can be so *out there*. But to die in a swimming pool . . . I expected more from him. Exploding onstage. Death with flair."

He'd removed the wig and scrubbed his face and now wore a white poet's shirt. Until AIDS, Mandy had been remarkably youthful-looking. The disease and worrying about it had chiseled his features to the bone. Even so, he was still a handsome man. Only death would take the spark from his marvelous blue eyes.

"You're looking at me that way again, Mei!" he said, plucking the sponge from her hand.

"What way?"

"Like you're picturing me in a coffin."

"Oh, stop it!" She grabbed the sponge back and rinsed it under the faucet in the sink. "Your stove's important. I told you that before. Looks like you haven't cleaned it since."

"Where's my food?"

"In the microwave. What is that green stuff?"

"Something Josh made. An elixir? Looks and tastes like hell but it works. I think his secret ingredient is Percodan."

While he shoveled in the food, she finished cleaning the stove.

"Who's Josh?"

"Adrian's younger brother."

"You're joking! Is he gay?" Adrian had been Mandy's second wife.

Salome spun around. "Good heavens!"

"Now, now. God moves in mysterious ways." He tossed the plate in the sink. "So where's the champers? Did you drink it all?"

"I forgot it."

"You are not of this world."

He uncorked the bottle and filled two flutes.

While Salome protested that she couldn't drink and drive, he again took the sponge away. Holding it like a basketball, he arced it into the sink. "Yes! Two points for Monroe!" Clutching her hand, he pulled her into the living room, set her down on the couch, then retrieved the two glasses of champagne.

"What shall we toast?"

"Good ch'i."

His eyes darted away from hers for an instant. "Whatever." Then his bonhomie resurfaced. "Here, here!"

They clinked glasses. Salome took the tiniest of sips.

"What's this about drinking and driving? I thought you'd be staying. Don't your parents still have a place on Jones up by Grace Cathedral? Not that you can't stay here, of course."

"Phyl wants me close to home. I was lucky she let me come up at all."

Suddenly, Mandy shot up from the couch and disappeared down the hall. *What now?* she thought, wanting to get on with the work.

A moment later he reappeared, talking into a cordless phone. ". . . uh huh, so many felons, so little time. Anyway, I've got the scoop on the late Palmer Fordam and won't talk to anyone but Mei." He paused. "Of course I have a tape recorder. I'm an entertainer!"

He grinned at Salome and pumped his free arm.

"Yeah, she's right here." He thrust the phone at Salome and mouthed "Phyl."

Salome looked from him to the phone in surprise.

"Phyllis?"

"Mandy said he'd planned to take you to a club Fordham used to frequent. Just be back early tomorrow morning. How does he look?"

"Handsome as ever."

Phyl sighed. "Well, anything you can do for him . . ."

"Sure. How's the investigation?"

A tense silence followed.

"Just do an extra good reading for Manderson."

"Of course," Salome replied tightly.

"And, Mei, I appreciate your discretion."

"What do you mean?"

"Your interview in The Echo."

"Oh. Sure." She'd quite forgotten about the newspaper.

"You must be pissed."

"Why?"

"Not very nice of Emily to use that old DMV photo of you. Now, give me back to Manderson."

Salome handed the phone to Mandy. Now he strolled down the hall, talking softly and sweetly, as if he and Phyl were still lovers. That he could reach her whenever he wanted said a lot about their relationship.

Love is strange, she thought.

Then she recalled the ridiculous old DMV photo. The Department of Motor Vehicles photographer had snapped her picture just as she'd opened her eyes wide and dropped her mouth in anticipation of a sneeze. And the poop had refused to take it over. Well, nothing she could do about it.

A place to stay the night presented no problem. Her parents did own a town house on Jones Street which had originally been her grandmother's. Family and friends stayed there when visiting the city for shows and shopping. A key was hidden in the molding at the front. Now, though, with all the action in Holyrood, she didn't really want to stay overnight.

Though curious to hear what Mandy had to say about Palmer Fordham, she really needed to concentrate on the feng shui, especially the transcendental work. Knowing Mandy, he'd be underfoot, chatting and drinking champagne.

She shut off the stereo then pulled a notebook and pen from her handbag and began making a shopping list of extras she could use. It would keep Mandy occupied but not exhaustively so, in Japantown.

Chapter 21

SALOME gave him money for cabs and the items on the list, and he cheerfully gave her carte blanche to do whatever she wanted. In some ways he was a typical male, delighted to have a woman do the grunt work. Still, she didn't mind in the least.

After finishing kitchen cleanup, she turned on all the stove's burners for a moment to clear the stagnant sha. Then she removed the bubble wrap from a lightweight mirror and hung it behind the stove at a slight angle to reflect the burners, symbolically doubling the number. This would increase his prosperity. Additionally, he would be able to see anyone entering the kitchen and wouldn't be startled while cooking. The idea being, the more contented the cook, the better the food, which in turn resulted in better health.

Standing in the doorway, she regarded the living/sleeping room, glad to have the extra enhancements on hand.

The mini blinds were broken and filthy and Mandy had simply left them as they were, drooping at the top of the windows. She took them down then cleaned the grimy panes until they sparkled—this would also benefit his eyesight. She hung new lightweight rice paper blinds easy to lower and raise. Being white and the color associated with this the children/creativity gua, the new ones would further enhance this area of his life, in his case, creativity. From the top of each window, she hung a twenty-millimeter-faceted crystal on an eighteen-inch red cord. At this eastern exposure, sunlight would hit the crystals in the morning and fill the room with myriad colors, thus raising the ch'i.

Next she rearranged the furniture, first by removing the cheap coffee table and putting it by the back door with the dirty blinds to be taken down to the trash.

The futon couch changed places with a tiny Formica table and two chairs that had been in the room's fame gua. She removed the dingy brown futon cover and happily tossed it with the other trash. Fitting the new red and gold cover over the many layers of cotton batting required some effort, but the result made for a spectacular change. Now he could see the entrance to the living room from an angle rather than having his feet toward the front door.

Next she covered the little dining table with a new green tablecloth. This being the family and health gua of the apartment and the room itself, green was the respective color, wood the element. She added a bonsai tree. Because it was so small, it didn't take up much space, while providing the necessary elements to enhance his health. Maybe he'd experience better relations with his family, his father having disowned him after Mandy "outed" himself at a family dinner.

As an added bonus, she hung a ceramic Celtic green man, abundant leaves coming out of his head, on the bare wall above the table. The virile, masculine image would also raise his personal male health ch'i.

Built-in cupboards to the right of the living room's entrance housed his TV and stereo and needed only a quick dusting. At some point, they'd been painted black, an auspicious color for this the room's career gua.

The wobbly table had compromised the room's balance and harmony, having been in the center, the *tai chi* area.

Maybe she'd find a sturdy replacement in the front room, since he did need a table.

Though the toilet and bath were clean, she checked the latter just to see if he kept stoppers in the drains. Sure enough, both the tub and sink sported rubber plugs, thereby reducing a "drain" on finances.

The entrance to the dressing room was in the helpful people gua. Since November, clutter had multiplied with a vengeance. Salome went to work.

First off, she cleaned the small window angled across the wealth gua and disposed of the dead plant on the sill.

The dressing table/vanity, for the most part covered with old hardened makeup, was in the career gua, just to the left of the door. She put the still-useable cosmetics in the drawers, disposed of the rest, scrubbed the surface, polished the mirror, and replaced the spent bulbs surrounding it. She set out sprigs of rosemary brought from home, crushing some of the leaves to disperse the aroma. Signifying feminine strength, the rosemary would support the unique expression of his yin nature.

He'd been discarding dirty clothes all over, including in the family/health gua. For Christmas, she'd sent him a three-foot-by-three-foot collage of old photographs of when he was vital and healthy—including campy professional stills—and had suggested that he hang it on either this wall or the wall in the living room, where the green man now resided. She cringed when she found it still nested in the torn Christmas wrapping, on the floor beneath a pile of dirty laundry. She hung it up on the wall.

On the wall above a rolling cart of gowns in protective wrapping were shelves of wigs, each covered by a dusty plastic rain hat. She found the underlying message both whimsical and ironic: Mandy's career had been rained on by AIDS. Yet, there was still hope. The rain bonnets could be removed.

She placed nine red silk rosebuds at intervals between the wigs, straightened the clothes jammed in the closet and collected more dirty clothing. The bills and other paraphernalia covering the floor she placed in a box. Checking the overhead light fixture, she found that one of the two bulbs had gone out. For good measure, she replaced both then moved on to the last room.

The problems in the front room, the apartment's overall helpful people gua, would largely disappear once he cleared out the boxes and odd bits of furniture. She did clean the bay window, then opened them at the top and bottom to freshen the stale air. Then she hung a metal wind chime of the sort ubiquitous in Chinatown, which immediately began singing in the breeze.

The delicate tones accompanied her as she cleared a space in front of the fireplace, in the room's family/health gua, pleased to discover a sturdy little table that would serve nicely in the living room. She polished the mantel and mirror above it, wondering what to place there to enliven the ch'i. A healthy plant would be nice but given the clutter blocking the windows, the room was too dark for a plant to flourish. But for a pine-scented candle and hefty wind chime for the hall, she'd about depleted her stock of enhancements.

However, in a kitchen cupboard she found a shallow green glass bowl. She placed it on the mantel, put the green candle inside, and lit the wick. The flame reflecting in the mirror and the clean pine scent instantly raised the ch'i.

For a moment she contemplated the clutter, blessing the spirit of the friend who'd left all his worldly possessions to Mandy.

Outside, the building storm cut loose. The wind chime began jangling erratically. Salome closed the windows and to her way of thinking, Mandy's friend had spoken. His belongings were not meant to uselessly block Mandy's ch'i but to be given away.

On the desk by the entrance she scribbled a note: "Call Salvation Army for pickup!"

After placing his "new" coffee table in front of the futon couch, she climbed the stepladder and hung a melodious wind chime on a twenty-seven-inch red cord in the middle of the hallway, within reach so he could swat it whenever he passed beneath.

Mundane work completed, Salome took a quick shower and changed into her robe. After the initial mantra, she began the transcendental blessing ritual starting in the kitchen and putting the full force of her mind on the health guas in each room.

By the time she finished at the fireplace in the front room, Mandy returned. She blew out the pine candle and told him to leave the bags by the door.

Then they began the tour. As they wandered from room to room, she could see his personal ch'i elevate in his delighted, somewhat awestruck expression.

"Who lives here?" he said breathlessly. "Why didn't I do this before? Salome, it's—Jesus—I can't wait for Jeremy to see this."

Per her request, he'd bought a brass bell to ring nine times in the morning at each health gua to call in the ch'i. A vase was found for the bright yellow daffodils. Salome set the cheery flowers on the new coffee table to trumpet balance and harmony in the center of the living room.

Finally, she hung the curtain of tightly woven blue and green beads at the kitchen's entrance. Like the windchime in the hall, the curtain would disperse the ch'i with sound and movement. Additionally, Mandy would be alerted whenever anyone entered the kitchen. Blue and green were also the colors associated with knowledge/spirituality, the kitchen's mouth of ch'i. Knowledge of nutrition would be stimulated, essential to one in such a precarious state of health.

"This is so *exotic*!" Mandy exclaimed, slinking back and

forth through the beads. "I . . . I," he sobbed, then unable to speak, dropped his head in his hands.

As he began to cry, she wrapped her arms around him.

A long moment later, they pulled apart. She expected him to be exhausted. He wasn't.

"First thing we *must* do is get you out of that dreadful garment! You look like an escapee from *The Crucible*."

He held her at arm's length, his face wet but the tears gone, his mood now exuberant and body odor strong. "Let's glamour you up! Tom-Tom left some really nice gowns."

"Mandy, slow down. I don't need—"

"Stop! Really, sweets, sorry about the gamy smell. Just part of the whole thing. I'm in the shower." He opened one of the cupboards and from a shelf inside plucked a clear patch. "My testosterone," he announced. "Now you go in my dressing room and find the perfect gown. It'll be in the section with smaller ones. They were Tom-Tom's. He'd be honored to have you wear anything of his."

"Shoes. I don't have shoes."

He rolled his eyes. "Not to worry. We'll find shoes. Just go change. Once I'm finished with you no one will look at your feet. None of the perverts I know have foot fetishes."

Salome opened her mouth to speak. Mandy immediately put a finger on her lips. "Go find a dress. I'll be out of the shower in a tick."

While he belted out "Good Vibrations" in the shower, sounding like an extra member of the Beach Boys, Salome switched on the overhead in the dressing room. She stepped out of her uniform and hung it on the closet door. Now wearing only a sleeveless silk shift, she shivered slightly in the cold room.

In the center of the rack, as if protected on both sides by Mandy's much larger creations, was a pocket of smaller gowns, some sequined, some covered in bugle beads, others colorful silks and satins, all short. Tom-Tom probably had good legs.

"Next one over," Mandy said.

Salome glanced over her shoulder. Mandy stood in the doorway, stark naked but for a towel turbaned on his head.

He spread his arms. "I know what you're thinking. Joan Crawford, right?"

Given the display of male genitalia, her thoughts never touched on the late actress and Salome laughed.

As if they were an old married couple, he sauntered into the room and checked out the contents of his closet.

"Ho hum. I hate being the boy. The clothes are so boring. Still, we've got to dress you first." He slipped on a hot pink satin kimono-style robe, moved the chair to one side of the dressing table, ordered her to sit, then went to work.

"Sweetheart, I am going to feng shui *you*."

Chapter 22

"THIS is expensive, Mandy," Salome whispered, peering over the top of her leather-bound menu, after they'd ordered drinks.

"Indeed, sweets, but it's my treat."

Having changed his mind about "being the boy," he chose another outfit altogether. He'd lost too much weight to pull off a voluptuous Marilyn Monroe look, so instead settled on a long-sleeved black polyester jumpsuit, black ankle boots, and a dark brown wedge-cut, Sassoon wig. In ten minutes, he'd done his makeup. The result: Diana Rigg in the sixties British television export, *The Avengers*.

"Please, let me take care of the bill. Or let's go Dutch."

"No can do."

"But—"

"Salome, I may live—rather, *did* live like a slob—and in a more moderately priced part of town than when I was working, but I made good money and some shrewd investments. Rather, Tom-Tom did. By day, you see, he was a stockbroker. So, I'm fine. I don't announce it to the world is all. And look what you did for me, gratis."

They sat by the window (in the relationship gua) of a charming rooftop restaurant on Nob Hill with a view of the north side of the city, myriad lights muted in the rain and fog.

Indeed, Mandy had "feng shuied" her. With the deft strokes of an artist, he'd made up her face, emphasis on her Asian features, and pulled her long black hair into a sleek ponytail.

After rejecting a number of gowns, he had settled on a blue and gold brocade satin Chinese dress with slits on both sides up to midthigh with matching shoes. The dress fit but they'd had to stuff tissue in the shoes. Gloating like a Henry Higgins, he declared proudly, "Nancy Kwan in *The World of Suzie Wong*. Tom-Tom would be so proud. He died before ever getting to wear the dress."

Though a little unnerved to be wearing the clothes of a dead man, she was quite fascinated with this glamorous dimension Mandy had coaxed from dormancy.

The waiter arrived with their drinks: champagne cocktail for Mandy, Perrier for Salome.

She raised her glass. "To Tom-Tom."

Mandy's eyes misted. "To Tom-Tom."

"Well, let's get started," she said quickly and brought out the little tape recorder he'd given her to put in the beaded handbag.

"So when did you meet Palmer Fordham?"

Almost instantly, he perked. But he was an entertainer and enjoyed being interviewed, no matter the topic.

"Sometime after he dropped out of the San Francisco Art Institute. Maybe ten years ago?" He blew out a breath and threw his head back, acting as if he was being visually recorded as well.

"My God, talk about drop-dead gorgeous. He hung out with both straights and gays but always with an eye for those with money. I don't think anyone was ever sure of him. Some people thought he was just a tease. Tom-Tom was smitten, I do know that. The feeling wasn't mutual, though. Palmer liked him because of Tom-Tom's investment tips which," Mandy said, rolling his eyes, "the fool simply gave away. He even bought a few paintings to keep Palmer interested. Paid way too much for mediocre, derivative art.

"But, honey, his lips. They were like silk pillows. Palmer Fordham kissed better than anyone. Bar none."

"You two kissed?" Salome asked, wondering how Phyl would feel when she heard that.

"How else could I give you such a literate description?" he snapped. After a moment, he took a breath. "Sorry. Didn't mean to be rude.

"Anyway, he used to hang out at certain clubs, especially Murph's, sketching people. We queens loved it. Other people weren't so hot. I remember one night. Someone in the audience took exception. Acted just like a rabid celebrity. Tore up the sketches then pounced on Palmer. Murph's can get rowdy but that's half the fun. Anyway, turns out the 'offended' was one a those "family values" Congressmen from back East!"

"What about someone who might have been a former lover?"

"Like I said, you couldn't really pin the guy down. Maybe we'll see someone at Murph's."

Despite Phyl's feelings, she had to ask, "Did you have sex with him?"

Mandy laughed. "In my head." Then he leaned forward and in a half whisper confided, "Don't know if it was good for him, but it was great for me!"

Their food arrived.

"Intermission, Phyl," Mandy barked into the tape recorder. "Me and Mei gotta eat now," he said and switched it off.

During the meal Salome told him about Michael O'Kelly being in Holyrood and Mandy confessed to having had a "secret crush" on him back in high school.

"I wouldn't try to refresh that relationship if I were you," Mandy advised.

"Why?"

"Truth?"

"Of course."

"I think he had a secret crush on me, too."

She stared at him for a moment, a forkful of grilled salmon halfway to her mouth. Then she laughed.

Mandy snickered. "Well, who wouldn't? I was a god!" Then he smiled impishly, "And, though I didn't know it at the time, a *goddess*."

Over dessert, they resumed the interview, the tape rolling.

". . . couldn't quite believe it when he called me the first of the year looking for Tom-Tom. Said he had a new project going and was looking for investors."

"What kind of project?"

"Coffee tables! Can you imagine, mermaid sculptures as the base. Plexiglas on top. Attractive, lightweight, inexpensive. Made in Taiwan. You know, the unusual crap for the masses. He already had some big import store, like Pier 1, lined up as the major distributor."

"World Wide Imports?"

Mandy shrugged impatiently. "Thing is Tom-Tom had been dead for months! Shows how much Fordham cared about old friends. I hung up on him. That was my last connection with Palmer Fordham."

It was a good thing they'd talked before entering the club in the Castro district. Murph's vibrated with thundering rock and roll, raucous laughter, and screamed drink orders at the long, stately bar Mandy said had been imported from Ireland along with the ornate fixtures and three busy bartenders raising and lowering bottles with dramatic effect.

On stage in the back of the room, (in the fame position, Salome noted), Rod Stewart and Mick Jagger clones lip-synced while leaping around playing air guitars.

A man wearing a pageboy wig, twinset, and pearls, a pleated skirt and flats walked by on the arm of a balding gentleman clad in tight black leather pants with a matching jacket unzipped to reveal a hairless chest. As she watched them pass, Salome noted an additional attraction: Ionic columns tattooed on each of the gent's exposed buttocks. She wondered if it was a code of sorts.

Mandy seemed to know everyone as they table-hopped. He introduced her as "Suzie. Suzie Wong." She was glad when they finally roosted at a small table near the stage.

Finally, the audience quieted and the show began. For the next hour they enjoyed the revue. Between the performances of Dolly Parton, Carol Channing, Barbra Striesand, and Liza Minelli impersonators, the gorgeous and glamorous paraded onstage, larking with the audience, their own particular personas carrying the moment. The only other times Salome recalled being in close proximity to such spectacular gowns was in the ladies' room at the Kennedy Center in Washington, D.C.

Assuredly, this wasn't the Kennedy Center but it was certainly fun.

When the show concluded and the cacophony resumed, Mandy's face was streaked with tears. Using his napkin, he daubed his eyes. She knew how much he missed being a part of the show, the excitement, performing, having an audience adore him. Giving him a moment, she went to the bar.

Slipping between two men—dressed as men—her eyes met those of the man on her right as she extended her arm to attract the closest bartender. She did a double take then froze.

"Do I know you?" the man slurred drunkenly.

The same voice had asked her about Hector's cioppino when she had made the delivery to the fire station.

She shook her head and, drawing the attention of a bartender, ordered a champagne cocktail for Mandy and another Perrier for herself.

Back at the table she said, "Mandy, don't look now but there's a guy at the bar who's a fireman in Holyrood. I just happened to meet him the other day. His name's Clay Bethune."

"Really? I know Clay. Haven't seen him in a while."

"Oh!"

"What?"

"He's coming toward our table."

A moment later, Clay Bethune, a full highball seeping at the edges, swayed over them.

"Clay! You old fire demon. Long time no see. Have a seat!"

Clay picked up a nearby chair and turned it so the back faced front then sat down. Very macho. With bleary eyes, he stared at Salome.

"Don't see you much these days," Mandy said.

"Got tired of the city."

"Where you living?"

"Santa Cruz. But I work in a little place called Holyrood." Suddenly, Clay pointed his glass at Salome. "I know you . . ."

Mandy said, "This is Suzie. Suzie Wong."

"Suzie? Huh."

"Actually—" Salome began.

But Mandy interrupted. "Suzie doesn't speak much English."

"Well, she looks familiar."

"Hey man! You hear about Palmer Fordham? Pretty awful. Wait a minute! He was living in Holyrood. You happen to run into him?"

"Yeah. A few times."

"Weren't you two an item once?"

Clay shifted his eyes toward Mandy. "Until he got rich. Didn't want all those high-powered old bitches knowing about his other life. You should see where he lived."

"Shit happens, man. Money starts coming in the front door, old friends get shuffled out the back."

"Yeah, well, I made sure he didn't forget about me."

"Heard he was beaten to death. Not a good way to go."

Clay grunted. Tina Turner came over the speakers belting out "We Don't Need Another Hero."

"I *have* to dance!" Mandy declared. He jerked Salome from her chair and began twirling her around the small dance floor.

"Look, sweets, Clay can be bad news. I'm getting a bad vibe."

"You think he might have had something to do with Palmer's death?"

"Hell, he can be a violent drunk but I don't know if he's capable of murder. At the moment, I don't like the way he's looking at you. Maybe it's time we headed for the barn. I'm getting kind of tired anyway."

When they returned to the table, Clay and his drink were gone. They collected their coats and handbags. On the way out, Salome looked for the fireman but didn't see him anywhere.

An hour later, after changing clothes and tucking Mandy into his newly positioned couch/bed, Salome hit the road, heading back to Holyrood. Sometime before midnight, she stopped at the Holyrood PD and dropped off Mandy's taped interview, to which she'd added, en route, information about Clay Bethune's possible relationship with Palmer Fordham.

Chapter 23

SALOME studied a photograph of Palmer's studio printed in Saturday's special edition of *The Echo*. Showing fine resolution, the picture had been shot from the doorway. Emily must have gotten hold of a negative from someone at the crime scene, either a civilian who managed to sneak in or a member of the team of investigators. She doubted the police photographer would ever jeopardize his position by sharing with the press. Phyl would not be amused.

According to feng shui, the top floor of a structure represents whatever is hanging over the occupants. In the case of an attic where items of the past are stored, the past will have a strong influence over the occupants. In the Perfume, however, the top floor had originally been a sunroom that, as evidenced by the photograph, the artist used as a work space.

Noting the mattress on the floor, she could tell he'd been sleeping with his feet toward the door (as Mandy had done) but, worse still, with no wall support at all, "adrift" as some practitioners referred to the placement.

By sleeping in the same space where he worked and without some sort of partition separating the two areas, he had put both his professional and personal life at risk.

Diagonally across from the door in the upper right-hand corner was what appeared to be the sculpted lower body of a fish. In an office or studio the relationship gua was considered the power position, most often where a desk or work station should be placed. Clearly the sculpture represented something quite important to Palmer. Was it the prototype of a pedestal for the mass-market coffee tables Mandy mentioned? The various coffee tables scattered throughout the room suggested such a conclusion. She had a strong feeling that this sculpture had something to do with his murder, had in some way disturbed a relationship of long-standing. She thought of Clay Bethune and his surly demeanor last night.

Putting the paper aside, she carried the mansion's blueprints over to the desk. Flipping through the sheets, she intended to study the basement again to determine where her grandfather would have constructed the concealed room. Her eyes suddenly fell on something she should have seen when she'd been sent the cash to feng shui the Perfume. On the first floor, off the dining room, was a tiny, three-quarter circle, like a pie with a piece cut out.

Just then the phone rang, the caller Emily.

"Barbara Boatwright's been taken into custody! Her fingerprints were found on a wineglass in the living room."

"Oh dear!"

"Is that all you have to say? As your spokesperson, I need more than that, Salome!"

"This is not a good time." No time was a good time to talk to Emily.

"Well, I'm at the police station and probably will be for a while. How about we meet for dinner?"

"I have other plans."

"Don't forget our deal, Salome."

After hanging up, Salome recalled Barbara saying on the phone that she hadn't seen Palmer since the middle of the month. Her prints being on the wineglass seemed to prove otherwise and that Barbara had lied.

She hated to think of her old friend as a murderer. Still, there might be some reasonable explanation. Maybe she'd just stopped in for a drink early in the evening of his death and had lied to protect herself—and her marriage.

A few minutes later, she turned her attention back to the blueprints. The three-quarter circle indicated a spiral staircase. However, she'd never seen one at the Perfume. As children, she and Phyl would have delighted in discovering and playing on such a feature. Of course, they'd have been unaware of the negative properties feng shui assigned to spiral staircases. A spiral caused ch'i to spin downward in a corkscrew motion, adversely affecting circumstances in the respective gua. Further, negotiating such stairs created disorientation and a feeling of insecurity.

Checking the other floors, she could find no corresponding marking and began to think the stairs had been planned but never actually included when the house was built. Interestingly, the marking was in the family/health gua.

STILL EARLY FOR A SATURDAY NIGHT, THE MU-sic at Scott's Bar and Restaurant was at a reasonable level and there was still space available at the bar and tables. Scott's catered to an upscale younger crowd, the patrons themselves rather than the menu being the main attraction. Salome looked around, even checked the outdoor patio, but didn't see Rita. She took a seat at the bar close to the waitress station, where Rita would see her as soon as she arrived.

The bartender, George Dawson, slapped down a napkin.

"Hi, Salome. What'll it be?"

"Actually, I'm meeting Rita Van Horn. Have you seen her?"

"Not tonight."

"Well, it's still early. Perrier for now. With a twist of lemon."

The waitress came up to the station and glanced at Salome. "Hi."

"Hi."

Then the waitress did a double take. "Hey! Aren't you the woman who found Palmer Fordham's body? I saw your picture in the paper."

"You recognized me from that photo?" Salome asked incredulously.

"Sure. Why not?"

George appeared with her drink and, having overheard, added, "I wouldn't worry about the heat being on you. Heard today they found Barbara Boatwright's fingerprints on a wineglass at the scene."

The waitress then remarked, "Well, couldn't accuse Palmer Fordham of age discrimination."

"What do you mean?" Salome asked.

"For about a week, he came in every night. At least every night I was working. Trolling, wasn't he, George?"

"I guess. But who isn't trolling in this place."

"Then I heard he was looking for a model," the waitress continued. "Maybe it was just a pickup line but I think he found her."

"When was this?"

"Just before I went on vacation. Two weeks ago. This couple comes in. The guy is really big, like a professional wrestler or something. The girl's totally awesome but in a sleazy kind of way. Like, the minute they sat down, Palmer was at their table. Thought there might be a fight at first. You remember, George?"

George frowned.

"Oh come on! She wore a T-shirt that said 'Hog Heaven.'"

"Awesome-looking women *work* here," he remarked with a charming smile.

The waitress actually blushed. "Anyway, he—Palmer that is—bought them a couple rounds then they left together."

"You see them again?"

The waitress shook her head. "That's the last time I saw any of them."

Salome felt a strong tug at her gut; intuition at work.

"You tell the police?"

She shrugged. "This is my first night back since vacation."

As business picked up, Salome began to wonder if Rita had forgotten or had maybe confused the restaurant. But she had suggested Scott's.

Finally, at about a quarter of ten, Salome paid her meager tab. "George, if Rita comes in, would you tell her I've gone looking for her. I'll be back shortly."

"Sure thing, Salome."

SHE DROPPED IN AT ALL THE RESTAURANTS then stopped at the Sand and Sea Gallery. The place was dark and shadowy without even a hint of light. That seemed strange. Normally, at least one painting in the storefront window was highlighted after the gallery closed. She went around to the back and knocked on the rear door. When no one answered, she headed for the Perfume Creek.

In a few moments, she stood looking up at the windmill at Rita's cottage. In the still, calm night, the windmill was motionless. Like the gallery, the house gave no indication that Rita was about. Even so, she knocked on both the front and kitchen doors. The garage apartment was currently empty. She walked around to the narrow street that fronted the creek-side houses. On the other side was a row of old-fashioned garages with pull-up doors, a pane of glass in each. These were rented by those who didn't have a garage or, as in Rita's case, had converted their garages to rental units. Peering in one, she found Rita's Lincoln Town Car. That didn't necessarily mean she was in town. She might have taken the airport shuttle to San Jose and maybe gone to one of her galleries in New York or La Jolla.

Clearly, Rita had had a change in plans.

She returned to Scott's. George told her Rita had not made an appearance. Not feeling hungry, she left.

For a moment she stood outside, watching couples and small groups heading for the bars and restaurants, their laughter tweaking a feeling of loneliness.

Why not engage in a little sleuthing? She walked home, climbed in her truck, and headed for the mountains.

HOG HEAVEN WAS A BIKER BAR. BEAUTIFULLY maintained motorcycles—Harleys, vintage Norton Atlases, and their Japanese counterparts filled the lot along with a few trucks. Steppenwolf's "Born To Be Wild," could be heard as she exited her car, preparing for the auditory assault.

The low light, dark walls, clouds of smoke, and the sharp *smack* of billiard balls from the two pool tables took her back to the Honolulu bar where she'd worked many years ago, a tavern patronized by GIs en route to or from Vietnam.

Most of the patrons were middle-aged men who once had terrified the average person whenever they hit the road. Now the same people held toy drives at Christmas. They were and always had been considered outlaws and, as such, treated with some respect. Like live ammunition.

Several waitresses wearing "Hog Heaven" T-shirts wove among seated customers and those standing around the pool tables.

A few people checked her out when she entered but no one disputed nor seemed threatened by her presence. But why should they? There was something in the eyes that always transmitted a comfort level in any place. Salome's time waitressing in Honolulu had given her "the essence." Besides, her middle-age bubble of invisibility was firmly in place.

She found a seat in the middle of the bar beside the waitress station, so marked by the trash bin beneath it, the smell of beer and cigarette butts rank. No one bothered enforcing the no-smoking ban here. The bartender, a redheaded woman who probably looked twenty years older in daylight, stood in front of her.

"Can I help you, honey?"

To order designer water in such a place would be a bit silly.

"A draft, please."

The woman moved to a nearby tap then presented Salome with a chilled mug on a beer mat. Salome paid and left the change on the bar. Then she spun around and regarded the crowd. The bartender was too busy to engage in conversation. Besides, Salome didn't know the name of the girl the waitress at Scott's had mentioned.

Patience was awarded when a short blonde matching the description hurried toward the waitress station and slid a tray with a half-dozen empty bottles on the bar. The bartender began plucking the empties off the tray. The waitress handed over a tab to be rung up and called out her order. While she dumped and wiped a couple of ashtrays, Salome introduced herself.

"I own the Perfume Mansion," she said after giving her name.

The young woman regarded her sharply.

"Look, lady, I'm busy."

"What's your name?"

"Brooke."

"This won't take long, Brooke. Why not get someone to cover for you for few minutes. The police will be talking to you soon enough." As an incentive, she added, "And they don't pay."

Brooke sighed then said in a resigned voice, "Just let me take care of this order. I'll meet you in the parking lot."

Believing she might slip out the back, Salome said, "I'll follow you."

A few minutes later, the two women left the bar.

Beside a massive redwood at the far west side of the property, Brooke fell against the trunk and lit a cigarette.

"You said something about paying."

Salome handed over a twenty. "For your time. There's more if you give me anything substantial."

The bill disappeared in the back pocket of Brooke's jeans. "Like what?"

"Like how did you know Palmer Fordham?"

"I don't want to get mixed up with the cops."

"Sure. I understand that."

"Who are you?"

"I told you. I own the mansion."

"You want to find out who killed him so you can get that out of the way and rent it again. Right?"

"You might say that."

"How'd you know about me?"

"Someone in Scott's."

Brooke smoked her cigarette for another moment. Then she told her story.

"We couldn't have been in Scott's more than a minute when suddenly Palmer appeared. I mean, he was really good-looking. Ken, my boyfriend wasn't very happy about it. But after Palmer bought us drinks, he convinced us to go home with him. He said he wanted to use me as a model for a couple of weeks, maybe longer.

"At first Ken didn't believe him and demanded money. Typical Ken. Didn't matter what I wanted. Anyway, we go to his place—yours, I guess. Totally awesome. Palmer's feeding Ken drinks. He showed us his artwork. Well, what can I say? I really wanted to do it. But I don't have a car and Ken said he wouldn't drive me down and pick me up.

"So Palmer said he'd give me a room in his house *and* pay me. Ken had a fit. No way, he said. So we start to fight. Thing is, see, Ken wanted something out of the deal. So, finally Palmer says we both could live in the guesthouse across the creek. If we'd take over housekeeping chores, we could stay there rent-free. I woulda done anything to get out of the ratty old trailer where we been living.

"Anyway, Ken takes me down there a couple evenings after he gets off work. Palmer makes a mold to fit me—my lower body—so I'm, like, this mermaid. It's really uncomfortable but Palmer pays me each time. He sketches me with my upper body in all sorts of positions—hands above my head, behind my head, across my chest. I tell ya, it's work. And boring! Ken keeps bugging him about when are we gonna move in the guesthouse. He's afraid the job'll be over before we get in. So Ken tells Palmer I can only come for a couple hours a week. But, if I—we—live in that house, I'll be available all the time."

She paused and crushed out her cigarette.

"Anyway, then we hear about Palmer getting killed. Next thing I know, Ken's gone. Now I'm stuck in that lousy trailer, no car, nothin'."

"Does Ken have a police record?"

She sighed. "Yeah."

"Any idea where he went?"

She shrugged. "Look, I really did plan on going to the cops but with Ken gone I figured I'd better keep my mouth shut . . . I mean, I didn't have anything to do with it."

"You think Ken might have killed Palmer?"

She hesitated. "No. I mean, why? He hardly knew the guy and why ruin an opportunity to live near the beach rent-free?"

Salome passed Brooke another twenty. "Thanks for your help. I know you don't want to talk to the police but you're going to have to—to eliminate yourself as a suspect. You understand?"

They walked back toward the tavern.

"So, please, don't think about taking off."

Then Brooke stopped. "There's something else—if you've maybe got another twenty."

"All right. What?" Salome pulled another bill out of her wallet but didn't hand it over.

"Well, you see, the last night I modeled, we finished about nine. Palmer walked us down to Ken's bike. He was carrying a big garbage bag full of crumbled sketches and stuff and put it in the trash.

"Later, after we'd been home for a while, I hitchhiked back down there. Ken was passed out. Anyway, I got that bag from the trash. I mean, he's a famous artist right? Even what he throws away might be valuable. Know what I mean? Then I hitched a ride back home.

"So the next day while Ken's at work I like smoothed out all the sketches. But I found something else. One a those home tests for HIV."

Salome shuddered at the ominous news. Brooke eyed the hand that held the money. Salome gave her the twenty.

"The test was positive."

A LITTLE WHILE LATER, SALOME STOOD ON THE stoop outside Phyl's cottage, hoping her cousin would answer the door.

En route she'd tried to reach Phyl by phone but at each number encountered voice mail. She'd slowly driven by the police station. Most likely Phyl was there but so were a lot of other people. In the packed parking lot were quite a few media vans. A number of people were outside, smoking and talking in small groups.

Eventually, Phyl would have to come home and Salome would be there when she did.

Chapter 24

NOTICING a movement at the curtains, Salome's excitement grew. A moment later, Phyl opened the door just an inch. Salome was in luck.

"What is it, Mei?"

"I've got some really important news."

"Uh, let's take a walk. I'll meet you at the end of the street." Abruptly, Phyl closed the door.

What's going on? Salome wondered. Why didn't Phyl just invite her inside?

A few minutes later, Phyl joined her. She wore an old army trench coat and a baseball cap pulled low over her forehead. They hadn't even greeted each other before two news vans squealed around the corner, braking abruptly right in front of her cottage. Standing in the shadows, they watched as two reporters and their camera people, lights bobbing, sprinted across the small lawn, competing to be the first at her door.

Phyl grabbed Salome's arm and pulled her briskly in the opposite direction.

"What's going on?"

"All hell's about to break loose," Phyl hissed. "So what's this news?"

Though anxious to learn of the "hell breaking loose," Salome began to relate what she'd learned from Brooke, about the planned move to Dora's cottage, and that Palmer had tested positive for HIV.

"I mean, the people he slept with are going to have to know so they can be tested, too."

They dashed across the street, headed toward the Perfume Creek. Traffic seemed to have picked up. But then it often did late on a Saturday night. However, more cars seemed to be headed into the village than out of it.

"Ask me," Salome said, "Dora's got a damn good motive to get rid of Palmer. He must have given her notice. Did you know she and Granddad were lovers?"

Phyl jerked her head around. "Where'd you hear that?"

"Mr. Boelkerke."

After a moment, they came to the footpath that meandered along the creek and in front of the houses, Mr. Boelkerke's about ten yards ahead. All the houses were dark but then it was around midnight. And there were no lights along the creek.

Phyl switched on a flashlight she'd brought, indicating the Perfume Creek had been the destination she'd had in mind when she left her cottage.

"Dora's house is just down the way. Why don't we stop in—or you anyway—and talk to her?"

Still gripping Salome's arm, Phyl said, "Do you know how Palmer died?"

"From what I saw—"

"Are you just trying to get your friend Barbara off the hook? You people with money always stick together."

"What do you mean? Did she confess?"

"She confessed to investing in a new project of Palmer's, making coffee tables. Sold her condo in Lake Tahoe for that purpose."

"Palmer told Mandy about the project. Did you listen to the tape?"

"Not yet."

Now she related what she'd learned in San Francisco, adding Clay Bethune to the list of suspects.

"Hell. I need think time. And some quiet." Then she started forward with purpose.

"Are we going to Dora's?"

"No."

"Then—"

"Just shut up, okay?"

They stopped in front of Dora's for a moment. No light shone inside. Salome started to speak then decided against it.

Phyl trooped across the footbridge with Salome at her heels. Almost immediately a picture came to mind: her own Japanese garden. The pagoda on one side of the pond, the Japanese man on the other looking up at the elaborate structure. Contemplating what might be? Was he envious?

Phyl pulled out keys, now noticing that the seal had been tampered with. "Damnit. Somebody's been in here! Or tried."

"Don't you have all the keys?"

"Not Palmer's," she snapped.

She opened the door then switched on a flashlight, piercing the black void beyond.

"Age before beauty," Phyl said, looking around furtively.

" 'Pearls before swine,' according to Matthew. Or was it Dorothy Parker?" Salome whispered, trying to still her apprehension with a little light banter.

"Just get inside!"

Salome hesitated, her sense of foreboding momentarily preventing movement. "Why are we here?"

"This is the last place any of those media parasites will show up tonight. I managed to sneak out of the station about thirty minutes ago. They want warm bodies. For the moment, the Perfume doesn't have any."

Chapter 25

ACCORDING to feng shui, the lowest level of the house represents the foundation of the lives of the occupants. In the case of a basement, it should be clean and free of clutter, otherwise the residents will be open to negative physical manifestations. Clutter creates sha, bad ch'i and sha represents clogged and stagnant energy.

Phyl closed the door, keeping the flashlight shining straight ahead.

Directly in front of them was a niche for servants to hang their hats and coats and a stand in the far right corner for umbrellas. Shelves were on the left.

Something tweaked Salome's memory but not enough for resolution. . . .

"I have to go outside for a minute!"

"Oh, please," Phyl moaned in annoyance.

"This is the first time since my seventh birthday that I've been through this door! It's important!"

Salome opened the door and took a deep breath of fresh air. Silently she chanted *om ma ni pad me om.* . . .

Behind her, Phyl switched on a light a few paces from the door.

A memory broke loose. She now recalled a small black and

green ceramic shard she'd picked up all those years ago . . . on the floor beneath the coats. When she'd dashed outside in terror, she must have dropped it in the creek.

Salome closed the door, pressing the button on the knob to lock it. For a moment, she stood quietly looking at the niche.

"Let's go on upstairs," Phyl said, moving to the right and down the passage toward the stairs that led to the kitchen. On either side were cluttered storage areas.

"No, wait."

After another long moment she said, "This is where it happened. Where I gained entry. It's here, Phyl."

"What do you mean?"

"The room of screaming children."

"Don't start that again. Let's go upstairs."

"Don't you remember?" *That ceramic shard I picked up . . .* "Phyl. It's here."

"What's here?"

"The way in."

She brushed past the coats on the right. "Why do you suppose there are so many coats? I mean, there's only Dora."

"She just never bothered to toss them."

The umbrella stand was ceramic and about three and a half feet tall and heavy. Salome rolled it to one side. The corner was shadowy.

"Shine the light over here."

With a loud click, Phyl switched on the flashlight and shone it along the floor.

"Look!" Salome exclaimed. A thrill of both excitement and fear prickled her skin. Her heart picked up its pace. Salome stepped on the now-revealed button.

A narrow portion of the wall slid open.

Phyllis's flashlight hit the mirrors, nearly blinding them both.

"Would you look at this," Phyllis muttered in astonishment.

Salome stepped on the button and the door closed. She touched it again. The door slid open. Phyl maneuvered around her and entered the room.

"Someone must have knocked over the original umbrella stand. It hadn't yet been replaced when we came down here on my seventh birthday. I found a shard and stepped on that button. When the door opened I saw myself in the mirror and screamed. That's why I thought there were screaming children in the room! Then, in my terror I stepped on it again as I ran away."

Phyl didn't seem to be listening. She ran her hand on the pleated pink satin cover of the round bed in the center of the room. Another bed adrift, Salome noted, then began exploring, as excited with the find as a child.

"Over here," Salome said. Phyl directed her light at an old-fashioned vanity like Mandy's but clean and featuring bottles of Worth and Chanel Number 5. Salome opened one of the drawers. Inside was makeup, neatly arranged and of recent vintage. Another drawer held candles and in another she found lacy underwear wrapped in tissue paper.

There were no lamps or a light fixture on the ceiling or walls.

"Guess this room was never wired for electricity," Phyl remarked as she examined the wall to the left of the entrance. There she found a walk-in cedar closet longer than the length of the room itself. "Mei! Come look at these clothes!"

The closet must have been fifteen feet long, a fortune in vintage dresses, shoes, hats, and handbags extending on both sides, most likely originally built to be storage for Lily Sebastian.

Suddenly Salome grabbed Phyllis's arm. "Did you hear that?"

They dashed back into the room to find the opening through which they'd entered now closed.

"Damn!" Phyllis exclaimed. "You didn't accidentally step on that button did you?"

"Of course not!"

"Maybe something fell on it."

"Yeah. Someone's foot."

"Did you lock the creek-side door?"

"Yes!"

"Someone's in the house," Phyl growled.

They both heard a scraping sound—like the umbrella stand being moved along the concrete and back into place.

Phyllis started pounding on the wall. "Hey! There are people in here! Come on! Open the door!"

For several minutes they examined the floor and wall from one end to the other, looking for another button.

Salome sat down on the bed, trying to conjure the blueprints, trying to keep calm. But her thoughts kept flying around. The flashlight suddenly blinded her.

"Get that light out of my face!" Salome demanded.

"What are you doing just sitting there? There's got to be another button or switch or something to open the door—maybe the mirrors!" Phyl dashed across the room.

Just a few seconds later she uttered a sharp cry. "Oh my God!"

Now she stood rigid, her light angled toward the floor on the opposite side of the large bed.

Phyllis moved closer then bent down. Salome heard the crackle of plastic, then moved over behind her cousin.

On the floor, swathed in a blue tarp was Rita Van Horn. "Quite dead," Phyllis announced. "I'd say, at least a day."

Salome sniffed the air and frowned. And it wasn't the corpse she smelled.

"Give me the flashlight."

"Why?" Phyl asked.

"Just give it to me!"

The light flickered. The batteries were getting low. But it didn't take much light to see the smoke billowing into their confined space through a vent at the top of the wall. Just on the other side would be the old coats and hats. A hat, she now realized must have been hung to conceal the air vent, further keeping the room a secret.

"Have you got your cell phone?"

Phyl gave her a sheepish look. "I just wanted to stay out of communication for a while . . ."

Both women dropped to the floor.

Smoke covered the ceiling and as it continued to pour in began pressing down.

Crawling past Rita's body, they both pressed the mirrored panels hoping one concealed an exit. But no such luck.

Salome scrambled over to the vanity, feeling beneath it and along the wall behind it for anything that might trigger the door to open. Phyl checked under the bed, even under Rita.

With no place to exit, the smoke now consumed half the air space.

Bending at the waist, the two women took refuge in the cedar closet.

"Being wood, this might not be the best place to be," Phyl said, coughing, after Salome closed the door.

"I can get us out of here, Phyl. I'll just have to figure out what I saw on the blueprints . . . and hope!"

"What the hell are you talking about?"

"Let's move these clothes!"

"What are we looking for?"

"A door, I imagine. You see, the outer door was for Granddad to use. How he came and went. Maybe there's some panel concealing another button we overlooked. But there was another entrance for Lily Sebastain. *Inside* the house."

"I don't have a clue what you're talking about but I believe you. Just hurry!"

The clothes pressing against their backs, they knocked on

the back wall, listening for a hollow place. Phyllis worked the left side, Salome the right.

Salome sniffed the air. Already smoke was creeping under the door.

Hurry, Salome, she ordered herself, working to suppress panic while trying to keep focused. Her eyes started to sting and water. The smoke muted the light from Phyl's bobbing flashlight. The gap between them was quickly shortening; they were running out of space. Time, too.

"Phyl? Find anything?"

"Nothing. Christ!"

And then Salome heard what she wanted to hear, that blessed hollow sound. Her hands moved rapidly along the wall searching out a doorknob, or an indentation which would enable her to slide a portion of the wall to one side, *anything*.

There was nothing. Her heart raced.

Phyl coughed. "Salome . . ."

"I'm trying, Phyl!" Finally, in frustration, Salome banged her fist against the cedar. To her amazement, a panel popped open right into her face.

"Here!" Salome cried. Cold, musty air entered the closet. Salome entered a completely black space, reaching blindly. Her hand connected with frigid metal.

"Phyl!" she shouted, her hand running up the curved rail. "A spiral staircase!"

Phyl shone the rapidly dimming light inside the confined area, which was only about four feet wide.

"Quickly!" Salome said.

"Where does it go?"

"The first floor—and hopefully to a room where we can get out."

Awkwardly, they moved up the corkscrew metal stairs, Salome in the lead. Finally, after they'd gone about twelve feet, Salome banged her head against the ceiling.

"Stop!" she yelled. "Move down a bit and give me the light."

"It's almost out of juice."

"Just give it to me!"

But the transfer wasn't successful. The light dropped, banging on the stairs.

Phyl cursed. "I'll go get it." Phyl cursed again. "Smoke's already coming in!"

But Salome wasn't listening. She felt along the ceiling, hoping for a latch or something, hoping that the concealed staircase hadn't simply been sealed at the top. Reason told her it hadn't because it had once been used. Maybe still *was* in use.

Phyl started coughing again.

Then Salome found a latch. She fumbled with it for a moment, but it was stiff with age. Finally, her fingers aching, she shoved it to one side. She pressed upward, straining, praying that a piece of furniture wasn't directly overhead.

At last, it seemed to give. Then with a snap, this bit of ceiling opened like a hatch.

"Got it, Phyl!" she shouted triumphantly.

A moment later, they crawled out and into a pantry with surround shelves. Just ahead was the passage that connected the dining room with the kitchen.

"We've got to call the fire department," Salome cried. "Where's Palmer's phone?"

Phyllis swore loudly. "At the lab. He only had one."

Behind them, smoke had begun to curl up from the spiral staircase, followed by a terrible growl as if emitted from the throat of some ungodly beast.

"Let's just get the hell out of here."

Then they heard shattering glass and shouts.

"I think the cavalry has arrived," Phyl declared as they ran down the passage to the kitchen. Two firemen carrying a fire hose had broken in through the pane of glass in the kitchen door.

"Phyl!" one of them said, startled. "What the hell're you doing here?"

"You can get in through there," she said, pointing to the door that accessed the basement stairs, smoke curling up at the bottom.

"Yeah, that's what whoever called said. Now get outta here."

"They tell you there's a body down there?"

Using the radio in the fire truck, Phyl connected with the Holyrood PD and the county coroner. Then she and Salome scurried down the embankment to the Perfume Creek and crossed the bridge to Dora's. Dora answered the door, wearing a nightgown and robe, clearly surprised to see them. But when she refused them entry, Phyl's anger finally found release. Nearly knocking down both the door and Dora, Phyl grabbed the housekeeper's head and sniffed her hair. The smell of smoke lingered.

Taking offense, Dora fought back and the two rolled around on the floor, knocking over a table and lamp while Salome groped around in the darkness, trying to find a light switch.

Amid the shouting and screaming, the cops started banging on the front, the street-side door. Salome stumbled through the dark to let them in, seeing two squad cars angled in the street.

After the two women were pulled apart, Dora was hauled off to the station, cursing and sputtering, at the moment arrested only for assaulting a police officer and suspicion of arson. Phyl dismissed the other cops and told them to wait outside for her. When they were gone, she bent at the waist, panting.

"You okay?" Salome asked, placing her hand on Phyl's back. Phyl nodded and a few moments later straightened, taking a deep breath. Obviously, she hadn't wanted the other officers to see her in distress.

"My God! That woman's got a grip like a weight lifter."

"You never did tell me what 'the hell breaking loose' was all about."

Phyl snorted, the nearest she could come to a grim laugh. "I think we just experienced it."

"Before. When those news vans stopped at your house."

She shook her head. "Wish I knew who told 'em I was at home. Well, I'd just gotten a call that someone in the coroner's office had leaked information about Palmer's autopsy. That he was killed by a poison dart probably tipped with curare. Rather sensational news for sleepy old Holyrood.

"Look, we better get out of here. I need to write out a search warrant for his place—"

Then suddenly, both women were startled as someone charged through the living room door.

Chapter 26

"I want my damn socks! Already paid in advance. Not much but still I paid and I want 'em."

"Herman! Get the hell out of here!" Phyl snapped.

Ignoring the command, he brushed past Phyl and Salome and headed straight for the basket beside Dora's armchair.

Before anyone could stop him, he began rifling through the basket.

"Herman, if you don't leave this minute I'll have to—"

He waved five socks in their faces.

"One's missing. Got two feet, don't I?"

Indeed, Mr. Boelkerke stood on two feet, though, like the rest of him, they were somewhat misaligned. Salome rooted through the basket, through other thick socks and skeins of wool. Then at the bottom, she pulled out a sock covering the darning egg. The sock still had part of a hole in the toe.

"That's it!" he exclaimed and yanked the sock off.

"Good night!" he spat and stormed out the door.

Salome and Phyl exchanged glances then both burst into laughter at the old man's antics, welcome relief after what they'd been through.

" 'Got two feet, don't I?' " Phyl mimicked.

When they finally stopped laughing and were starting to

leave, Salome realized she still held the darning egg. Phyl moved to close the living room door.

Before returning it to the basket, Salome examined the inlay on the wooden oval. It was a beautiful object, probably an antique. While passing her fingers over it, she discovered that it separated in the middle.

She unscrewed it. Inside the darning egg's hollow interior was a brown, tarry substance in plastic wrap. And a key.

"Phyl! Come look at this!" Salome cried, goose bumps erupting on her arms and legs.

Phyl rushed over. "Son of a . . ."

Using a sock from the basket, Phyl held the handle and examined the items in the interior. Salome began to wonder if Dora had used a blowgun and where she would hide *that*.

The wind suddenly picked up. Salome heard the bamboo chime outside *thunking* an earthy melody, quite different from the high-pitched metallic song of her own chimes hanging in the arbor.

Almost immediately, she experienced a slight buzzing in her head, accompanied by more gooseflesh, familiar as one of those "Ah ha!" synchronistic moments. She went outside and standing on tiptoe, lifted the wind chime from the hook by the door. It consisted of nearly two dozen pieces of bamboo in varying widths and lengths. She avoided touching any piece while carrying it.

Phyl frowned. "What are you doing?"

"I've got a hunch . . ."

A moment later, after finding a ballpoint pen beside a notepad near the telephone, they both regarded the narrow blowgun Salome had coaxed from the interior of a bamboo rod with the aid of the pen, having held the rod with a sock so as not to leave prints. Then there was the key that matched the one to the creek-side door in Phyl's possession, and the tarry substance in plastic wrap.

"Catch of day," Phyllis remarked grimly. "Now. Everything back as it was. Until I have a search warrant, this evidence has not been found! *Capice*?"

"What evidence?"

THE FOLLOWING MORNING DORA'S COTTAGE was legally searched and the incriminating items "found." (Later, the lab would confirm that the tarry substance in the darning egg was curare.) Yet, even when confronted with the evidence, Dora refused to speak.

Then Phyl had an idea. She waited until just before dinnertime then went to Dora's cell at the station.

"How you doing there, Dora?"

Dora didn't even turn her head. Maintaining a rigid posture, she stared at the wall.

"Just had some news." She'd decided to drop her bomb then leave. Though she didn't know Dora well, she did know the housekeeper's area of vulnerability.

After a deep sigh, she declared, "Salome's decided to destroy the Perfume. She's got this idea in her head that since the truth might never be known about who killed Palmer and Rita, the Perfume itself will be poisoned—her words—and must be torn down. These feng shui people have some funny ideas. But, like she said, only the truth can save it.

"Don't know about you, but imagining that wonderful old mansion reduced to a pile of rubble just breaks my heart."

She thought she detected a slight shudder pass through Dora's body then left.

EARLIER IN THE DAY, SALOME AND DORA weren't that far from each other, though in another sense were worlds apart. Salome sat in the chair beside Britta O'Kelly's desk, giving her statement about last night's events. When she finished and prepared to leave, Britta said, with a sparkle in her eye, "Know what, Salome?"

"What?"

"Shanna, one of my grandchildren, is coming to visit for a couple of days. She's a journalism major at Arizona State. Now I don't know if it's because of all the hoopla going on around here or if that crystal I hung in the window where you told me to has anything to do with it. Could be she plans to write a story about what's been going on around here for her school paper. But, either way, she *is* coming."

Salome smiled and gave Britta a hug.

WHEN DINNER ARRIVED, DORA ANNOUNCED that she wanted to talk to Phyllis. Over the next couple of hours, the truth emerged.

Indeed Palmer had given her notice, paving the way for Brooke and Ken to move into the cottage. Dora made her plans the last night Barbara Boatwright had visited Palmer. While cleaning up, she decided to hide Barbara's empty wineglass for later use.

He was sleeping in the studio when she killed him by blowing a poison dart into his neck. Once he was dead, she slipped on latex gloves, carefully removed the dart, and flushed it down the second-floor toilet. She pocketed his keys and wallet and wrapped him in a tarp he'd used to cover his fish sculpture. Then she dragged him downstairs, positioning him between the sofa and the French doors. She wrapped herself in the tarp to protect herself from blood splatter and using a hoe-fork brought in from the toolshed, battered his head and torso until her arms ached.

She wrapped the hoe-fork in the tarp and went back to the toolshed near the garage on the north side of the property. Using a hose, she washed off the hoe-fork and tarp. Then she stuck the tool in the ground a few times to dirty it and put it back in the shed. She folded the wet tarp and took it down the kitchen stairs to the basement and hid it in the secret room. The garbage had already been collected so she'd have to wait until next week's pickup to dispose of the tarp in a neighbor's bin.

Then she went back upstairs and entered his office, where she checked his wallet to see how much cash he had, glad to note that he had plenty, though she had brought extra with her. She called Beach Bistro and altering her voice slightly, ordered takeout for two, requesting that they not include plastic cutlery. She took money from his wallet and put it in an envelope. Then she went to his file cabinet and pulled out the folder containing the life insurance policy. She'd met Babette Fordham at Christmas and while serving them Christmas dinner had overheard them talking about the policy—one of Palmer's Christmas gifts to his sister. She set the folder on his desk.

In the past few years she'd never known Beach Bistro to call back and confirm his order. Still, she took the cordless phone with her just in case and went to the double front doors and propped the envelope on the ground.

Next she returned to the studio and collected the bottle of wine and the glass he'd been drinking from earlier in the evening and set them on the coffee table. Then she retrieved the glass Barbara had used from a far corner in the pantry and added wine from the open bottle.

Soon after that bit of staging, the doorbell rang. She waited until the car pulled away before she collected the order. Making certain the front doors were locked, she took the food into the kitchen. Having worked up an appetite, she ate some then dumped the rest down the garbage disposal letting it run while she washed two forks and put them in the dish drainer on the sink.

Back in the living room, she regarded her handiwork. For an added touch, she set the cordless phone on the floor by the coffee table, then kicked it slightly.

By staging-within-staging, she had created a couple of scenarios. One involved Barbara Boatwright, the other a robbery gone bad as might have been perpetrated by Ken and

Brooke—though she was able to describe them, she didn't know their names. Certainly Ken looked and acted like a person capable of brutal murder. The insurance policy, prominently displayed, would also cast suspicion on Palmer's sister.

She was doing the cops a favor, she said, giving them a choice and believed the real cause of death would not be discovered.

Through the kitchen door she went up to the patio and threw the now-empty wallet over the embankment into the creek, as Ken might have done. She started to do the same with Palmer's keys, then decided to keep his key to the creek-side door in reserve. The remaining keys followed the wallet.

Once home, she'd laundered her clothes, then dropped into bed.

Then about 5 A.M. she'd awakened in a cold sweat, alerted that she'd forgotten something. She dressed quickly.

Of course! The French doors. She should have left them open. She'd seen Ken exit the living room via the French doors while Brooke was with Palmer; had seen him on the patio looking down through the trees at her cottage. His fingerprints might still be on the interior and exterior doorknobs. Having tossed Palmer's wallet and keys, she should have thought to leave at least one of the doors open as if, after killing Palmer, Ken had left via the patio, then tossed the keys and wallet.

With the fog as a cover, she'd hurried across the footbridge, let herself into the basement, dashed up the stairs to the kitchen and out the kitchen door to the patio. Inserting her key, she unlocked one of the French doors and pulled it open. Then she retraced her steps back to her cottage.

AS FOR RITA, ON FRIDAY SHE HAD BEGGED DORA to let her inside the Perfume to look for a stash of paintings she wanted catalogued. She'd said she knew Dora had to have an extra key. She promised not to tell anyone, that it would be their "little secret," but she just had to find those paintings. At first Dora refused. Then Rita told her *she* would be the new owner of the mansion, that Salome had agreed to sell it to her—which meant, she'd also own Dora's cottage. If Dora would help now, Rita would keep her on. If Dora didn't, well, she'd just have to sell the cottage and Dora would be out on the street.

They met at the creek-side door after dark Friday night. Dora had her blowgun prepped and they hadn't been in the basement but a few moments before Rita succumbed to a lethal dart. Dora wrapped the body in the same tarp she'd used during Palmer's murder and left it in the "special" room. During the next storm she planned to dispose of the body in the creek, where it would be washed out to sea.

How she'd acquired the exotic poison revealed another interesting chapter in the Perfume's history. It all began with Dora's grandparents, Teodora (for whom she'd been named) and Jorge Pena.

Lily and Connor Sebastian had met them during a tour of Brazil and brought the couple to the U.S. as house servants. Jorge taught Connor how to use a blowgun, make darts, and cure them in the poison for hunting. When the Sebastians moved from Hollywood and into the Perfume Mansion, they naturally brought Teodora and Jorge. Lily didn't want servants living in the same house, so they were settled in the cottage across the creek and the footbridge built.

Throughout, Jorge had had a source in Brazil send curare for Connor to use for hunting. The tradition continued into the next generation when their daughter, Maria, married Arthur Whalen and Teodora and Jorge retired. Maria and Arthur, Dora's parents, took over the care of the mansion.

Dora's mother showed her the secret room and taught her how to use the blowgun and prepare the poison, mainly for protection should she ever need it. Even after her parents retired, Dora continued to receive a monthly supply of the poison. Dora considered the protection of the mansion to be her sacred duty, instilled in her by her own parents. Whatever threatened her, threatened the Perfume itself.

REGARDING THE FIRE............

Alerted by their voices, Dora had watched Phyllis and Salome cross the footbridge and enter the mansion and had followed them to see what they were up to. Discovering that they'd found the secret room, there was only one thing she could do. She set fire to the old dusty coats and hats and for a moment considered incinerating herself as well. Then she realized that by doing so, there would be no one to call the fire department. She didn't want the fire to go out of control and burn down the entire mansion—just the one room and those inside. Even if it was discovered that she'd made the call, she could always say she'd simply smelled smoke coming from across the creek.

She'd hurried back to her cottage, made a quick call to the fire department, then threw her clothes in the washer and changed into a nightgown, not even thinking that the smell of smoke still lingered in her hair.

Later, her feelings for Salome having warmed, Phyllis stopped in at Salome's and, over a cold beer, related the details of Dora's confession.

Chapter 27

SALOME sat on a couch in her living room stroking Shishi while waiting for Emily to arrive for an interview. Her thoughts weren't on what she'd say but, rather, focused elsewhere. Her father had nearly succumbed to another heart attack upon learning of the fire. Murder in the mansion was bad enough but a fire could have completely destroyed the venerated structure.

She'd returned the journals to the cabinet, leaving a note that her grandfather's handwriting had put her off and so she hadn't spent more than a few minutes with each.

When she'd surveyed the fire damage with Phyl, what had struck her most was not so much the gutted secret room but something unseen. Per her usual practice, she'd entered the basement with her eyes closed. The energy felt lighter, no longer menacing, *purer*, if that was the right word. The fire must have burned out the sha, the lingering evil. Though she and Phyl could have lost their lives, maybe in some strange way the fire had been for the best. For one thing, their shared brush with death had dramatically improved their relations.

Phyl had allowed her to perform a brief blessing ceremony in the basement. A thorough ritual cleansing of the entire structure would have to wait until both murders and the arson investigation were concluded. For now, the Perfume was evidence. And as such, Phyl's.

Salome felt guilty for neglecting the Perfume for so many years. Since she would likely be in D.C. when it was released, she would fly back to Holyrood and supervise every aspect of its renewal: from cleaning to painting to rebuilding the lower level. She planned to plant a palm tree in the missing relationship gua to align that space with the rest of the house and hang round mirrors on the inside walls on each floor to symbolically fill the void.

One other feature of the Perfume bothered her—the spiral stairs which, to their good fortune, had provided Salome and Phyl's escape. Still, being hidden and shut off, the energy would continue boring a hole in the Perfume's family/health gua. Most likely, Lily Sebastian had used the stairs to access the secret room through her storage closet. Did she die of natural causes? Salome doubted she'd ever know, but Lily's husband had been a hunter who used a blowgun and curare-cured darts, as Dora had confessed, and Phyl confided to Salome.

It was easy enough to imagine Conner discovering the route to the secret room and catching Lily there as she awaited a tryst with Joshua. He might have shot her with a dart, removed it when she was dead or dying, then left her on the bed and retreated up the spiral stairs.

Salome thought about those who'd lived in the Perfume. While they had to have had wealth to do so, that hadn't been enough to keep marriages from dissolving—for which the missing relationship gua shared blame.

Only after the full complement of transcendental work would the Perfume be ready for occupancy.

She'd told no one of her decision to split the rent money with Phyl. Certainly this would complicate matters, but hopefully, only regarding bookkeeping. It just seemed the right thing to do.

Shishi suddenly darted off her lap. An instant later the doorbell rang.

The kitty trotted to the front door. "Good radar, Shishi," she said, following the feline.

She wasn't looking forward to the interview, but most likely this would be the last. Everyone knew she and Phyl had narrowly escaped death and Emily wanted details.

When she opened the door, she immediately wished she'd taken more pains with her appearance. All the blood seemed to drain from her upper body.

For a long moment Michael O'Kelly and Salome stared at each other, neither breathing.

"So, who's going to blink first?" Salome finally managed, though the words had to fight their way around her heart, which seemed to have lodged in her throat.

"Told Emily I wanted to conduct the interview. If you don't mind."

On unsteady legs, Salome stepped aside and motioned for him to enter.

"You look wonderful, Mei," he said. "Not at all like Aunt Livia's description—which put you somewhere between one of the witches in Macbeth and something that washed up on the beach."

"She always had a good eye."

They both laughed and the initial awkwardness vanished. Then, to her surprise, he thoughtfully pulled off his shoes.

"You bash your head escaping from the fire?"

"Oh that," she said, lightly touching the bandage. "A different accident."

A few moments later both were settled in the living room with tall glasses of Kirin beer, Salome in scuffs, Michael in his stocking feet.

He raised his glass in a toast. She noticed his hand shaking slightly.

"You all right?"

"Not really. I just can't believe I'm actually sitting here

with you. It's surreal. And there's something I want more than anything."

"What?" she asked. He must mean a kiss, she thought, and figured she'd be reduced to a pool of protoplasm once their lips met.

"More than anything I—I, God it's so stupid. I want a cigarette."

So much for romance, she mused, at the same time a little relieved. "Uh, when did you take up smoking? You were always such an athlete and stickler for training."

"The day I left Holyrood. Bought my first pack at the San Francisco airport. Finished it off before I got to Boston. Of course I quit ten years ago."

Shishi decided the moment had come to examine this new person and jumped up on the sofa between them, staring at Michael.

"That's Shishi. Go ahead, give him a pet. He's much better than a cigarette."

After the initial stroke, Shishi climbed aboard, deciding Michael's lap was fine place to begin an acquaintance.

Lucky kitty. Suddenly, Salome couldn't think of a thing to say.

"After boarding school I got my undergraduate degree at Harvard. Then went to the B-school. Dad provided plenty of cash, payment for me to stay away from the West Coast."

He took a drink then looked at Salome. "What about you?"

"Finished high school in Hawaii. Lived with one of my mom's sisters. She owned a florist shop in Honolulu."

"You go to Stanford?" he asked. They'd both planned to attend Stanford and after graduating, change the world.

"No. Just sort of hung out in Hawaii. Came back to visit my family a few times but didn't move back to the mainland for quite some time."

Neither said a word for a moment.

"What about college?"

"Went to a community college but never got a degree."

"Jesus, Salome, you were in the National Honor Society!"

"So what? Life changed radically after, uh, that night."

Michael heaved a sigh, then gently putting Shishi on the floor, sat forward, his elbows on his knees.

"I'm so sorry. God!" He ran a hand through his thick gray hair. "You know who informed on us, don't you?"

"Your brother."

"Yeah, but who told him?"

She shook her head.

"Billie Ruth."

Salome's mouth dropped open. "I knew she didn't like me but that's, well, treacherous."

Michael finished his beer. "Look, why don't we do this over dinner. I need something stronger than beer and have to confess, I don't know diddly about interviewing. It was just an excuse to see you."

"You didn't need an excuse, Michael."

THE "INTERVIEW" RESULTED IN MORE THAN AN article in the paper. The years melted away and Michael changed his mind about a quick escape from Holyrood after the sale of *The Echo*. He didn't even mind staying at Aunt Livia's. But then, when the national media hit Holyrood once word got out that the First Lady had been painted by Palmer Fordham and that Palmer had been HIV-positive, Damon O'Kelly had quite the time singing and farting for the cameras. Livia had whisked him away to an undisclosed location.

Salome worked at Otter Haven during the AT&T golf tournament. Dressed in her maid's uniform, pleated plastic rain hat, ordinary raincoat, and a pair of harlequin glasses studded with rhinestones, she was able to come and go—right through the front gate—without being bothered. Certain journalists were prowling for celebrities staying at the resort and Salome hardly appeared to fill the bill. The tabloids pursued leads to a sex scandal involving Palmer Fordham and the First Lady. Of course, having created the lurid story themselves, they were chasing their own tails. Still others pestered Phyllis and the Holyrood PD for more information about Dora Whalen.

As best she could, Salome stayed away from the circus.

When Mandy called to share the news that his biopsy declared him to be free of colon cancer, Salome, Michael, and Phyl drove up to San Francisco to join him in a celebration at Murph's. Not only had his health improved but he'd been hired to participate in the documentary, *Queens, Dying Royalty?* The filmmaker attended the party, following Mandy around. Clay Bethune was there, drunk and surly as the last time Salome and Mandy had seen him. Mandy didn't care. He wore a long black evening gown and his Princess Diana wig and tiara, reveling in the sheer joy of the moment.

Salome, Phyllis, and Michael stayed the night at the Waterhouse town house on Nob Hill, each in their own room. Phyllis and Michael had been pretty wasted and Salome, not being much of a drinker, helped them both to bed.

BY THE TIME SHE PREPARED TO LEAVE FOR D.C., Salome and Michael had uncovered layers of mutual compatibility. But he didn't trust his feelings. Both his failed marriage and the trauma of that December night so long ago had left him not only scarred emotionally, but damaged physically. He admitted that his brother had kicked him so severely—leaving his face and upper body without any obvious wounds—that he pissed blood for a week and ended up in the emergency room at Tufts with peritonitis. One of his testicles had to be removed.

On a beautiful clear day while Salome was taking care of outside chores before her departure, Janelle Phillips showed up, wearing a smile and a golden tan.

"Salome! How nice to see you."

Salome glanced up from weeding her Japanese garden.

"Hello, Janelle."

Salome resumed her work. Janelle looked around, shifting her weight from foot to foot.

"Well, thought I should tell you that I sent the money for the feng shuing on Palmer's birthday. That morning I wanted to be sure you wouldn't just keep the money and not do anything. I hung around watching for you to leave your house, then followed you to the end of the Bluff. Honestly, I was surprised to see you outside on the promontory not long after. Then I saw the police head over . . . and, of course, heard later he'd been murdered."

"So you left town without providing me with an alibi."

"Palmer and I were lovers for a while. I just couldn't take a chance that Tommy would find out."

"So where'd you go?"

"Jamaica."

"Just get back?"

"Well, yes. Thought you'd fill me in on what happened."

Salome straightened. "I don't have time. You can head down to the offices of *The Echo* and read the back issues."

"Oh. Well, all right then." Her smile had lost some wattage, and was about to lose more. "Well, have a nice day."

As Janelle turned to leave, Salome said. "There is one bit of information I can share with you and, I suppose, you really do need to know, if you don't know already."

"Really? What's that?"

"Palmer was HIV-positive."

DURING THE DRIVE TO THE AIRPORT, MICHAEL said, "I lined up a couple of contractors to work on Aunt Livia's B and B. By the time you get back it'll be a real showplace."

"You didn't tell her, did you?"

He laughed, deep and hearty just as she'd remembered over the years.

"If she knew I snuck you in to feng shui the place when she took off with Damon, there'd be another corpse in Holyrood. No, she's just glad I'm paying for the work."

He reached over and squeezed her hand. "Seeing you again has really been costly, Mei," he said. "But worth it."

She gave him a knowing look.

"Ch'i moves in mysterious ways."

Miriam Grace Monfredo

*brings to life one of the most exciting periods
in our nation's history—the mid-1800s—when the passionate struggles
of suffragettes, abolitionists, and other heroes touched the lives of every
American, including a small-town librarian named Glynis Tryon...*

__BLACKWATER SPIRITS__   0-425-15266-9/$6.50

*Glynis Tryon, no stranger to political controversy, is fighting
the prejudice against the Seneca Iroquois. And the issue
becomes personal when one of Glynis's Iroquois friends is
accused of murder...*

__NORTH STAR CONSPIRACY__   0-425-14720-7/$6.50

__SENECA FALLS INHERITANCE__

                                            0-425-14465-8/$6.99

__THROUGH A GOLD EAGLE__   0-425-15898-5/$6.50

*When abolitionist John Brown is suspected of moving counter-
feit bills, Glynis is compelled to launch her own campaign for
freedom—to free an innocent man.*

MARGARET COEL

THE EAGLE CATCHER

When Arapaho tribal chairman Harvey Castle is found murdered, the evidence points to his own nephew. But Father John O'Malley doesn't believe the young man is a killer. And in his quest for truth, O'Malley gets a rare glimpse into the Arapaho life few outsiders ever see—and a crime fewer could imagine...

❑ 0-425-15463-7/$6.50

THE GHOST WALKER

Father John O'Malley comes across a corpse lying in a ditch beside the highway. When he returns with the police, it is gone. Together, an Arapaho lawyer and Father John must draw upon ancient Arapaho traditions to stop a killer, explain the inexplicable, and put a ghost to rest...

❑ 0-425-15961-2/$6.50

THE DREAM STALKER

Father John O'Malley and Arapaho attorney Vicky Holden return to face a brutal crime of greed, false promises, and shattered dreams...

❑ 0-425-16533-7/$6.50

THE STORY TELLER

When the Arapaho storyteller discovers that a sacred tribal artifact is missing from a local museum, Holden and O'Malley begin a deadly search for the sacred treasure.

❑ 0-425-17025-X/$6.50
